SHARON MARSHALL

DEEP RIVERS

A NOVEL

ICAN PRESS

DEEP RIVERS

This is a work of fiction. Names, characters, places, and incidents are products of the author's imagination or are used fictitiously and are not to be construed as real. Any resemblance to actual events, locales, organizations, or persons, living or dead, is entirely coincidental.

Copyright © 2024 by Sharon Marshall

All rights reserved. No part of this book may be reproduced in any manner whatsoever without written permission except in the case of brief quotations embodied in critical articles and reviews.

Cover Design: Original photograph by Sharon Marshall and Dall E generated image of a river

First Printing, 2024

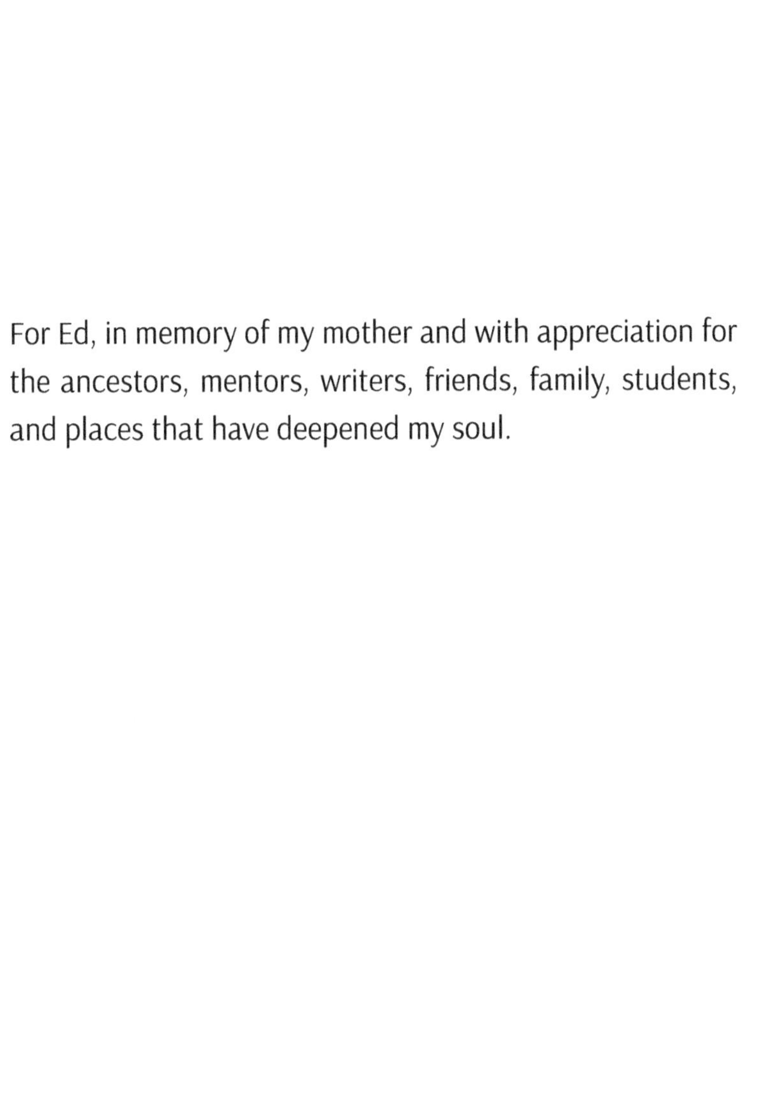

For Ed, in memory of my mother and with appreciation for the ancestors, mentors, writers, friends, family, students, and places that have deepened my soul.

CONTENTS

CONTENTS

CONTENTS

CONTENTS

CHARLES RIVERS, APRIL 2000

Charles Rivers hunched over an enormous metal desk in his windowless office on the 6th floor of the academic center grading yet another student paper. *Where's the thesis statement?* he scrawled in jagged red script on a loose-leaf page that was as thin as his patience after reading Kameron Johnson's 500 words on legalizing marijuana. He dropped the pen onto the desk, its dark gray surface ink-stained from nearly two decades of just such moments. The urge came over Charles to go out into the hallway to find someone he could complain to about his students. But it was that transitional hour between the day and night sessions which meant there would probably be no one around.

Instead, he took a deep breath, consciously inhaling through his nose, remembering the alternative medicine guru on Pacifica radio who said nose breathing increases stamina. He closed his eyes, stretched out his long legs in their khaki trousers, the left one an inch shorter than the other from his war injury, and he breathed in again, this time feeling the air press against the inside of his ribcage. He leaned back in the worn five-wheeled metal office chair that matched the desk. And presently on the black screen behind his eyes, he conjured up an image of a blue sky, leafy trees, and the circle of track with its chain-link fence surrounding the Central Park reservoir, the oblong body of water in the center of New York's eponymous Park. He was setting the stage for the appearance of Rosetta Ocean, who soon materialized, half-naked in skimpy running shorts and a sports bra that barely covered her bouncing breasts. She was running with the beautiful posture and sure footing of a Kenyan marathoner, singing along to music plugged into her ear, her dark brown skin glistening with sweat, her face at once animated and serene.

He let out his breath and took another, anticipating the vision of what came next. But he leaned back too far in the chair; it tipped, and Rosetta Ocean disappeared as he jerked forward and the chair rolled backward, hitting the wall with a dull thump and adding another mark to the gallery of tiny gashes and dark smudges behind the desk. Charles stood up and raised his arms over his head. His right shoulder ached, and as he stretched towards the ceiling to loosen his muscles, he rewound the tape of the day--grading, faculty meeting, classes. That's when he realized how hungry he was and remembered the tuna sandwich he left in the mail room refrigerator that morning.

He went out into the deserted hallway and passing the dark closed doors of faculty offices and the gaping doorways of empty classrooms, he heard the slight syncopation of his footsteps as his cordovan wingtips struck the polished floor. The mail room door was locked since Yolanda and Joan, the department secretaries, had left for the day. Luckily, he had a key, and as he pulled his keys from his side pocket, they jangled on the key ring his son Jason had given him as a Father's Day present when he was in elementary school. "It has a monogram, dad," Jason said. At the time it boasted a black italicized raised *R* for Rivers, but now it was just a steel coil curving around and through half a dozen keys, a couple of them orphaned forever from whatever doors or cabinets they once opened. Charles wondered where Jason was at that moment, and he felt a sudden tightness in the same spot in his chest that minutes before had expanded with his breath. To relieve the tightness, he ran his forefinger against the jagged edge of the slender mail room key, a brief corporeal distraction that helped suppress thoughts of Jason.

Charles inserted the key into the polished steel doorknob, twisting and angling for the sweet spot in the cylinder. The tumbler wouldn't budge, and just when the impulse to kick the door came over him, it opened from inside, and Rosetta Ocean stood in the doorway, a sheaf of student papers clasped in her left hand.

"Oh, Professor Rivers!" she exclaimed, her voice bright with amusement. She stepped back from the door and further into the tiny room to let him in. She was wearing a black bulky oversized sweater and skinny denim jeans, her voluminous natural hair pulled into a thick puffy bun on the top of her head.

"Ms. Ocean, what a surprise! I didn't expect to see you here."

"I've been meeting with students," she said, letting go of the doorknob and jumping a little when the door slammed shut behind them with a metallic clang. He did not expect anyone to be in the locked mail room, especially not this younger woman he made love to many times in his mind but had rarely found the opportunity to speak to. As she gazed up at him suddenly everything in the room, the wall of battered wooden mailboxes, the water cooler, the half refrigerator, the ancient mimeograph machine with its jug of toxic blue ink, melted away and everything inside Charles Rivers rushed towards Rosetta Ocean with her smiling black eyes, smooth cocoa skin, valentine cheekbones, and tiny ears studded with pearls that appeared to be the same color as her perfect teeth. He had been so lonely, so weary, so hollow from the inside out, but now summoned by her beautiful countenance something like laughter bubbled up inside him, and he found himself returning her red lipstick smile with a huge grin.

"You work too hard," he said.

"Some of them need a lot of support."

"Yes, but don't let the college take advantage of you. They do that, you know. They get young people in here and they feed off your altruism. They think they don't have to pay you a living wage because you care."

"Trust me. I'm not that young," she said.

She looked like a teenager, but she had been working there for a number of years since she entered the graduate program, and if he recalled correctly, she had returned to school after taking time off. He had been on the English prize committee the year she graduated and won honorable mention for a story about a protagonist, not unlike herself, he surmised, who grew up poor and black in Youngstown, Ohio.

"That's even worse. I'm serious, how much do you make as an adjunct?" She looked down at the floor. "My advice—get out of here as soon as you can. Believe me, I should know how they use and abuse people. I've been here since the seventies. You probably weren't even born then." He smiled again. It was less spontaneous this time because he was afraid the last part of his remark sounded disingenuous.

"I was born."

"You can get a better job teaching high school in Westchester. Over fifty thousand a year."

"Why haven't you?"

"You know what they say about an old dog and new tricks. Anyway, I'm looking forward to an early retirement in a couple of years. And when I retire, I plan to sail around the world, find a deserted tropical island, settle down with a beautiful woman, and populate it. Interested?"

"I doubt I'll be fertile by then."

"You're flattering me. My retirement is not that far off... How old do you think I am?"

"Sounds like a trick question."

They both chuckled. She was even prettier when she laughed, her black eyes crinkling, turning up at the edges, and giving off a sunny beneficent light. He remembered the first time he noticed her sitting in the back of the room at an English Department faculty meeting, listening with barely concealed amusement as the usual suspects—the associate and full professors she had studied with—assumed their customary battle stances. He couldn't stop looking at her, which was unusual because she was dark, and it was reflexive for him to turn away from or glance past dark-skinned women. Dark himself, he was often teased as a child and called "tar baby" and "blackie" by the kids on his block. And although he considered himself a champion of his people and white folks as a group made him uncomfortable, he had always preferred his women light.

But the pale European prototypes on which he based his assessments of beauty faded away in the rich skin tone and the lush proportions of Rosetta's face. Every time he saw her, he wanted to smile, and he marveled at how cheerful and energetic she appeared. Once he saw her dash out of a classroom and *run* like a carefree child in a playground back to the office she shared on alternating days with other adjuncts, bounding out again a few moments later, hugging a large black spiral attendance book to her chest.

"Besides, I already have kids," she said.

"You do? How many?" At that moment, besides desiring her, he envied her—her youth, her children, the years she had yet to live.

"Two boys, five and seven, and actually, nobody knows it yet, but I'm pregnant." After the word pregnant, the corners of her mouth turned down and the pink pillow of her lower lip protruded. He looked down at her belly. She shook her head.

"Just a few weeks."

"Congratulations," he said faking cheer as the geyser of happiness that had bubbled up inside him abruptly died down.

"I don't know. It wasn't planned." She bit her lower lip, turned away, and looked towards the old mimeograph machine.

"You're fecund."

"I guess you could say that."

"Just the sort of woman I'd be looking for," he tried to joke.

"A breeder?"

"That has terrible connotations. Healthy and fertile. Your husband is a lucky man."

"How do you know I even have one?"

"Given the circumstances, I sure hope you do," he said with a weak laugh.

"Yeah, I do. But I'm not sure how I let this whole family thing happen, you know. I was supposed to grow up and become a writer. Now I just make peanut butter sandwiches and teach freshmen how to avoid sentence fragments."

"Well, writers create the illusion of life. You've created it in the flesh. And now I'm sure you have plenty to write about." She shook her head slightly. "And if your boys are as handsome as you are lovely..." He knew he was going overboard, especially after what she had just said, but it was one of those times when he couldn't stop himself.

"And you?"

"I'm no writer."

"Children?"

"I have a son, Jason, he's twenty-two; he's had some problems. I'm not sure where he is right now." Rosetta cocked her head slightly and gave him a sympathetic look. When the subject of Jason came up, he always tried to speak in neutral tones and not betray the anguish that like a disease of the blood had caused him many private episodes of indescribable pain. "It's a long story," he shrugged, but he was no good at shrugging. The weight he carried was too heavy and now, like an anchor, it held him fast in the sediment of despair.

"I'm sorry," she said looking at him with so much compassion he felt like he might drown in it. He turned away, and instead of undressing her in the bushes, which was the second part of his Central Park fantasy, now he wanted to tell her the story of his anguish. But the thought of opening up made him feel even more stuck. Rosetta touched his elbow lightly and looked up at him with concern. Her touch was gentle and curious, but his brain turned it into a lightning bolt.

"I better get ready for class. I still have a couple of papers to correct. Good talking to you." He took a few steps backward and pivoted towards the door. "Have a good weekend," he said, suddenly not sure what day of the week it was. It wasn't until he was back in his office that he remembered the tuna sandwich.

For nearly a quarter of a century Charles had been teaching at the college where he himself enrolled in the heady days of open admissions, when after grass-roots protests and a takeover by Black and Puerto Rican students, the institution finally opened its doors to any student who graduated from a city high school. He had forfeited his own high school graduation by enlisting in the army two months before receiving his diploma. But when he returned from Vietnam where he'd spent nine months before sustaining the injury that sent him back home, he met a young professor who taught at the college, and she encouraged him to go back to school. He ended up marrying her, and she persuaded him to get a master's degree in English, of all things, and when he finished it, he was hired as a full-time lecturer, in part, because she was on the faculty.

Early in his teaching career, he had felt a sense of liberation. He became another person in the classroom, no longer stunted by prejudice, poverty, and self-hatred or torn apart by what he had come to realize was the senseless violence of war. He was just short of six feet tall, a sinewy 160 pounds, but after his tour in Vietnam, the person he saw in the mirror had shrunk into a kind of cubist jigsaw puzzle with visible fissures and missing pieces that might scramble or collapse into an unrecognizable pile of fragments at any moment.

In the classroom, the pieces came together and formed, at least temporarily, a coherent whole. He grew again to his actual stature and the walls of the room seemed to disappear as he sometimes gestured dramatically with hands as supple and articulate as a conductor's, even though the left one was missing its ring finger.

Teaching had transformed him. The Harlem boy who jumped from the frying pan into the literal fire by going to war to escape his surroundings became the man who survived it, and that man became the student of life the times demanded, and that student became a teacher who used the lessons he had learned to guide others. His students had liked him, the older ones and students of color found a role model for negotiating the tricky path to graduation, and even the working-class whites who never had a Black teacher came to respect him.

But now, at the beginning of the new century, a more restrictive policy had been instituted by the university. That, and having been a widower longer than he had been married, as well as the many years of struggle with his only child had come to make the classroom feel confining. Charles found himself becoming distressed by the classrooms themselves. The pitted cinder-block walls painted an oily beige, and the ugly clutter of the metal and plastic chairs reminded him of the police stations where he picked up Jason on a number of occasions.

It was true that the students made the spaces come alive, but sometimes their stories and dreams and the trust they put in the institution and in Charles overwhelmed him. Lately, he worried that the university and maybe even he was failing them, and that made it harder for him to teach with the enthusiasm he had brought to the task in his youth.

He sometimes wondered how his life would have been different, how he might have been able to move, live, and teach somewhere else if he'd had better credentials. His department was full of scholars who were well-known in the academy and in the world, whose scholarship and activism had earned them the status of public intellectuals. He was not one of them. He had never finished the Ph.D. he began at his wife Madeline's urging shortly after their son was born because writing the dissertation coincided with the beginning of her illness. Once she died, he not only struggled to keep going, but he also struggled to believe in himself the way she had believed in him.

Tonight, having felt the spark of connection with Rosetta Ocean in the mail room, he was acutely aware that his classroom was a box with a single door, no windows or natural light even during the day, and that the glow of the fluorescent substitute was filtered through metal panels that resembled prison bars. Once when Jason was about eleven, he found one of those light panels near the garbage cans outside his school. He brought it home and hung it up in his bedroom in their apartment near Central Park in West Harlem and called it abstract art. Charles had been impressed by Jason's artistic eye and interest in art; Madeline, whose mother was a self-taught painter, loved art as well, and trips to museums had always been part of their family time together. But these days Charles tried not to look at that panel when he passed Jason's empty room because it reminded him of imprisonment, his own figurative confinement, and the actual incarceration of so many others, maybe even Jason.

The students—there were seventeen of them tonight—were writing a response to an essay in the reader, "I Want a Wife," by Judy Brady. The questions he asked them to answer, *Do you want a wife? What qualities would that person have?* were an exercise in masochism, though the essay was part of the unit and written by someone described as a feminist in the introduction. It's what he got for being lazy this semester and following the syllabus in the annotated Instructor's Edition like one of the clueless white graduate students he often saw at the front of a room of students of color when he passed their classrooms. To be fair, though, he was trying to do something different. To respond to the guidelines of the new English composition director—and to challenge himself by teaching with new materials even though the old ones had worked perfectly well in the past.

He paced back and forth in front of the blackboard as some of the students screwed up their brows and chewed the tops of their pens. Most of them were adults. Not the usual eighteen-year-olds you might expect in a first-year writing course. The evening classes were full of returning and sometimes academically under-prepared students that the stricter admissions guidelines had been designed to discourage. Most of them had enrolled in college to make something better of lives they were already in the process of living. They had jobs and children and health problems and car trouble. They were single and searching for love; they were married and seeking divorce; they were suffering on account of no-account boyfriends, children who were failing in school, former husbands who owed them child support, wives back in Bangalore or St. Petersburg. They had lost brothers, mothers, fathers, grandparents, children, friends to AIDS and gunshots, crack and cancer, prison, death squads in Nicaragua, the Cultural Revolution in China, the graveyard stretch of the Atlantic Ocean between Port Au Prince and Miami. They had memories of green countrysides and smoky crowded cities that he had never seen, and many of them were ignorant of the history he had lived as a Black man born in 1949 and living his whole life, except for his tour in Vietnam, in America.

Some of them had a hard time detecting irony in Brady's essay. English was not their mother tongue. They did not recognize the tongue tucked inside her cheek, and they asked with great puzzlement how a woman could possibly want a wife.

"Do you want a wife?" Before class he found himself wanting somebody else's wife. Lusting in his heart as Jimmy Carter had famously put it. Madeline had been dead for over fourteen years. But he was still haunted sometimes by images of her skeletal body in the ICU. He saw her clawing at the IV, blood black and clotted like macabre lipstick around the hole that was her mouth, her eyes rolled back like a broken doll's, her face a skull.

It was harder to remember her before she got sick. He didn't know why. Maybe because now that he had passed fifty, he was starting to feel the impingement of death himself. He had most likely lived longer than he had yet to live. Sometimes though, when he was running, or just about to fall asleep, or standing in the kitchen with warm water running over his hands as he did the dishes, he would envision her as she was before the beginning and the end of that devastating illness. He would catch a glimpse of her as if he were peering into the Aleph in that story by Borges that begins with the death of love, a story he had first read as a graduate student in a Latin American literature class Madeline had encouraged him to take. She would be reclining on the curve of the world holding Jason in her arms, or she would be restlessly pacing and ardently talking on the telephone with one of her activist colleagues, or she would be standing at the massive mahogany dresser that his mother, a former domestic, had inherited from one of her rich employers, combing the thick coils of her distinctive "Birth of Venus" red hair.

Madeline would look and smile at him, an understanding would pass between them and Charles would hear and feel in his heart the resonant marriage of horn and piano of John Coltrane's "Peace on Earth."

There really hadn't been anyone since Maddie. No one significant, anyway. No one he could trust or who really interested him as a person. There was a colleague from another campus he had met at a conference and dated for a while and it looked like they might get married, but she did not especially like children and Jason never warmed to her. He slept with a few other women over the years. He and one of the single women in his building who worked for an airline had kicked it every now and then until she moved to Atlanta. And then when things got really bad with Jason, he couldn't bear to open himself up to anyone anymore.

How had he endured once Jason left behind the innocence of childhood—playing catch and Frisbee in Central Park, the YMCA basketball league, trips to Yankee Stadium and the natural history and art museums, science projects they worked on together, the hotdogs with ketchup, not mustard? How had he endured when at age thirteen Jason started coming home late from the homes of his private school classmates reeking of weed and stumbling from alcohol? Or when he got expelled from that school and then kicked out of the public middle school Charles had managed to enroll him in after he started selling weed supplied by one of his white prep school cronies? How had Charles endured a few years later when Jason began locking himself in the bathroom to smoke crack and hanging out with a group of local young men who had gotten the message that there was no other future for them except to sell escape and death to others in the community who had been let down and wounded the same way they were?

Why had Jason, who showed early talent as a visual artist, turned to drugs? Was he just born that way? Was it that fall from the monkey bars that lead to a concussion when he was seven? Was it his mother's long illness and death? The A.D.H.D. diagnosis that came shortly after it? Was it feeling different in the hood because he was Black and middle class and different in school because he was not white and rich? And when Jason left home seeking escape into any reality other than the one he had been born into, how had Charles endured the guilt of feeling that somehow it was his own trauma, fear, anger and loneliness that caused his son to flee?

Charles had kept himself busy. He devoted himself to the teaching--college skills and the writing classes. He took course overloads and taught six sections a semester. He was an anomaly among the tenured professors, harried adjuncts and arrogant white graduate students. He went in almost every day. He stayed up grading papers almost every night. And he ran six miles in the park every morning before taking the bus to campus.

It was not unusual for Charles to spend more than an hour on a single student essay. He made a life and living in the liminal space between his students' lives and language and the writing standards the university touted as their ticket to a new and better way of life. When he was not teaching, when he was not in class, pacing, cajoling, hectoring, or in the office grading papers or advising students, he went into a kind of sleep mode, like his new computer when the screen went black, but the power was still on. And that was good, because actually, he wasn't much of a sleeper.

A student raised her hand. Quintasia. Every time he read or said her name, Charles wondered what her mother had been thinking when she named her child. He pictured a young single girl bestowing on her baby the loveliest sounds she could imagine since she probably had little else to give her. He wondered if she knew that "quint" meant five and that "asia" was a land mass. It bothered him to think that despite the euphony of its syllables her mother didn't realize the burden a name like that might add to those of her baby's sex, race and class.

"Do you want us to quote from the essay, Professor Rivers?" she asked.

"Yes, if you find something she is saying that you'd like to respond to," he answered, hoping as he always did when he spoke to her that the other students would not hear the adrenaline in his voice.

"I mean if you need it to make your, ah, point." He was intrigued and yet frightened by her, and he wasn't sure why. It wasn't just her body, though her voluptuousness made him dizzy, as if there were actually five of her and she was the carnal fantasy that her name suggested. Like some prehistoric Venus, she was almost too much woman, the bosom, the hips, the thighs that stressed the seams of her knit skirt. She was large, but firm, heavy but much too shapely and well-proportioned to be described as fat. She was in her mid-twenties, he guessed, but there was a roundness to her Sugar Daddy brown face that made her appear younger, though not cherubic or sweet.

Quintasia. Maybe he was wrong about her name being a a burden. She seemed to have a high opinion of herself and she carried herself with confidence. She was certainly one of the smarter ones —that was clear. When she spoke to him, she managed to sound respectful and resentful at the same time. He wondered why when she asked a question, as any student might, he felt as if it were some sort of interrogation that instantly put him on the defensive. And why did his answer, no matter how basic, seem to count, at least in his mind, for so much?

Many years ago, he experienced similar feelings of intimidation *and* attraction in Maddie's Intro to Sociology class when she challenged a comment he made about Black women. Those feelings made sense in terms of the power dynamic. She was the professor, and he was the student. The roles were reversed here. What power did Quintasia hold over him? Why did he fear her questions but crave her attention? And why would she never fully meet his gaze?

He knew she worked in a bank. He tried to imagine her there, the badge on the collar of her blazer—Ms. Quintasia Williams—but the image was too surreal. He also knew she'd been enrolled in college before. Upstate. Alfred University. She announced that during the first class.

"I shouldn't even be taking this course. I already took freshman English, and I got an A. They messed up my transcript."

Now, satisfied with his response, she went back to the page. He noticed that she had lifted her heels out of her shoes to balance the open textbook on her lap. Her knees trembled slightly, and her heels quivered as though they had wings. She was so solid and yet so ephemeral. And in that moment, she seemed to embody what he longed for physically and what eluded him emotionally. He quickly turned his back to the class and scribbled the homework assignment on the board.

"Five hundred pages?" a student shouted out, exaggerated incredulity lacing his voice. The class tittered.

"No, of course not. I mean five hundred words." Charles turned to them and laughed along with them at his own expense. It released some of his tension.

At the end of class, he asked them to hand in what they had written. Quintasia made a big production of ripping the paper out of her notebook and tearing the jagged edge off the page. He found himself staring as she painstakingly pulled the strip of paper along the perforation. Another student, Carlos, asked if they could leave. Charles said, yes, and all of a sudden there was the commotion of standing and ripping and book packing and people asking where they should leave the papers. Charles said on the desk and don't forget to write your name and then the class was empty except for him and Quintasia who slowly and deliberately packed her bag in the same careful way she had torn the edge from the notebook page. Charles went behind the desk and started gathering up his things.

"You want to speak to me, don't you?" Charles was taken aback.

"Was there something on your mind?"

"No, professor. There's something on your mind." She sighed heavily, impatiently. "And you know, it's the same old thing. I guess it don't matter how smart or old a man is," she said, glancing with distaste at his four fingered hand. She buttoned her black leather coat. She tied the sash and pulled it tight so that it cinched her waist. He walked over to where she was standing.

"What is it?" He knew it was foolish to ask the question, but he felt helpless not to, compelled somehow to drive the conversation to whatever conclusion it might come to.

"Like you don't know. The way you always be looking at me."

"What way?"

"That way. You think I don't feel your eyes burning my clothes offa me?"

"You're very attractive." He said it without intending to.

"Well, I think you're very unprofessional and that maybe I should tell my girlfriend or maybe I should tell your boss."

"Your girlfriend?" His voice went weak.

"That's right. I *have* a wife. I'm not interested in no man, especially no *old man,* okay? And you better not try to hold it against me. You better give me a fair grade, or you know what I'm gonna do!"

She threw her bag over her shoulder, pushed aside a chair in her path, and marched towards the door. Her broad leather-covered butt moved up and down as she walked. Charles didn't want to notice, but he did. After she disappeared into the corridor, he stood motionless for a long time. He felt as if he'd just been gutted like some glassy-eyed fish, that she had ripped out his entrails as slowly and carefully as she had torn the jagged edge from the page of her composition, and that she had dragged them behind her out the door. After a minute or two, he recovered himself. He went back to the desk and shuffled the papers into a folder. His hands shook. He examined them as if they belonged to someone else, wondering if they were an old man's hands yet. He wanted to hide them somewhere. But his hands were not the culprits. His eyes were. Nothing like this had ever happened before. No student had ever spoken to him like that. Suddenly he was very, very angry—at Judy Brady and her essay about wanting a wife.

He shoved the papers into his attaché case. "Goodnight," Rosetta waved and smiled as she passed by the open door. He did not respond. He was silenced by his shame and loneliness and not just his inability to hide his desires but the embarrassment of having them. He feared that what he had said to Rosetta was inappropriate, too. He imagined the worst, word getting back to his Chair. But then he remembered who the Chair was. Probably *not* going to be a problem there, he decided and almost smiled. Bishop had a reputation.

When Charles got home, he did not switch on the hall light. He pushed the button on his ancient answering machine and stood in the dark listening to his messages. It would not have surprised him if there had been a threatening message from Quintasia's girlfriend or Rosetta's husband, "Stay away from my wife." But there were no such messages. "Hi, Mr. Rivers this is a reminder that you have an appointment with Dr. Rosenburg at ten a.m. tomorrow." Message two: "Dad. Are you there?" Then the message cut off and the machine spoke: "There are no more messages. Press one to save this message. Press two to replay this message." He stabbed at the keypad to replay the message. "Dad. Are you there?" He replayed it again trying to discern from the background noise where Jason might be. At least it wasn't a collect call from a jail or prison.

"Where? Where are you, Jason?" Charles sat down heavily on the couch, sinking into the worn cushions, and feeling the hard frame against the back of his calves. The room was dark but the glass coffee table in front of him was faintly illuminated by the streetlights and the bright windows across the boulevard. Charles kept crystal glasses and a decanter of scotch on the coffee table. And now he poured himself exactly two fingers of whiskey. The first sip seared his tongue, and as he continued to sip he began to feel warm in that hollow space inside. Once he drained the glass, a calmness came over him and restored him to a state of equilibrium that had more to do with the ritual of imbibing than the actual amount of alcohol he consumed. He closed his eyes and leaned his head against the cushions, pushing away thoughts of Jason, Quintasia, and Rosetta Ocean. If he could maintain this stillness, this blankness, he would be able to get through another night.

| 24 |

ROSETTA OCEAN, MARCH 2000

She knew she would never forget the acrid smell of the paper hospital gowns. They were bright blue, an unnatural shade like the aqueous uber-indigo of concentrated laundry detergent. The gowns reeked of chemicals, or maybe their odor was intensified by each woman's scent of fear, as naked under the thin gown tied with a skinny plastic sash, she slowly moved through a series of connected waiting rooms by taking the vacated seat of the woman ahead of her. There was no clock on the wall to measure the waiting time. There was no TV hanging from an awkward mounting arm in the corner of the room. Planned Parenthood was clearly under-funded; the most recent magazines were over a year old. To say that time stood still and that the expressions of the unwilling and unwittingly pregnant women, who seemed to range in age from 15 to 45, were grim, was the grossest of understatements. Grimmest of all was that of the mother of the youngest girl. Dressed in a cheap business suit and fake oversized pearls, she seemed concerned about taking the time off from work to accompany her daughter. She glanced at her watch repeatedly, and craned her neck to check on the progress of the queue, her face rigid with a kind of granite discipline one imagined she hoped her daughter would learn one day. The girl cried quietly into her hands after a loud petulant outburst in the counseling room during which she had threatened to run away.

Rosetta could not stop smelling that odor; she couldn't stop looking around her. And she couldn't stop looking down at her wedding ring, noticing how the dull gold contrasted with the warm molasses color of her skin. How many of the other women were married? She looked surreptitiously to her left and right at the hands of the women closest to her. This was something you did when you were single. Or at least before you were ready to welcome a first child. She was already a mother. Twice. She adored her children. But they had been planned. They had arrived according to a schedule and exactly three years apart when Will was still doing well in his job as manager in the office supply company.

Rosetta sat in the last row closest to the door. Will was in the main waiting room. What was going through his mind? He had not seen the enlarged image of the embryo on the ultrasound screen or heard the strong, steady amplified beating of its developing heart.

She wondered if it was a girl. She would have named a girl Eleanor after her mother who died of an asthma attack when Rosetta was seven. Eleanor was not a popular name. But for Rosetta, Eleanor was all that was left of her mother. Eleanor was snuggling together to try to stay warm in the big lumpy bed with the skimpy covers in their draughty railroad apartment; Eleanor was the heavy scent of cooking grease that clung to her mother's clothes from her work as a waitress; Eleanor was the way her mother pronounced her name with emphasis on the Rose—*Rose* Etta and how she placed a glop of green hair pomade on her left wrist to dip into and oil Rosetta's scalp as she parted and tugged on her hair with a wide toothed comb. Eleanor was lukewarm baths together in the yellowed pitted claw-footed bathtub because hot water was scarce, and a scratchy washcloth rubbed across her back until her skin tingled. Eleanor was watery white hominy grits just the way Rosetta liked them, sprinkled with two teaspoons of sugar, a streaming, melting margarine sun in the center. Eleanor was standing on tippy toes to kiss her mother goodbye in the schoolyard because Eleanor was so tall. Eleanor was the day her mother didn't pick her up from school. Eleanor was not talking or laughing or playing for almost a year. Eleanor was a book she read in 7th grade about the former first lady Eleanor Roosevelt and how she helped poor people and wrote a declaration of human rights. Eleanor was the way her mother Eleanor Ocean and Eleanor Roosevelt became one person in her mind, and the way that person had come to embody love and all the qualities Rosetta associated with motherhood and caring about the fates of others and being a humanitarian woman of justice.

Eleanor. What was she doing? You did not name a child you were about to abort. And you especially didn't name it after your dead mother. She had been afraid to say it, but now she said that word out loud in her mind. *Abortion.* It was an ugly word. Such an ugly, ugly word. Even uttered silently it was a sharp knife scraping the back of her throat. When she was struggling to decide what to do about the pregnancy, she forced herself to look up the definition—the way she urged her students to look up words they assumed they knew in order to discover new meanings that might help them in their writing. The Latin past participle aborri meant to make disappear, which made her think of the whispered euphemism she had heard while growing up—"She got rid of it." And now in her mind she made the dangerous experiment of applying that phrase to herself, holding her breath to see if it would make her change her mind. But the guilt and sadness it quickened were not enough to dissuade her now that she had made up her mind, or to question her or any other woman's right to make that choice. If she wasn't willing to go through with it, she wouldn't have come this far. Now she would make the pregnancy disappear; she would get rid of it, and then she would go on as if it had never happened.

"Excuse me," Rosetta looked up. A lanky white girl with a hapless expression and asymmetrically chopped blond hair was trying to get past her. She was boyish and unattractive, and Rosetta wondered unkindly who had knocked her up.

"Trying to get a magazine," she said. She had a flat midwestern accent and large crooked teeth vying for limited space in her mouth. The table with the magazines was near the door. Rosetta sat in the middle of the row. She pressed her thighs together and swiveled them to the side. The girl squeezed past hers and three other pairs of knees that were barely covered by their paper gowns. Rosetta needed something to occupy her mind, but she had not thought to bring a book and when she glanced at the magazine table as she entered the room, nothing had caught her eye.

The girl's teeth made her think about the dentist, and she remembered the magazine she used to read in the dentist's office —*Highlights for Children*. The covers were all the same. Plain and nearly monochromatic, so dull you'd think the magazine had to be boring. But she became so enthralled by the puzzles and stories inside that she'd forget where she was, and she would be startled when it was her turn to enter the treatment room and climb into the dentist's big chair. Did they still publish it? Maybe she could get a subscription for the boys. She thought about her old dentist. Dr. Brown. And his first name: Oral—like Oral Roberts, but a dentist! She and her cousins, whom she had gone to live with after her mother's death, had found that hilarious and instead of Brown, they referred to him as Dr.

Oral. She'd heard from friends at school that dentists could give you laughing gas, but Dr. Oral never offered it. She was a teenager before she was given anesthetics for dental procedures. She always had a high threshold for physical pain. Maybe that was one of the reasons she was so gung-ho about natural childbirth and why she had chosen local and not general anesthesia for what was happening today.

Emotional pain was something else. She was not sure how much more of it she could take before the aquifer of daily sadness spilled over and drowned all the happiness she ever expected to experience in her married life. She pictured Will reading the copy of the Daily News he'd bought on the way there, and for a split second she replayed the tape of his reaction when she told him she was pregnant.

"We can't have another baby. We can't afford it. You can't stop working. And my unemployment is about to run out. I can't ask my parents for any more money."

Can't, can't, can't. She would have been willing if Will had been. She went for a week or two thinking that they would go through with it, and she was happy about it. They would work it out. People always did. But then Will got a bad migraine. He was in bed for two days. She had to keep the lights dim and the boys extra quiet and spoon-feed him like an infant. She realized she was in no position to take care of three children and a sick husband. She was sorry she had told some people, including that guy at work, Charles Rivers. Why did she tell him? It was a moment of weakness. Now when she saw him again, she would have to explain.

CHAPTER

THREE

CHARLES

Charles eyed the stack of papers he needed to read before his evening class with customary apprehension. He was not looking forward to their responses to the questions at the end of the Judy Brady essay. He picked up the first one—Keisha Brown's. The too skinny girl with the pockmarked cheeks who looked a little like Mary Wilson from the Supremes because she wore her hair in sort of a throwback version of a bouffant. It was an odd anachronistic combination with her big hoop earrings, skinny stonewashed jeans and close-fitting tee shirts. In the beginning of the semester, he had them read "Theme for English B" by Langston Hughes and had them write a page, well two pages, that "come out of you." She wrote about living in homeless shelters with the five-year-old daughter she gave birth to when she was fourteen. Later in the semester she brought the little girl, who had a very bad case of eczema, with her to her student conference.

"And who is this lovely little lady?" Charles asked.

"Why you gone be all shy now? Tell him your name."

"Bianca," the little girl said softly in a husky voice.

"That's the name of a character in a very famous play by William Shakespeare. Did you know that? She was a beautiful and gentle girl." He smiled and the little girl stared at him as though she couldn't make out the meaning of his facial expression.

"Well, that don't describe you, do it? Because you don't know how to stay out of trouble." Bianca looked down at her feet. She wore miss-matched socks and worn pink sneakers with no laces.

"What kind of trouble?"

"She always be fightin. I mean, she get into fights."

"At school?" Bianca nodded almost imperceptibly.

"What grade are you in?"

"Kinnygarden," Bianca whispered after a long pause.

"Why are you fighting?"

"Dey be callin me snakeskin and pee-pee the homeless girl." She uttered the words very quietly but there was no plea in her voice. These were just the ordinary facts of her life. Charles was not sure how to respond.

"Children can be very cruel," he said, the relentless teasing he had undergone as a child in the back of his mind. She gave him another uncomprehending stare. It made him do a quick mental assay of the definitions of the words he had used in the sentence.

Keisha's response began like this: "You might find this hard to believe, but I can't think about what qualities a wife would have because I don't know anybody who is a wife. I seen wives on TV, but I have sense enough to know that they are not real." Charles made a squiggle under the words "I seen."

"The females I know are their own wives. They do for themselves. Like I do."

Charles pushed the papers aside. He decided to get a cup of coffee on the lower level of the building. Striding into the corridor, he passed the English Department office and he waved to Yolanda, the secretary, and saw Bishop, the Chair, ushering a young woman into a side office. Charles took the escalator on the east side of the building where a huge vertical window formed the outer wall of the academic center. As the escalator slowly descended he thought about Keisha's response to the question. He thought about his mother who had been a wife, but of an abusive husband, his father, and how she had to do for herself and everybody else including the white people she worked for even before his father died. Now she was in a nursing home with dementia but the years of constantly working and putting the needs of others before her own had left their mark on her. Often when Charles visited her after only a few minutes, she'd say, "Go on, now. I got work to do," and she'd keep repeating it until he left.

When Charles arrived at the lower level, he stepped off the slow-moving stair into the hectic eddies of students and faculty converging on the food court. He strode past the long line for the sandwich counter, realizing when he reached the coffee urns at the other side that the "student" on the deli queue wearing a fat navy-blue backpack was actually Rosetta Ocean. He glanced back but she was ordering and had her back to him. He felt a pang of embarrassment and regret for what he'd said to her in the mailroom the week before and for not responding when she had waved goodbye. He thought about what he could say to make up for those things as he filled his paper cup with murky brown liquid, pushed the stainless-steel bar that released a bluish stream of skim milk from the plastic teat of the milk machine and mashed a plastic cover over the mouth of the cup. He stepped out of the way of a student behind him, and coffee in hand, he went to stand near the bank of cashiers waiting for the chance to speak to Rosetta.

"Eating for two?" he asked, smiling as she approached. She was carefully balancing a sandwich wrapped in thick waxed paper and a bottle of apple juice lying on its side on her tray. She looked up, startled.

"Professor Rivers." The way she said his name sounded more like an observation than a greeting.

"Are you having that here? I'm taking a break from correcting papers. Can I sit with you?" She nodded but she didn't smile. He missed her smile and realized that all that thinking about what to say or not say was really about how to elicit it.

In the stadium sized room teaming with students at long tables, they were lucky to find a table for two against the back wall across from the large windows that looked out on the fortress-like walls and brick pathways of the academic center. One of the chrome-legged chairs was rickety and broken. Charles sat on that one.

"You ever eat in the faculty dining room?"

"Too stuffy and too expensive. And let's face it. I'm not really faculty. Just an adjunct." Her mood was strange. He'd never seen her so somber. He wanted to ask her what was wrong, but he sipped his bitter coffee instead. He was happy just to be with her. She took a bite of her sandwich. Her lips were full, but her mouth was not wide. The sandwich was large. It was a bit of a struggle. She wiped her mouth with a napkin afterwards, chewed and swallowed, "I'm not eating for two."

"I didn't mean to—a"

"No, I mean, I couldn't do it. I couldn't go through with it. My younger one just started kindergarten, and my husband..."

"I'm sorry."

"It's okay. Life's tough," she said, and then she smiled. For a moment he feasted on that small smile—took a big bite of it as if it were a chocolate chunk cookie and let the sweetness he craved from it melt on his tongue. "It was terrible, terrible," she said, "the worst, the hardest thing I ever had to do." He watched her remember. Her eyes clouded up. Her face contorted. He had enough sense not to tell her that she didn't have to do it because that was what he instantly believed, but he did not want to lose his connection with her—to respond with reproach to what she had confided would be the end of it. And who was he to advise or judge her? He did not know the first thing about the truth of her life. Every semester his students wrote tired arguments on both sides. He had heard them all. He believed it was a matter of personal choice. He was not too old or too sexist to believe otherwise. For years, he forbade the topic, and then he relented. It was an issue always in the public consciousness, especially as the political climate and rhetoric in the country became more conservative; the students had to come to terms with it at one point or another, he reasoned. There was no use ignoring it, but he tried to get them to focus on and analyze the language of the debate: murder, right to life, pro-choice, pro-life. Still, he was sensitive about it because he did not want any of his students to be traumatized in class. Every semester or so some young woman would come to his office in tears, attributing her absences and lack of concentration to the trauma of an unplanned pregnancy. At first, he was astonished that they would actually come and tell him—that they would confide in him as Rosetta had confided now.

But unlike Rosetta, they were usually very young, single, poor, and without resources. She was married, after all, and then he wondered what was wrong with her husband. She seemed so sweet, generous and motherly. There must be something really off with him or the marriage he decided, and that made the fissure that had opened in his estimation of her character repair itself a little. But Charles was at a point in his life when he could see or thought he could see the end, and what he longed to do now was make more life, not destroy it. This woman had destroyed it. And he knew something about destroying life. He also knew how hard it was to sustain it. He felt angry at Rosetta and sad for himself because his image of her had been altered and this glimpse into the complexity of her situation would make it difficult for him to fantasize about her and romanticize who she was.

Why did you tell me this? He wanted to demand angrily, but he saw that she was suffering and that she had asked herself the same question. He said instead, "Sometimes we have to make hard choices." She looked at him gratefully, eyes brimming and luminous in that way he'd come to recognize. He patted her hand awkwardly and was somewhat disturbed to feel a sexual spark the instant their hands touched because in that moment he was only trying to comfort her. She excused herself without finishing her sandwich, and he sat for a while thinking about what just happened.

He rode the elevator instead of the escalator back to his office on the fifth floor. There was less chance of running into a student or colleague that way. When he first got his faculty office, soon after the "riot-proof" building was finished in the wake of student protests, he'd considered it a coup. Now he thought of the windowless cubicle as a kind of tomb, but one from which he would luckily escape alive because of the university's retirement plan. The tiny office was filled with the clutter and detritus of years of teaching: rows of textbooks on metal bookshelves in no logical order, stacks of old papers students never claimed, a picture of Jason graduating from 6th grade wearing a garish blue cap and gown, the pointing finger poster of Malcolm X high on the wall behind the desk, just barely hanging by one cracked loop of masking tape. He sat down again at the big metal desk and picked up the next paper in the pile. Carlos Mejia's. His thoughts turned to Jason because there was something about Carlos's restlessness and idealistic impatience with everything that reminded him of his son.

Except for the unfinished message Jason left on his answering machine last week, Charles had not heard from him in months. He didn't know where he was. Whether he was incarcerated or free. Alive or dead. He couldn't be dead, he decided. He had left that message. But maybe he left the message because he was in trouble. And maybe that trouble had led to his death.

Charles remembered taking Jason to *The Treasures of King Tutankhamen* at the Metropolitan Museum of Art and how fascinated Jason was with the mummies and the idea that they were buried with all the things they would need in the next world. What did Jason take with him when he descended to his other worlds? Was he equipped with *anything* that would help him survive?

"You can't blame yourself for everything that happens to your kids. They live in the world." A school principal had once said that to Charles when it was discovered that Jason was selling weed to classmates at school. That was true, but Charles blamed himself *and* the world. He should have been able to equip Jason better. He should have outfitted him more extensively, the way they should have better equipped Charles and his platoon when they went to war. He should have given Jason more armor, made him tougher, more of a man, someone who could endure and not try to escape from pain, especially since he had lost his mother when he was so young.

But how do you do that? How does a Black parent do that without totally traumatizing the child and sending the message that he is not safe or even welcome in the world? How when you feel unsafe and unwelcome are you able to cope with more than just your physical and psychological survival? How can you be expected to claim your place in a world that denies your existence or that allows you to live only if you kill parts of yourself that make you who you are? Isn't it easier to just anesthetize yourself, chill out, check out, or take risks with the life no one values anyway?

If Jason were dead, Charles would know it, wouldn't he? He'd feel it somewhere inside or there would be a sign. Some sort of sign. Right? *Wrong.* He didn't believe in that foolishness—in omens and signs. Unlike many of his ancestors and Black contemporaries he had not been raised up in the church. He had seen how superstitions held people back. His father died because he had an irrational fear of hospitals. He saw them as places where people went to die, not to get treatment that might keep them alive. Charles put his faith in common sense, in things that could be verified and proven. His mother, who wouldn't set foot in a church, was ruled by superstitions.

If you dropped a knife a man was coming to visit. If you put your purse on the floor you would lose all your money. If a bird flew into the house, or you laid a broom on the bed, or washed clothes on New Year's Day, someone in the family would die. Some unfortunate coincidences had probably led people to believe those things, but metonymy was not destiny and correlation was not causation. That was something Charles always tried to get his students to understand.

Once, years ago, he opened the door to his office and found a starling strutting on his desk. It must have flown in through the vents in the ceiling. The bird appeared to be black but close inspection of its feathers showed them to be as iridescent and rich with color as a peacock's. Charles expected the bird to fly away frantically when he came close, crashing into the walls like

Sky Budgie, Jason's blue pet parakeet that had regularly escaped from its wire cage when Jason tried to feed it. But the starling just continued to lift one wrinkled, skinny, orange, four-toed foot after the other as it trod across the papers on his desk. Charles had gone off to find a maintenance person to open the vent and somehow free the bird, but when they came back with a ladder the bird had vanished as mysteriously as it appeared. Madeline was already dead, and subsequently, no one else had died. The bird did not even defecate on his desk. If anything, its appearance was a boon rather than a portent of misfortune because Charles had been astonished by the extraordinary beauty of an ordinary black bird.

Somehow Charles got through Carlos's paper and then the rest of them despite his lack of concentration. He dreaded going to class; he was afraid of what would happen if he looked at or didn't look at Quintasia. But as soon as he walked into the room, he saw she wasn't there. For a split second he felt relief, followed by worry, but then he looked at the class, saw their expectant faces and recovered his purpose.

"How were the papers, Professor Rivers?" a skinny Asian kid named Sheldon asked.

"Terrible," Charles only half joked. The students laughed and groaned.

"Alison, have you ever met a comma you didn't like?" Alison, a white girl in her twenties with dyed black hair and blue tattoos, grinned.

"They're cute," she said. "Like little curvy periods."

"Yeah, but they're not periods. They are not, what we call, end punctuation." Alison shrugged as if to say, why should anything end?

"Mr. Rivers, can you explain why they call periods full-stops in Jamaica?" Obadiah, a car mechanic in his forties, asked.

"It's the British influence."

"In Hong Kong, too," Sheldon said.

Charles started passing back the papers. The students craned their necks and reached out eagerly.

"Okay, so if there's a squiggle under the sentence or some part of it that means something was not working there," he said. "I want everybody to choose one of those sentences to put in the sentence hospital on the board. Just go up and write it on the board." He reached into his black attaché case and brought out a box of chalk that he had bought himself because there was never any in the classroom. "Here's the chalk."

JASON RIVERS, SEPTEMBER 1993

His father tried to save him many times. One was that Outward-Bound trip to the Arizona desert for troubled teens when he was thirteen. Who knew nights in the desert could be so cold? When he thought desert, he thought hot. He remembered the first night they were in their sleeping bags, lying in a circle like the spokes of a bicycle wheel, their feet pointing towards the charred remains and chalky ash of a campfire. On Jason's right, there was the milk white boy with the potty mouth from Minnesota. On the left, the Mexican kid from L.A. who claimed to be the leader of a gang. Peanut butter from their shitty excuse for a dinner was still stuck between

Jason's molars, and his tongue repeatedly performed a failed excavation mission to get it out. Someone kept farting. Probably that fat kid from Ohio with the wrong kind of hiking boots. Someone else started a fart countdown--5, 4, 3, 2, 1 and made a joke about blasting off into space. Jason wondered what it would be like to actually blast off into space—if it got you high. The ground was fucking hard as concrete, and a layer of goose feathers stitched into nylon fabric wasn't going to change that. The sky was like a ginormous planetarium curving around them so that they could see and feel that the earth really was Christopher the fuck Columbus round. Jason kept having olfactory weed hallucinations; he was not lying with rocks in his back in the parched Arizona desert but sitting on a stoop on in his neighborhood smoking a blunt and chillin with his niggas. The kids where he lived in Harlem used to make fun of him because he talked white and went to a private school, but in 8th grade he became cool because he always had money and he always had weed. In spite of the cold and the rocks he started drifting off to sleep on the soft cloud of his imagination and soon his mother's face appeared —the vision that came to him every night just before his eyes closed. *Mommy.* When he was little, they played a game as she bent over him to kiss him goodnight; he'd tap her cheeks with his index finger pretending to count her freckles. She'd surprise him during the count by turning her head and pretending to nibble on his fingers. Then she would hug him long and tight and plant a big kiss in the middle of his forehead. Right before she died, he promised that he would be a good boy. But he was small, and he didn't understand that he was saying good-bye for the last time and besides what kind of promise was that? It depended on your definition of good. And that was bound to change. He guessed that being forced to go to the desert with other kids who were supposedly fucking up, wishing that the taste in his mouth was from a Reese's Peanut Butter Cup and not some dry ass sandwich, meant that he had not kept his promise.

But still he didn't understand why he had to go away just because he smoked weed. The parents who sent their kids there were a bunch of hypocrites! Like they had never smoked. Like they could cop some lame Clinton plea that they didn't inhale. Like they didn't drink. Like they enjoyed doing homework and like they wouldn't have played video games 24/7 if they had been invented back in the day. He knew for a fact that his parents smoked before he was born. And his dad poured himself a glass of scotch every night. And okay, his parents probably did like homework. They were both professors, but that didn't mean he was supposed to go that route too. The trip to the desert was supposed to teach him a lesson. Make him tough. Like being in the army had toughened up his dad. Not. His dad tried to act tough. But the man whimpered like a puppy in his sleep every night. And it wasn't just about his mom. That war shit makes you mad crazy. He, Jason, a "troubled teen" knew enough to know that blowing up people don't make you a man. His father had to have things a certain way and would lose it if something was out of place or messed up his routine. Once when Jason was little and he spilled his milk at the table, his father jerked the chair from under him and he landed hard on his butt on the floor. His mom rushed to pick him up and told his father that if he ever did that again, she would leave him. After that when he got angry he would go in his office and knock all the books off of the bookshelves. And then the next day he would put them all back.

In Jason's opinion people just needed to chill. To just shut up, calm down and smoke some chronic. And he was not going to put up with that bullshit private school anymore. What could they really teach him? Like he wanted to go to Harvard or Princeton and be a super wuss. Like tagging was some kind of capital offense. And that look on his father's face when he came into the police station that night and he, Jason, was sitting there next to his friend Nathan, and Nathan's white mother was reeking of alcohol and blubbering to the bored look-ing cop that her son was a good boy. His father looked like he, Jason, had dropped an atomic bomb on Harlem or something. But to the cops he tried to present himself like a dignified professor and shit. And the whole time those pigs were probably thinking *who does this nigger think he is*—talking like a dictionary. Even the Black ones. And that's what made him, Jason, feel bad about the whole thing. Not what he did, tagging that subway station was fun, but that they dismissed his pops like that and like it was just the same old shit, but a different day and they were just your everyday common niggers. He wanted them to know that his father didn't approve and that it wasn't his fault and that his dad was one of those people who was trying to make a difference, except that nothing really makes a difference unless you have a lot of money and you're white.

CHARLES, SEPTEMBER 2001

He opened the door without asking who it was because he knew when the doorbell rang late at night it could be Jason. He did not know what shape Jason would be in. How he would look. What he would smell like, whether he would be alone or with some broken down girl or woman. He always opened the door. And no matter what condition Jason was in, his heart always surged with the same emotions—insane unquestioning love and intense unquenchable guilt, anger, and fear. Fear that he would let him in. Fear that he would slam the door. Fear that the cycle would never end.

He was taken aback when it was not Jason but Keisha from his spring writing class with her daughter, Bianca.

"Professor?"

"Miss—"

"It's just me, Keisha from your English class. Last semester. Remember me?" She gave him a plaintive look. Then she quickly looked down at the floor.

"Oh, Keisha. What a, what a...surprise. What can I do for you?"

"Can we come in?" She said to the floor.

"In, oh, yes, please, come in." He stepped back and Keisha, who was all of five feet tall and less than a hundred pounds, rushed in with a large woven laundry bag and the little girl, who was chubby and almost as tall as she was. The girl looked sleepy and confused. She was wearing pajama pants under a dirty red coat and her pink sneakers didn't have shoelaces. It was September and still warm. Why was she wearing a coat?

"It's pretty cool in here," Keisha said, approvingly.

"Where are you coming from so late?"

"We was in a shelter, but we had to leave. I mean, I had to get my baby girl out of there, you know, because it was like a riot, people started fightin and shit cause they accused this one woman of stealing something and before the guards could stop her she just went crazy and started pulling people out they beds claiming they was hidin something."

Charles looked at Bianca. She wore the impassive expression of a child who had retreated from a reality that was constantly betraying her, but her eyes were alive with what looked like fear and a kind of wonder as her mother recounted the story.

"I got real scared because somebody started shootin. They ain't, I mean, they not supposed to have no guns in there," Keisha shivered. Charles tested the probable truth of this story against the calculus of doubt he developed dealing with Jason.

"How did you know where I live?"

"You told us in class. You *in* the phone book."

In the phone book, yes, he thought, so why didn't you call.

"We don't have no place else to go," she said quietly. "We couldn't go back to where we was stayin before, and I thought you might be looking for somebody. You know. A woman."

She raised her head and looked him full in the face then. The bare light bulb in the hallway ceiling illuminated cruel pitted acne scars on Keisha's cheeks and when he recognized a certain look in her eyes the floor seemed to quake beneath him.

"Looking for a woman?"

"Well, Quintasia--"

"Quintasia? What does this have to do with Quintasia?"

"She said you horny and the reason why you made us read that essay by Judy was because you want—"

"She told you what?"

"She said it in class before you got there. And a lot of people laughed but not me."

Embarrassment lit up Charles' insides and twisted his tongue into a coil of speechless filaments. He wanted to shove Keisha out of the doorway and slam the door in her face.

"I'm not—isn't there somewhere else you can go?"

Keisha looked down at the ground, assuming again a demure and innocent expression.

"No."

KEISHA BROWN, NOVEMBER 1995

Bianca wouldn't stop crying. Everyone was looking. Keisha was on the Uptown 2 platform at 42nd St.

"Damn girl, can't you shut that baby up," someone said behind her. She was coming back from taking Bianca to see Aunt Shirley in Brooklyn. The platform was crowded. A girl and a boy about Keisha's age were making out against one of the poles. The boy's hands were deep inside the girl's puffy jacket.

"Y'all better stop for you get yourself one of those." Keisha wheeled around to see who was speaking. A homeless man with matted hair and an armful of newspapers grinned back at her. The couple ignored him.

"Mind your business," she said.

"This is my business cause you in my home." He grinned again. He took a step towards her. She raised her hand to ward him off. He shrank back. "I ain't gonna touch her. Don't be getting all salty. Them lungs of hers, now that's a weapon."

Bianca was so heavy—four months old and eighteen pounds. She ate too much. She was always hungry.

"That one big baby. She huge," Aunt Shirley said. "Who's the daddy? The Incredible Hulk?" Shirley laughed at her own joke, and that upfront gold tooth of hers that Keisha always hated gleamed. Keisha felt herself retreating, going back to the place inside where she usually stayed unless she had cause to venture out. She wondered why she had brought the baby to see Shirley. She should have known there would be no warm welcome or tenderness there. Shirley was not her kin. She wasn't someone who loved her and could love her baby. There wasn't anybody like that. She was just one in a succession of foster mothers Keisha had lived with since she was eight and the last one before they sent her to the group home.

The diaper bag was heavy too, and it hurt her neck. The nurse at the clinic tried to get her to keep breastfeeding. But she was scared. Bianca was so greedy. *It's better for the baby.* But Keisha was afraid because Bianca was always sucking. She was afraid the baby would eat her up. She weighed less than a hundred pounds herself. She knew it was bad to be that hungry because you were never going to get enough.

She was eleven when she went to live with Shirley. And the reason why it felt like family and maybe the reason why she had gone there today was because there were two other girls. Carmen, another foster child who was half-Puerto Rican, and Jessica, who was Shirley's real niece. She remembered how Carmen taught them Spanish curses and how once when Shirley wasn't home she suggested that they take their clothes off and get in bed together to practice kissing. Carmen was fourteen and she was warm and soft. Keisha found out later that men have different bodies. A grandmother lady came up to her speaking Spanish.

The lady's eyes were sweet. She was not a *puta.* She chattered away as though she didn't realize that Keisha didn't understand her.

"She won't stop crying," Keisha said.

"Hungry?" The woman asked in English.

"She always hungry."

But the milk was gone. Keisha showed the woman the empty bottle. Bianca wailed. Keisha shifted the weight from one foot to another. The train did not come. The woman put the pacifier pinned to the fabric of the baby carrier into Bianca's mouth. The pacifier fell from her mouth and dangled from the string. The ululation contin-ued. The woman shuffled off with an embarrassed smile that didn't hide the discomfort around her heart. People leaned over the tracks and looked anxiously for the train.

"Somebody need to shut that baby up," Keisha heard some woman say behind her. She looked across at the downtown side and it seemed as though everyone, even across the tracks was staring her down wishing she would disappear. She wanted to disappear. She wanted to throw Bianca onto the tracks or stuff her into the trash.

"That's what happens when babies be having babies," the woman said.

CHARLES

Charles hung Bianca's coat on one of the plethora of wire dry cleaner's hangers in the closet by the door. He took them into Jason's room.

"Just for tonight," he said. But his words seemed a weak protest against the huge red, white and blue woven bag that Keisha dragged in behind them, stuffed, it would appear, with all their earthly possessions. The room was a small rectangle, facing the air shaft between the two sides of the six-story pre-war building. It was a young boy's bedroom, straight out of the fifties, arrested at a stage before adolescence, with a twin bed, a battered maple dresser and matching desk and chair, the seat bleached and worn smooth. There was also a bedside table with a cowboy on a horse lamp that hadn't worked or been plugged in for years. Madeline had found the furniture in mint condition at the Salvation Army on 8th Avenue when Jason was three or four. The lighting panel and several of Jason's unframed Basquiat-esque abstract drawings were tacked to the walls, the edges yellowed and curled, along with class photographs in frames, another photo of Jason at age nine standing on a basketball court next to Wilt Chamberlain and coming up to his knees, and a picture of Madeline pushing Jason on a swing near the Lenox Avenue playground in Central Park, the coils of her hair flying behind her as she shoved the swing. The room was hot and close. Charles saw Keisha eyeing the small air conditioner wedged precariously and at an angle between the top of an old-fashioned sash window and the paint encrusted sill, cardboard taped to the sides as a seal. The landlord was supposed to replace the windows in all of the apartments, but he was taking his own sweet time with Charles since he was one of the rent-stabilized tenants who had not been bought off or run off so the apartment could be renovated and the rent quadrupled.

"Do the air-conditioner work?" Charles looked at Keisha and frowned. But he switched it on anyway. Hot air smelling of mildew and soot came through the vents as the machine noisily began to function. Charles couldn't remember the last time it had been used. But the fight he had with Jason one night when he had tried to carry it out of the apartment and sell it to get drugs was still fresh in his mind.

"Let me get some sheets," Charles said.

"This your son's room," Keisha said.

"You know my son?" Charles asked, on guard because Jason had brought all kinds of people into the apartment over the years.

"You got his picture in your office."

Charles went to another closet in the long hallway to look for sheets for Jason's bed. He was not exactly sure where the cleaning woman, Maria, who used to come once a month, put them. He was careful not to disturb the items on the top shelf for among them was the silver revolver in its hard-locked plastic case that he had confiscated from Jason the last time he had been home. The sheets were on the middle shelf, neatly folded and stacked. When he came back to the room, Bianca was sitting on the floor next to the bedside table sucking her thumb and stroking the blacked chipped mane of the lamp cowboy's pony. Keisha was studying the pictures on the wall.

"He a artist?"

"He wanted to be."

Charles pulled the comforter and the old sheets off the bed. It had been a long while since Jason had actually slept in it. The last times he came home, he ended up crashing on the couch in the living room.

"She died right?"

"Who?"

"Your wife."

"A long time ago." Keisha grabbed the sheets from him. They had a musty smell and pictures of G.I. Joe on them.

"They old," she said, but she quickly pulled the almost threadbare fitted one over the sagging mattress and neatly spread the top sheet over it. It was a simple act, but her competence startled Charles and for an instant he saw someone other than the hesitant and distant student he remembered from his class who could never seem to write more than a paragraph. She folded the corners hospital style and once she had finished, she stepped away from the bed and looked up at him. "That's how they made us do it at Stoddard. You know, the group home." Charles nodded feeling uneasy, recalling Jason's failure to learn any such lessons during his stays at various drug programs and treatment centers. They had tried to teach him the "life skills" he would need to function, but he was too preoccupied by his retreat from life to pay any attention.

Charles woke earlier than usual on the morning after Keisha showed up at his door because when he rolled from left to right, flinging his left arm across the width of the bed, the way he usually did in that final hour before daybreak, he felt something occupying the space. "What?" He jerked up, fumbled with the lamp switch and half-expected to see Jason. Then he remembered and recognized Keisha as the light came on. She was drawn up in a fetal position —her knees nearly touching her chin, her spine a fretted half-moon, the blanket below her waist and between her knees. She was naked, except for dingy skimpy underpants. Above the elastic on the small of her back she had a tattoo of her first name in black ink and curlicued letters. He backed out of the bed, testing for the floor behind him, caught between an immediate loathing and an attraction/

fascination that made him hold his breath. Though she had borne a child, she still had the body of one, at least in terms of its size. He couldn't see her breasts, but the curve of her hips was slight. Her shoulders, thin and narrow, seemed to rattle with she breathed. There was a patch of soft black nappy hair at the nape of her neck under the stiff helmet of her perm. His impulse was to stroke it. Instead, he thrust his hand behind his back, and she woke up suddenly, as if he'd actually touched her, and sat bolt upright in bed.

"No, no, no don't you touch me. You better not touch me. I'ma tell. I'ma tell your mama..." Charles was taken aback at first. But he realized she wasn't really awake. She did not see him and was not speaking to him, but to some threatening presence in her dream. Where was the little girl? He listened for her breathing in the next room. But he couldn't hear it over the laboring exhalations of the air conditioner. He did not know what to do. If he attempted to wake her up and calm her down, he would have to acknowledge to himself that not only had a former student insinuated herself into his apartment, she had also actually crept into his bed. And what was he supposed to say to her? Everything is alright? Go back to sleep? She started breathing quickly and then she was flailing and screaming as if actually fighting off an attacker. He grabbed her arms.

"Miss Brown, you're having a bad dream. Please wake up."

"Get offa me!" She yelled, striking Charles with the back of her hand.

"Miss Brown!" She stopped flailing and opened her eyes. It took a few seconds for her to get her bearings.

"Professor Rivers? Where I'm at?"

"In my bed."

"How'd I get in your bed?"

"I don't know. That's what I wanted to ask you."

She looked down at her nearly naked body and glanced up at him. He shook his head. It was a scene that would have signaled a comic turn in a movie. But the moment was serious, as they both, in their own way, paid homage to the subconscious motivation that might have brought her there.

"Where Bianca?"

"In my son's room."

"Lie down with me," she whimpered. When he heard the neediness in her voice, Charles felt the hairs stand up on the back of his neck. He looked at his wrist to check his watch, as if he'd find an escape from her there, but he hadn't put it on yet.

"I'm about to go for a run," he said in a plaintive voice that almost matched hers. He was a creature of habit. He had his routines. Matters with Jason had disrupted that somewhat, but they could not alter his essential nature, his means of survival. Doing the same things, and in the same way, made him feel that everything was under control, that his life was significant, and that he was, strangely enough, actually alive.

Running was chief among those things. In the morning it was always the same. He got out of bed, peed, put on his running shorts, laced up his shoes and was out the door. He did not wait for the stinking urinal of an elevator; he could run down the worn marble stairs twice as fast as it could rise and then carry him back down. Often the routine included running around or jumping over the bodies of drunks and drug-addicts that populated the neighborhood who sometimes found their way inside the building and fell asleep or nodded out on the landings. Running was what kept him from ending up with them. Running was what kept him from thinking about how Jason was probably lying in some hallway somewhere just like them.

But now Keisha reached out and grabbed him by the wrist, pulling him back to the bed with the strength of a demon girl. Earlier he had been aroused, but dread had dampened that. He wondered if he was going to have to call the police. How could he explain this? They would think he had somehow lured her there. Had he lured her there? Not literally, but was his loneliness some kind of siren call that had led her to him? *No, that was ridiculous.*

"Lie down with me." Her face was stormy, and somehow beautiful, preternaturally charged with energy that was about to radically disperse. He shut his eyes and let himself be pulled downward onto his own bed. He told himself there was no resisting the force of her emotions.

"Daddy," she said into his right ear. "You my daddy," she whispered. She burrowed herself into his arms trembling, sputtering, and rooting as if to find her way back into a womb no daddy could possess.

He held her for a few seconds feeling everything stiffen but his member, and then he gently pushed her away.

"Miss Brown, you need to get a hold of yourself. Are you hungry? Tell you what. You get up and get dressed, and I'll make you and Bianca some breakfast."

"It's mad early," she mumbled in a pissed off teenager's voice that was very different from the one she had used just moments before.

"Yes, but we're up now," he said in his crispest professorial tone.

"I'm sorry, professor. I'm just real tired. It's so hard out here trying to do everything and take care of my daughter and find a place to live and make things better for us..." her voice trailed on.

He gave her a penetrating look, not asking but wondering if coming here was part of a conscious scheme to "make things better" and not just a spur of the moment decision.

"Of course, Miss Brown. I imagine things are very difficult for you. I myself was a single parent for a long time and..." What was he doing? He was not required to tell her his history. He had revealed too much already.

"You always talk like that? Even at home? Where your son at now?"

"We don't need to be talking about my son. Now put some clothes on."

He went into the kitchen and looked around. Nothing had changed. The same old aging refrigerator, spray painted in spots where the original white enamel had worn away, the stove with the broken back burners he'd never bothered to have fixed, and the gray faux marble patterned Formica topped table and chairs that had been his mother's.

He'd seen the same set on sale for an arm and a leg in the window of a vintage store in the East Village. Everything was familiar, but he was lost. He opened the cupboard and looked in for a long time thinking not about breakfast but about the stew he had somehow gotten himself into, about the trouble he had invited in through the front door. It wasn't a conscious thought, but maybe if he stared long and hard enough a portal would open to another world somewhere where he could leave the troubles of this one behind.

"You got cereal?" He turned and saw Keisha standing in the doorway. He was annoyed by the provocative way she was leaning against the door jamb, posed like a pin-up girl, and dressed now in a red silk wrapper patterned with green vines and delicate white flowers, her right leg exposed up to the thigh and crossed in front of the left one. "This from Japan," she said seeing him eyeing the wrapper. "I got it at the Goodwill." Charles turned back to the cupboard and brought out a box of Raisin Bran.

"This is the only cereal I have."

"That's old people cereal. You ain't got no cornflakes?"

"Well, I'm old and beggars can't be choosers, young lady." She had the nerve to harrumph. How did the shy, desperate, homeless girl become a Hollywood vixen with an attitude in a matter of minutes? She seemed to have as many personalities as Eve in that fifties movie with Joanne Woodward.

"That just ain't no good breakfast."

"What's a good breakfast?"

"You got eggs?" He opened the refrigerator. "You got bacon?"

"No, I don't eat pork."

"You a Muslim or somethin?"

"Just never had a taste for it. And what's with the third degree?"

"What?"

"Why all the questions?"

"You say you gonna make breakfast; I'm just trying to help you out."

"Oh really, now!" He found himself smiling a bit at her sassiness. In class she had been a mousy little thing scratching out words in a smaller than standard notebook in the back of the room. Now here she was invading his kitchen and ordering him around.

"I have pancake mix," he said.

"You got syrup?"

"Pure maple from Vermont."

"Vermont," she said. He had a sense that she'd never said the word before. "I like Log Cabin." She came in and slid onto one of the three chairs at the kitchen table. The seat was split and yellowed and dirty stuffing poked out in places. She was so tiny her feet barely reached the floor.

Charles was good at making pancakes because Jason loved them. Besides, all that was required to make the batter was measuring out the mix and adding water from the tap. When Jason was little, they went to Vermont for a summer vacation one year. They went hiking in the Green Mountains and took a boat tour on Lake Champlain. Jason stuffed himself with maple sugar candy shaped like leaves and pine trees and tiny old-fashioned men and women, and then he got a stomachache and soiled his pants in the rental car.

Keisha was so mercurial and changeable that he could almost imagine a young Jason sitting there, and as he often had in the past, he found himself trying to pinpoint the exact moment that he knew he would no longer be raising Jason to achieve the normal things in life but fighting a constant battle just to keep him in this world. *Where was the frying pan?*

"I don't like cookin," Keisha said.

"No?"

"Probably cause nobody ever taught me how to do it."

"Your mother didn't teach you?" Charles was distracted, trying to contend with a situation that had turned his routine upside down. He was concentrating on watching water from the tap flow into the measuring cup until it reached the thin red ¾ cup line.

"My what? You know I ain't got no mother, Professor Rivers. You ain't read my papers? You sure marked them up a lot." He looked up from the sink, somewhat stricken.

"Well, yes, of course, but I have so many students, Miss Brown." She shook her head slowly. She wasn't buying that excuse.

"Something you wrote on one of my papers once made me think you, like, cared and maybe understood me. So you was just goin through the motions then, huh?"

"I'm not sure what you're talking about Miss Brown." She was looking down at her tiny foot, twirling it around and staring at it like an infant fascinated by an appendage it doesn't realize is part of its own body. The expression on her face was blank now. He watched the twirling foot. What's coming next? He thought. "I'm sorry." Why was he apologizing? "I don't remember, now. What did I say?"

"You said, I know what it's like to lose someone who means the world to you." And then he did remember. He even pictured the essay lying on his desk at home, the yellow light from his desk lamp shining on the slightly wrinkled handwritten page. Her mother had died when she was three. She didn't say but it sounded like AIDS. They had been living with her grandmother in the projects in Brownsville. A few years later her grandmother was robbed at gunpoint in the elevator and had a heart attack. That's when they put her in foster care.

"I remember now," he said. "And I meant it." She glanced up at him and then back down. That's when Bianca came into the room, dressed in a Rainbow Brite nightie, clutching the cowboy lamp with the bucking bronco, the yellowed rawhide stitched shade poking her in the face, the worn cord trailing behind like an absurd tail.

"What you doing with that? That's a lamp, girl, not a toy! You better put that back for Professor Rivers slap you!" Keisha screamed. Bianca looked towards Charles in a silent appeal.

"The lamp belongs on the bedside table." Charles said gently. Bianca stared at Charles as if she were mute, clutching the lamp to her chest, her cheek pressed against the shade. He stared back and a silent communication passed between them. Bianca turned around and padded towards the bedroom in her bare feet, but not without casting back a sharp glance at her mother.

A few seconds later she was back, standing close behind Charles as he attended to the pancakes in a cast iron skillet.

"Get outta his way," Keisha yelled when Charles moved to lift a pancake from the skillet to the plate. Charles looked over his shoulder to see where Bianca was standing, and the pancake slipped off the spatula and onto the floor.

"Look what you made him do!" Keisha screamed, lunging from her chair, grabbing Bianca and smacking her hard upside the head.

"Miss Brown!"

"She don't listen!" Keisha hit her a second time. Bianca uttered a low moan that got louder and more tremulous as tears filled her eyes. "Shut up! Stop that noise. Stop that crying right now or I'ma give you something to really cry about."

"Please don't hit her," Charles said, stepping in front of Bianca to protect her. "And you don't have to talk to her like that. There are better ways to talk to children."

"You don't know how bad she is. She never listens. She ain't grown. She act like she grown, and she don't listen to me."

"She's acting like a little girl," Charles said as he picked up and threw the pancake in the trash. "She's a *child*,"

Charles drew out the word, hoping his measured tone would dilute her sudden rage. He was jarred by how quickly her mood had shifted from sadness at losing her mother to anger directed at her own child. He searched her face for clues that might explain the sudden change. Her anger had raised the acne scars on her cheeks into a kind of topographical relief that disturbed the harmony and attractiveness of her features. She was a pretty girl, but he was surprised at just how ugly she had become in that instant and paradoxically how small she appeared folded into the bright red kimono, given the volume and vitriol in her voice. Chastened, Keisha looked down at the floor and what should have been obvious came to Charles, emotionally she was clearly still a child herself, vulnerable to any thought or emotion that took hold of her and lacking in the self-control she seemed to expect from Bianca.

The sense of dread that had begun to overtake him the minute he opened the door and saw Keisha standing on the worn tiles in the tepid light of the hallway, had now become a kind of incessant buzzing inside him, like the sound of an burnt out light bulb about to go dark.

"It's okay," Charles said to Bianca. He patted her on the shoulder and her trembling brought back his father's angry words, the humiliating cuff and sting of his blows, and the welts they had raised on Charles' body. It always pained him when he saw Black parents and caregivers belittle, yell at, and hit their kids out of the fear that the children were becoming too full of themselves or behaving with a kind of freedom and agency that would be denied them by society as they grew older. And it was especially painful when it was a knee-jerk response out of all proportion to the child's misdeeds, or just the usual way of parenting, as it was in Keisha's case right now.

Maddie explained how the whippings and the rants were remnants of slavery; prophylactic switches torn from the lynching tree to frighten, correct, protect and punish children by parents afraid for their futures. Black parents needed to get control of the one element in their lives *that they could* control—their kids—because if they didn't, some white person who didn't care whether those children lived or died would certainly do it for them. But she had tried to impress upon Charles and anyone else who would listen that constantly dangling the noose of that parental anger, woven as it was from the twisted rope of racism, would shrink the child's spirit and cause him to become so small that he would be hidden even from himself. She tried to explain that doing that would be doing the white man's killing for him.

Keisha morphed yet again. She reached out and pulled the sniffling Bianca towards her and asked in a sweet voice, "You got a television, Professor Rivers?"

"In my bedroom," he said, wincing a bit and taking a deep breath.

"She can watch it?" Charles nodded. "Come on," Keisha said, pulling Bianca out of the kitchen. Soon Charles heard the Sony turned up to a volume he'd never thought possible.

"For god's sake! Turn it down," he yelled. After a few minutes Keisha slipped back into her chair at the table as delicately and demurely as a Geisha, her eyes traveling around the room and sizing up everything in it. By stashing Bianca away in the bedroom, she got to be the curious child and the sole object of Charles' attention.

Charles glanced at Keisha but avoided engaging her in further conversation as he studiously finished cooking the pancakes and set a plate of them in the center of the table. He rarely had company and he tended to use the same plate, knife, fork and spoon that he washed and left in the dish drainer next to the sink after every meal. He found utensils in the jumble of flatware in a drawer next to the sink and took plates from the top shelf of the cupboard. He got the syrup, noting the dried amber drops near the spout, resisting an impulse to lick them off. When he brought these things to the table, he saw Keisha had begun munching on a pancake that she had folded over in her hand like a pizza slice.

"I'm so hungry, I couldn't wait," she said grinning with her mouth full. Keisha quickly piled her plate with more pancakes and poured a sea of syrup over them.

"What about your daughter?"

"Get in here, Bianca," Keisha yelled, continuing to chew her own food. Charles went to the bedroom to fetch Bianca, who was sitting on the floor at the foot of the bed sucking her thumb. When he brought her back to the table, Keisha picked up the knife Charles had placed by Bianca's plate and held it up, pointing it towards Charles like a miniature sword. "Why you give her a knife? She don't need no knife. She don't know how to use no knife, professor."

The first stack of papers of the semester was waiting for him on the desk in his home office. He had intended to get to them after he came back from his run and read the *Times,* which he bought every day along with a container of coffee from the corner bodega. But now here he was standing at the sink washing the dishes from Keisha and Bianca's pancake breakfast. It was Tuesday. He was on a Monday, Wednesday, Friday schedule this semester, and he was cutting back, slowly weaning himself from his five day a week habit as he moved towards retirement. He hadn't planned to go to campus.

In fact, the plan was to run over to the Hudson River and past the boat basin to look at the boats in the harbor and start working out the details in his head. He was going to spend his retirement building a yacht and sailing. Never mind that he didn't know the first thing about boats, couldn't swim more than a doggy paddle, and hadn't built much besides model cars and planes out of balsa wood with Jason. He got the idea late one night when he couldn't sleep, got up, poured himself another glass of scotch and switched on the TV. He found himself watching *Lifeboat* and he became fascinated with the idea of surviving in the open sea and living with the rhythms of the tides, the wind, the stars and the marine inhabitants of the deep--romantic fantasies he had never known or acknowledged that he possessed. It was a movie about war and the wiliness of an enemy, but that's not what interested him. Once you'd been to war, you realized that movies and books and art that somehow tried to represent the experience and make some kind of moral statement almost always fell short. It was like mistaking a mannequin for a person or even a glass of water for the ocean. They were works of the imagination. For civilians. Because one thing that being in a war did was annihilate your imagination. Reality became more horrific and fantastic than anything you could imagine. The most difficult thing being your own death, but once you had died without dying, participated in killing and witnessed the shocking transformation from "he was just alive to now he's dead" of comrades, you no longer needed a faculty to project yourself into the unknown. You knew.

Tallulah Bankhead, the female lead, reminded him of Madeline, who was also feisty, husky-voiced and from the South. Except she was a light-skinned, red-haired Black woman, a mixture of African, Caucasian and Indian blood, from Ahoskie, North Carolina. Madeline had been full of Black pride as well as Southern charm but when she came north and saw how her people were treated in the so-called liberal Northeast, she became consumed with Black rage. Her grandfather had been a Garvey-ite, and although he and his rural clan had no intention of returning to Africa, Garvey's message of self-determination resonated with them especially since they owned a good deal of the land in their county and had been self-sufficient and mostly oblivious and miraculously unharmed by the white minority in their environs since the end of slavery.

Charles had no use for the pious simplicity of Joe, the Negro character; he viewed him as little more than a castrated caricature that revealed more about the depravity of the white American psyche than the characteristics or circumstances of any real Black man. What he identified with was the flame of longing that would surely smolder inside a real person whose very humanity was denied. He understood the yearning to be fully alive, to fully express oneself and to fully inhabit all known and unknown territories of being and feeling and acting in the world in the short time allotted to us in this life. That's why he wanted to build the boat and venture out on the open sea.

Charles glanced at the red plastic wall clock; like the kitchen furniture, it was a relic from another time shaped like a cat, with a curved tail for a pendulum. It was still early. Only 8:45. There was still a chance that he could recover at least some of his intentions for the day. Keisha and Bianca were in his room watching television. When he finished cleaning up, he would politely but firmly invite her to gather up her things and find another place to make things better for herself and her child.

He switched on the radio he kept on the kitchen counter; it was tuned to WBAI, the New York listener sponsored Pacifica station.

"Oh, we have breaking news. It looks like a plane has crashed into the World Trade Center."

"Mr. Rivers! You gotta come see this," Keisha shouted from his bedroom. "A plane just flew into the World Trade Center."

"That fire real?" Bianca asked in a loud whisper. No one answered her. Charles stood in the doorway gripping the molding of the doorframe while Keisha crouched near Bianca who was sitting cross-legged at the foot of the bed staring at the TV screen. Even still images of explosions and fires made it hard for Charles to keep the memories of the war (that didn't make him a hero, or a proud veteran, but a pacifist) shut away in the classified file cabinet in his brain. A loud noise like a car backfiring could quickly melt his defenses like Napalm denuding a patch of jungle and take his mind back to a time of terror.

"Professor Rivers, what is happening?" Keisha asked.

"I don't know," he said, trying to keep his voice steady.

"I don't like this movie," Bianca said.

"This ain't no movie, girl! This is the news."

"Remember, she's just a little girl." Charles said in a voice that sounded distant to his own ears.

"I know but I hate it when she say stupid stuff."

"We just saw another one," the TV announcer said. "Oh my god, that looks like a second plane. Another plane just flew into the second tower. We just saw another plane coming in from the side."

Bianca jumped up, pushed past Charles and went into Jason's room. She picked up the cowboy lamp and clamped her arms around it.

"This was obviously, or it would seem to be a concerted attack against the towers of the World Trade Center."

She came back into the bedroom and sat down on the floor at the foot of the bed clutching the lamp. Keisha looked up at Charles. He shook his head. The announcers were trying to sound professional, but it was clear that they were terrified.

"Who would do that, Professor Rivers?"

"I'm not sure."

"Are we gonna die?" Keisha asked.

"No, of course not," Charles said. But he wondered if this was the beginning of an attack on the country that would lead to some kind of full-scale war.

"I need some cigarettes," Keisha said.

"Smoking is one thing that *will* kill you, Miss Brown."

"Yeah, but not today. You don't understand. I'm stressing. First the fights in the shelter, now these planes." She was as agitated as a junkie now which led Charles to wonder if maybe she was one.

"I don't allow people to smoke in my apartment. My son used to suffer from asthma."

"Your son ain't here." Keisha gave him a "what kind of man are you" look, as if she were channeling Quintasia, then she got up and went into Jason's room.

Minutes later she appeared in the doorway dressed in jeans and a turquoise tee shirt with the words "Dancing Queen" outlined in silver studs, many of them missing.

"Again live at this moment. There was a gaping hole. An airplane shaped hole, a gigantic hole...." The broadcasters continued.

"I'm a be right back, okay?" She looked at Bianca who had slipped her thumb in her mouth again and still had her eyes fixed on the screen where smoke was pouring out of the twin towers. "You gotta stop suckin that thumb, girl."

Bianca took her thumb out of her mouth long enough to say, "I'm scared of the fire."

Keisha disappeared down the long hallway. On the way out she noticed Charles' wallet on a table by the front door. She turned to see if Charles was looking. He wasn't. She slipped a couple of bills out of the wallet and hastily stuffed them in the pocket of her jeans.

Charles watched Bianca, who seemed unfazed by her mother's quick departure, stroking the lamp, eyes glued to the screen. The door slammed and both Charles and Bianca jumped a little. Charles looked towards the door, sighed, and then looked down at Bianca.

"Let's see if there's something else you can watch on TV," he said, picking up the remote and flipping through channels that were all broadcasting the same horrendous images. Finally, the exaggeratedly cheerful voices of child actors filled the room and bright primary colors flashed onto the screen. "How's this?"

"Barney."

KEISHA

Keisha walked into the bodega on the west side of 112th Street and checked out the selection of cigarette brands, each in their own little slot behind the counter. She didn't quite remember when she started smoking. And it wasn't like she was a pack a day smoker, but sometimes when she got stressed out and she could borrow one or had the money she'd reach for a cigarette.

"Give me a pack a--" she started. But then she faltered. She pictured the smoke from the explosion she has just witnessed on the TV screen and somehow imagined that if she lit up, another explosion, one that might actually blow her up, would be triggered at the end of her cigarette. She looked in confusion at the large middle-aged man behind the counter who was wearing a white apron over a print guayabera shirt.

"You want Newports?" he asked.

"No, I changed my mind. I don't want no cigarettes. You should turn on the TV," she said. "They blowing up the World Trade Center." He snorted. *Another crazy one*, he thought, as he started arranging the Mike and Ikes and Jawbreakers in the candy display case. The bell on the door tinkled as Keisha found her way out. Once outside she looked about in confusion, half-expecting to see the landmarks she had come to know around the shelter near 14th Street. She did a 360 like Dorothy seeking home in the *Wizard of Oz* and when she spied the north end of Central Park, two blocks away on 110th Street, she started walking. Moments later she found herself in a confrontation with a livery cab that had screeched to a stop and was honking madly as she jaywalked across 112th Street.

"Fuck you! I'm a fucking pedestrian!" she screamed, adrenaline fueling her footsteps. Once she crossed 110th Street and entered the park she had trouble finding her bearings. She was not that familiar with the north end. She had taken Bianca to a playground near the entrance at 59th Street a couple of times and then over to the zoo near Fifth Avenue, but this was the first time she had been this far uptown in the park. She wondered what direction she should go in. Left and against the directional arrows stenciled onto the bicycle lane, or right? Or should she just go back to Professor Rivers' apartment since she had said she was just going out for a smoke? If she went back, he might ask her to leave right away and then what would she do all day? She decided to go left, which led her past a steep stone staircase leading into a forest. She wasn't *that* adventurous, so she stayed on the sidewalk adjacent to the road that wound through the grassy area bordering the trees.

A string of hardcore joggers ran past her with tight stomachs, muscled legs, and rhythmic breaths. She wondered if they knew about the World Trade Center. She didn't know where she was headed, but just going *somewhere* felt good. She could feel all the bunched together and confusing thoughts that had made her so jittery in Professor Rivers' apartment spacing out in her head. She felt a little guilty for just leaving Bianca. But she would be back soon, and Bianca would be safe with the professor. He was a good person, and she didn't know too many good people. And it was better for her to be away from Bianca when she got like this--when she felt so lonely and hungry and scared inside and when every thought in her head was a bomb waiting to explode.

When she felt like that and she looked at Bianca, what she saw was a fat little monster wedged between the doorway of what her life was and what it was supposed to be. She saw the faces of the boys and men who had forced themselves on her and the ones she had invited to love her but didn't melting into one indistinguishable face and many rough hands.

Nobody had asked her if she wanted to have Bianca. She just came up pregnant while she was in the group home. She wasn't sure who the father was. It could have been one of the boys who made a joke out of the 24-hour supervision, or Teddy, who was a worker there who had promised to protect her from the boys who continually harassed her but had ended up cultivating her trust only to get what he wanted for himself. Girls were always getting raped or seduced at that place and there were rumors that some of them were even pimped out by the staff. When it became apparent that Keisha was expecting, nobody questioned Teddy or any of the boys who might have been responsible. She was called a slut and sent to another home for pregnant teens back in the city.

That's why when Keisha looked at Bianca sometimes and she saw a feature or an expression that reminded her of one of those boys she would hold the burning tip of the cigarette against Bianca's skin and listen to the monster scream.

The path was heavily wooded now. It began curving up a hill. Keisha decided to go down a flight of stone steps that led back to the roadway where she saw the shiny mirror of the lake and a boathouse that looked like a picture from a book of fairy tales. She walked along on the side of the road below the wooded area. The air felt cool, and there was a faint musty smell of decaying leaves. A couple of bicyclists and a single Rollerblader came careering down the steep incline ahead of her. Soon she heard the sound of rushing water. She followed the sound into the woods. If she didn't know better, she would have thought she'd left the city and had entered a forest in the country somewhere because of the dense trees, the thick undergrowth, and dappled light.

She knew what a real forest was like. The group home was in the boonies in upstate New York.

She stood still for a moment listening to the sound of water. It seemed to speak to her and say, "Don't be afraid. It's not the end of the world." She walked on and then she saw it, the miniature waterfall, cached and flowing between two jagged and enormous gray rocks. There were beer cans, tiny blue plastic weed packets, cigarette butts and crumbled potato chip bags scattered about on the stone path, but they didn't detract from the beauty of the scene. *A waterfall, a waterfall.* She sat down cross-legged on a large boulder facing the gushing stream, wishing now that she had bought the cigarettes, but content and soothed by Mother Nature. The very thought made her smile to herself it was so damn corny. She remembered the poem by Emily Dickinson they read in Professor Rivers' class about nature being the gentlest mother and it made her think that maybe if she spent more time in nature she could be more like the kind of mother Professor Rivers was telling her she should be.

"There's another one not too far from here."

Keisha was listening to the waterfall with her eyes closed. She opened them to see a skinny white guy in his twenties standing across from her looking like some stealthy caricature of an Indian in an old movie. He had dirty blond matted dreadlocks, and he was wearing a filthy suede tunic and ripped up jeans.

"Scuse me?"

"I said, if you like this waterfall. I can show you my other one."

"*Your* other one? This Central Park. Last I heard it was public property."

"You wanna see it?"

"No, that's okay." She should have been afraid of a mangy looking white dude appearing out of nowhere, but sitting had calmed her, and in her time, she had fended off scarier characters than he appeared to be.

"I could show you things you never thought you'd see in what they call Central Park."

"No thanks. I came here to be alone."

"You might think you are, but you're never really alone here."

"Well, I want you to leave me alone, now. Do you even know what's going on outside of here? They crashing planes into the World Trade Center. It's probably like the end of the world."

He didn't answer right away, but after a few seconds he cocked his head to the side as though trying to distinguish a particular sound from the background noise in his mind. Then he began to recite: "The World is too much with us. Late and Soon. Getting and Spending, we lay waste our powers. Little we see in Nature that is ours. We have given our hearts away, a sordid boon!"

Keisha drew back even further from him and frowned. *Just what I need another crazy-ass motherfucker messing up my day.*

"It's Wordsworth," he said.

"Who?" Keisha shot him a disapproving look; her eyes lingering on his cowboy and Indians get up. She stood up and tried to make a quick getaway, but her foot slipped on a tiny plastic bag that had settled into an indentation on the rock and she wobbled. The guy was at her side in an instant. He grabbed her elbow and kept her from falling. She shivered when she felt his dirty calloused fingers on her skin. She wrenched her elbow away and made a dash for the stone stairway that led back to the North Woods path.

"Dancing Queen," he called out, referring to the words on her tee shirt, 'I'm not going to hurt you. Seriously, I wouldn't hurt a fly, or even a cockroach."

Keisha looked back over her shoulder. *Humph!* She had heard those words before. That's what people said when they *were* going to hurt you. But she had also learned never to show her fear.

"Do and I'll bust your ass, white boy."

"I do not believe in violence," he shouted, standing on the boulder she had been sitting on as she sprinted up the steps. Then, tuning into another channel and accessing another recording in his brain, he shouted after her, "Nonviolence is the answer to the crucial political and moral questions of our time; the need for mankind to overcome oppression and violence without resorting to oppression and violence. Mankind must evolve for all human conflict a method which rejects revenge, aggression, and retaliation. The foundation of such a method is love."

She called back, "You need to tell that to whoever crashed them planes into the World Trade Center, MLK!" She felt safe once she put some distance between herself and the guy and was above the waterfall on an asphalt path that seemed to wind through the woods. It was scary the way he threw out quotes like that, and she wondered what was wrong with him, but she also felt strangely proud because she knew he was quoting Martin Luther King, Jr.'s Nobel Prize acceptance speech because they had read that, too, in Professor Rivers' class.

Some of the trees had started to turn and the ground was covered here and there with bright red and yellow arrow shaped leaves. She felt a strange sense of exhilaration as she continued along the path realizing that she was moving farther and farther away from Bianca. She was not really sure why she went to the professor's house; it was on impulse. The fight in the shelter was bad, but she exaggerated about the gun. Maybe it was because she missed being at school. She didn't have the money to go back this semester. She didn't file the Pell Grant form on time because she was waiting to hear about her housing application.

When Quintasia told her about how the professor tried to hit on *her* something took hold in the back of Keisha's mind. She started thinking about him doing the same to her. She tried to imagine what his apartment looked like. She pictured his face and the kindness and sadness in his eyes behind the stern expression he wore in class. And then she tried to imagine what it would feel like if he put his arms around her. How she would just let go and relax and fall asleep because she really was, just like she told him, so tired. Whenever she complained about another chore, Miss Betty, one of her foster mothers used to say, "You too young to be tired." But she figured she was probably born tired, fighting to stay alive inside her mother who wanted to have an abortion. Her grandmother told her many times what she'd said to Keisha's mother, "Peggy, you need to have this one. You got rid of all the others. I need me at least one grandbaby."

The first time her granny told Keisha that story she had no idea what she was talking about. Later on, it hurt her heart because even though her granny was trying to tell her how much *she* loved her, the flip side was her mother never wanting her to be born. And what was so messed up about that now is that she felt the same way about Bianca.

CHARLES

Charles went into his front room, the one he used as a library, and he peered out of the window to see if he could see Keisha coming out of one of the bodegas on the east or west side of Adam Clayton Powell Boulevard. *It shouldn't take this long,* he thought. But he didn't see Keisha. What he saw was a clean-cut thirty-something man in a dark suit with a newspaper under his arm striding down the avenue in polished wingtips past the younger men, faces obscured by hoodies, who were standing on the street corner waiting for business. Below his window, a heroin user in a state of suspended animation slumped back on the tailgate of a gray Ford Windstar, and a woman from up the block whose curvaceous butt he had admired on a number of occasions was walking her dog, a little yapping pit bull mix, and wearing a green velour track suit.

He looked towards the park, wondering if he could see smoke or any other evidence of the destruction that was going on downtown. But the sky was as clear and blue as an image on a souvenir postcard. The park was still a rich summer tapestry of green with only the slightest hints of fall color. It appeared to be a normal day. He wondered where Jason was. He would call him if he knew. He would call his mother also, if she were still able to talk on the phone and recognize his voice. She was in a nursing home, only a few blocks away, but it might as well have been on another planet considering how alien he appeared to her when he visited her there. He remembered the attack on the Twin Towers seven years before and wondered if the same persons were responsible. Six people died in that attack, and the father of one of his students was among those injured. It was clear that this one was far worse than the first one. He had changed the channel because he didn't want Bianca to see the people jumping out of windows to escape the flames.

He went into his office where he could follow the events on his computer. He logged on to CNN.com, constantly tapping his foot to contain his apprehension as he watched and clicked through information. He learned that there had also been an attack on the Pentagon, that the bridges and tunnels had been closed, that airports had been shut down and flights had been suspended. He gobbled up the information as it became available. He couldn't leave his desk. He kept replaying the moment of impact. He needed to desensitize himself by watching the images on his computer screen so that his own memories of heat and screams and thunderous fire did not take over. He couldn't stop wondering where they would strike next. Maybe he should go out and get supplies. He was shocked when he checked the clock and saw that it was already past noon. Then the thought seized him—Keisha's kid was still in the bedroom. It had been over three hours! Where the hell was she?

He went into his bedroom and saw that Bianca had fallen asleep at the foot of his bed with the cowboy lamp beside her and her right hand inside her underpants. Her mouth was open, and he saw her tongue, pink as a cat's, trembling a little with each breath. Tiny beads of sweat had collected on her brow and her chubby brown cheeks had a ruddy overheated glow. He had not noticed before, but she was an angelic looking child, plump in a pleasing way that made her look healthy despite the fact that the skin around her mouth, and on her neck and arms was covered with rough darkened patches that reminded him of an elephant's hide. As he got closer, he noticed a series of little white circles on the light brown skin of her exposed thigh. They looked like scars from chickenpox.

Where the hell was Keisha? He turned away from Bianca as if he expected to find Keisha standing behind him. He looked back at Bianca, blinking rapidly as he tried to process his thoughts. Maybe this was all a ploy. Maybe Keisha left her child never intending to come back for her. And maybe the tragic events of the day had provided her with additional cover.

"We're going to go out and look for your mother," he shook Bianca, who was snoring audibly. She responded by putting her thumb in her mouth and sucking it vigorously. He shook her again.

"You need to get dressed so we can go find your mom." Bianca snatched her thumb from her mouth and sat up on the bed rocking from side to side like an ocean buoy.

"Where my clothes?" she asked. Charles looked around then located and pulled the red, white and blue bag, woven out of low-grade plastic fibers, towards the bed. He'd often seen women and kids in the neighborhood lugging or dragging these bags to the laundromat, and this one was stuffed as though such a trip was imminent.

"What I'm sposed to wear?"

"I don't know. Pick something."

"Keisha pick out my clothes. She say I don't know how to match."

Charles looked at her in dismay. He didn't know the first thing about dressing a little girl and he was loath to start poking around in the woven bag and find himself as deep into Keisha's possessions as he suddenly was in her life. Bianca gave him a "you're the grown-up" stare, and he reluctantly started going through the stuff in the bag. It wasn't just clothes. He pulled out a manila envelope stuffed with papers, a steam iron, a marbled composition notebook, a math textbook, a separate plastic bag of shampoo and soap and toothbrushes, and a bunch of ragged and in some cases coverless, paperback children's picture books, including one bright with Sesame Street characters about Elmo. Eventually he was able to find a pair of hot pink bicycle shorts and a faded white tank top with a sad cascade of ruffles across the front.

"How about these?" Bianca started pulling up her nightgown.

"Wait, I'll give you some privacy," Charles said. Bianca looked at him blankly. He quickly exited and checked the streets for signs of Keisha. When he came back a few minutes later, he saw that Bianca had managed to stuff herself into the clothes, which he realized were way too small. She had left her nightie in a colorful pool on the floor. She'd also managed to put on her shoes, but they were pointing outwards at a sort of comic dancer's turned-out angle. Charles saw that she had put them on the wrong feet.

"Come here, let me help you with your shoes," he said. His voice was unexpectedly tender. Even though he couldn't be more annoyed by the situation, sympathy for the little girl welled up in him, "Sit down. Where are your socks? Oh, I guess I was supposed to find the socks."

Charles was not accustomed to taking the elevator, but he waited for it on account of Bianca. He had no idea where he was headed, but somehow once they got to the street, he felt sure they'd find Keisha. He held Bianca's puffy little hand as she went from the top to the bottom of the ten steps on the stoop one at a time, tensing up her fingers as she reached for the next step. *Jason.* It was not so much a thought as a kind visceral sensation as he remembered what it felt like to hold a small child's hand. They headed south towards 110th Street. Central Park seemed to shimmer like Oz in the midday sun. People were milling about on the streets as if waiting for the next shocking thing to happen. Charles' neighbor, Mrs. Campbell, a dour church lady with a metal cane and penchant for elaborate satin and tulle hats festooned with ribbons, rhinestones, lace and dyed feathers, was coming up the block with one of the four or five foster children always in her care. The thin, handsome, plum-colored boy, who looked about twelve, was struggling to pull a rickety shopping cart full of gallon bottles of water stacked onto two twenty-pound bags of white rice. Charles nodded, his customary greeting to neighbors he met on the street, and Mrs. Campbell replied with a grim once over of Bianca.

"That your grandchild?"

"No, I'm just babysitting."

"Humph!" Mrs. Campbell grunted, her eyebrows rising in the direction of her celestial home as she moved on without another word.

JASON

"My mom just told me somethin really fucked up."

"Your mom is fucked up. I'm trying to sleep. Leave me alone."

"You are always in the worse mood in the morning."

"Shut up, it's not morning."

"Planes flew into the World Trade Center."

"Yeah, and monkeys will fly out of my butt and down your throat if you don't leave me alone."

"Your dad lives in New York."

"Thanks for the information, bitch."

"You are abusive."

"You're an idiot."

"You are sooo mean."

"It must be cause I do drugs. Leave me alone."

"Y'all should come see this," the girl's mother drawled from the next room.

"See, I told you."

Jason rolled over in bed. He had been dreaming that he was back home, and that people were running away from the Empire State Building like in that old King Kong movie. He hated waking up. He hated realizing where he had ended up— with dumb-ass Gracie Ellen and her mom, Donna, in a Section 8 apartment in butt-fuck West Virginia. If he'd had to explain to anyone how exactly he had gotten there, he wouldn't be able to. They were dumb white hicks that he met on the Internet, and they had nothing in common except the desire to get high every day. Jason was the man of the house now that Donna's husband and son had moved out. A Black dude from New York. How crazy was that in a town where there were only about ten Black people? But at least he wasn't in jail or sleeping on the steps of a church or in a bus station—all of which he had done since the last time he'd been home.

Sometimes he thought about talking to his dad, but he didn't know what he would say. He called him one night a few months ago and got his answering machine. He had started to leave him a message, but he was drunk and high and had taken a lot of pills and he got all tongue-tied after the beep. He was ashamed to tell him where he was now and what he was doing. Maybe he could just say he was part of an alternative economy. But his dad would know what that meant.

His dad had tried so hard. He got him into good schools. He did all of the things you were supposed to do. He saw that now living with Gracie Ellen and her mom in this hick town, eating ramen noodles every day and getting fucked up on pills and weed and beer and whatever just because. Just because. Home was kind of lonely after his mom died. He started hanging out a lot at his friend George's humongous apartment on Riverside Drive playing video games and messing around while his parents were on Wall Street or wherever making tons of money. Everybody would probably think that the first time he smoked weed or drank would have been in his own neighborhood in Harlem, but nah, a lot of those private school kids were actually way more precocious than the kids who lived in his building and on his block. He was in fifth grade when he started drinking at George's house and one day when he was like twelve, George's brother Alex told them to come into his room. He had a bong and he told them to take a hit, and you could say the rest was history.

He put the pillow over his head so he couldn't hear Gracie Ellen, but she kept screaming at him to come look. He dragged himself up and went into the sparsely furnished living room where Gracie Ellen, with her thin slightly crooked body; she had a curved spine from scoliosis, was standing in front of the chunky portable television chewing on a clump of her limp blond hair.

"You ever been in them towers?"

"Plenty of times."

"How far is it from where your daddy lives."

"Very far."

"You think he's alright?"

"Why do you care?"

"He's your daddy."

"If I cared would I be here?"

"I'm just saying."

"Keep your mouth shut."

CHAPTER

ELEVEN

CHARLES

Charles was frantic. Keisha had seemingly disappeared into thin air. He had dragged Bianca up and
down 7th Avenue into all the bodegas and corner stores.
Then they hit Lenox where they climbed down the stairs
and peered onto the platform past the turnstile at the
110th Street subway station, then ducked into Wonder
Chicken and Pizza and witnessed money and drugs
changing hands; Charles tucked his head into the Mac
Liquor store and pushed past carts full of wet clothes
in the Ipanema Laundromat. She was not in the Lenox
Pharmacy, or the Parkside Dry Cleaner where he got his
shirts done, and where the Korean woman behind the
counter recognized and smiled at him. He ventured into
the beauty supply store next door, its shelves stacked

with hair dyes and relaxers, swatches of straight glossy human and synthetic hair hanging from a display board behind the cash register.

They searched the cramped aisles of the Met Foods where people were waiting on long lines behind shopping carts filled with bottled water and canned food. No Keisha. They walked another block and passed by the usual group of men hanging around outside of Fred's Wines and Liquors talking above Earth Wind and Fire singing an old jam about the way of the world on a duct taped boom box one of them carried. And then Charles saw her. She was sitting on the benches and smoking in the playground of the Martin Luther King, Jr. housing project on the east side of the street.

He dragged Bianca across the downtown and then the uptown lanes of traffic, eyes trained on a young woman on one of the benches with her back to the chain link fence. But as soon as they entered, he saw he was mistaken. It was an older woman watching a toddler scoot about on a toy fire engine. Charles surveyed the playground—the children's play area, basketball and handball courts and the thirteen-story brick half hexagon of a building set back in a field of patchy grass, its matching wings on either side like sheltering arms or a proscenium for everything that went down below.

Bianca had tugged at his shirt and pointed to the swings behind a low chain link fence beyond the jungle gym.

"What? We don't have time for swinging. We have to find your mother. We didn't come to play."

"She burn me," Bianca said.

"What are you saying?"

He scowled at her. She hitched up her shorts and showed him the pattern of white circles he had noticed earlier along with a couple of fresh scabs on the sweaty skin of her inner thigh and when he looked closer, he saw patches of skin sprinkled with what looked like tiny red pin pricks. "Your mother did that?" Bianca said nothing more. Her bold unbroken gaze was her answer. It sounded in Charles' mind and ears as if she had shouted through a megaphone, especially since he had grown accustomed to her staring at the floor or the ground, or looking away when he looked at her. He thought of the beggars who maimed their children and sent them out with begging bowls. *What kind of scam was this? What kind of game was Keisha playing? What kind of payment was she attempting to exact from him?* He was a sympathetic guy. He was sensitive to the plight of young women like Keisha. He understood her situation in the context of their history as Black folks in America. He was doing his part to change things by trying to educate his students about structural racism and human rights. He was doing his part by trying to arm them with literacy.

"She burn me," Bianca said again. And suddenly the sight and smell of charred roasted flesh overtook him and he looked at Bianca from a faraway place in his brain. She continued to stare at him, waiting for a response, and the steady beam of truth from her eyes became a searchlight into his soul. It shook him. The vision passed. His right hand began to tremble slightly, as if he were the one guilty of burning her and it was his hand that had inflicted the wounds.

Another child who was not his child had once fixed him with the same infrared stare that had tested the warmth of his heart and the parameters of his compassion. It was in Saigon before he had been sent to the jungle when war was a happy adventure and he felt fit and invincible from surviving basic training. During their transport he and other soldiers had come across a group of Ameri-Asian children. One of them, a boy with round black eyes, thick curls and copper skin had grabbed his hand and asked in pidgin, "You my father?"

Now Charles looked around, as if to break the spell that Bianca had cast upon him. He saw a young teenaged boy in a team jersey dribbling a basketball, an elderly man dressed in a mismatched suit and pants proceeding slowly past the entrance to the playground, two young women pushing strollers talking to each other one of them saying loudly, "And I'm like, are you for real, nigga? How I'm sposed to buy Pampers with this?"

Charles turned back to Bianca. He bent down and picked her up. He felt a slight twinge in his back. He carried her over to the swings. They were empty except for one occupied by a young girl with a big pregnant belly that she sat clutching like a beach ball. He helped Bianca onto a swing. Her feet didn't reach the ground. He gave her a push and another when the swing returned.

"Higher," she said, giggling. It was the first time he heard her laugh.

KEISHA

She bummed a cigarette from some foreign girl with white-blond hair who was wearing clogs and carrying a backpack on the front. And now Keisha sat on a bench almost blissfully smoking, watching scruffy ducks bob in and out of the murky waters of a pond near the west side of the park. Consequently, she was only mildly surprised and no longer afraid when the crazy guy dressed like a TV Indian appeared beside her on the bench. She figured she was safe because there were other people around them, walking their dogs and running, apparently unaware that the world was coming to an end.

"You all over this park."

"Wanna dance, dancing girl?"

"I tole you I want to be alone."

He jumped up from the bench and started shaking the upper part of his body as if responding to the beat of invisible congas.

"You know what? You crazy."

"I know where you can get some," he said.

"Some what?"

"What you're looking for."

"How you know what I'm looking for?"

He held two fingers up to his lips and pretended to take a drag.

"Where?"

"Come right this way."

Keisha did not know why she decided to follow him. He led her back to the path and then into the woods she had avoided when she first entered the park. They trudged along a winding dirt trail for a while, immersed in greenness and silence punctuated by birdsong. Then suddenly they emerged into an opening where a young Black man wearing dark shades and dressed impeccably in a red and white sports jersey, white sweats and a red and white snapback cap was studiously smoking a blunt and leaning on a large rock overhanging the park.

"Dancing Queen," the TV Indian stepped back, presenting Keisha to the brother in sunglasses, as if for inspection. He stared at her for a long minute through opaque lenses and she felt herself shivering although she wasn't cold. He offered her a hit. She took it hungrily.

"Ever seen this view?" He nodded towards the rock. Keisha shook her head. Suddenly she was scared. He beckoned to her. "You can see all a Harlem from here."

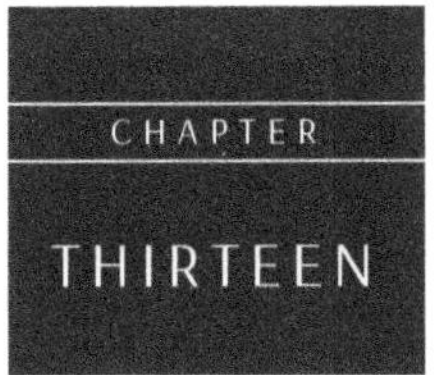

ROSETTA

When Will finally came home, the kids were watching a video in the living room while Rosetta sat at the foot of the bed in her bedroom trembling and stuffing her fists into her mouth to keep from crying. She had taken Ryan and Evan to school and then rushed back to collect them as soon as she'd heard the news in the morning. They spent most of the day gorging on cookies, fighting over the beanbag chair, and watching Nickelodeon while building and rebuilding an elaborate Lego structure that they knocked down with a toy plane. Rosetta kept them from seeing the footage on TV, but by the time she had picked them up, Evan, the second grader, had heard what happened. From time to time they popped into the bedroom asking for drinks and whether more planes had crashed into buildings. At one-point Ryan burst in jabbering about helicopters and pulled Rosetta to the living room window where they could see black Air Force choppers circling like raptors searching for prey. Rosetta had hidden the remote and she kept the sound of the news broadcast low in the bedroom. When she heard Will's key in the lock she jumped up from the bed and flung the front door open.

"Thank god! Thank god!" She pulled him into the foyer. His hair, face, and the gray business suit he was wearing were covered with patches of white dust.

The kids screamed, "Daddy!" and rushed towards him, but hung back when they saw how he looked.

"Why do you have that powder on you?" Evan said.

"Daddy, are you a ghost?" five-year-old Ryan asked.

"Why didn't you call?"

"I don't know what happened to my phone. I took it out to call. Everyone was running and then I didn't have it anymore."

"A pay phone?"

"Lines were too long. I just. I just walked. I just wanted to get home as fast as I could."

"Were you in the building?"

"No, no, I stopped to get coffee. My appointment was at nine. I was almost in the building, but I wasn't in the building," he said, "But I saw..." and then he began to weep.

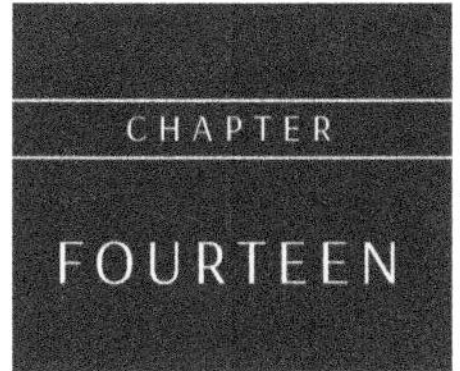

CHARLES

Keisha did not come back. That night Charles put Bianca to bed again in Jason's room, assuring her that her mother would be there when she woke up. But it felt like he was trying more to convince himself than Bianca, who just stared in that way of hers. He spent most of the night pacing up and down in front of his computer, haunted by the horror of the day's events and troubled by the President's words about war. His four-fingered hand started twitching the way it did when his mind drifted into the enemy territory of his war memories. He thought of calling the police about Keisha. But he told himself she would probably return shame-faced in the morning, and that it would be hard to get them to take her disappearance tonight seriously in the flood of calls about missing persons from the World Trade Center. He had classes the next day. He wondered how many students would show up and if any of them had been personally touched by the tragedy. He got an email from his cousin Harry in Atlanta asking if he was okay. And when he responded in the affirmative, he thought about Jason, half hoping that somehow, he would try to call home.

In the morning he got up and dressed for his run. Maybe Rosetta Ocean would be out today. He hadn't seen her all summer. She probably went away to Maine or Martha's Vineyard or someplace like that with that husband and those kids of hers. It was crazy the way she was always on his mind. When he jerked off in the shower thinking about her would take him over the edge. She was way too young for him, and she was married. Married. He had to keep telling himself that. But except for the time when she told him about the abortion, she seemed like such a poster girl for hope. Hope was hard to resist when you got to be his age, when you'd been through what he'd been through, when you'd lived so long without it.

He was at the front door with his Walkman plugged in when he remembered there was a child asleep in the other bedroom. He hesitated; then he shrugged it off. It was early, not even 7 a.m. He'd be back before she woke up. Maybe he'd even spot Keisha somewhere out there, and doggone it he was damned if he'd let Keisha screw up his routine yet another day.

When he returned from the run, he felt energized despite everything that had happened and the general malaise and uncertainty that was always the background music of his life, now made louder and intensified by events outside of it. The regulars had mostly all been out there. Runners deal with stuff by running. He was cooling down, listening to Stevie Wonder, jogging slowly after the sprint he liked to do before exiting the park at 110th St, and about to go into the bodega to buy the *Times* when he noticed something on his stoop that wasn't there when he left. It was not uncommon for drug addicts or homeless people to find temporary ac-commodation on those steps. But this was not a person. He came closer and saw that it was the cowboy lamp with the frayed cord from Jason's room perched on the top step, the yellowed shade with its unraveling rawhide stitching at a tipsy angle. *What the!* Charles swore and all the endorphins seemed to drain from his body. He ran up the steps, grabbed the lamp and stabbed his key into the lock of the heavy metal front door. As he opened the second door, he saw Bianca huddled in the open doorway of 1A with Mrs. Campbell leaning on her cane bending down towards her, then looking up as the door opened, the signature scowl on her face.

"She lookin for her mother. One of my boys found her sitting in her pajamas on the stoop. How you left her and let her come outside like that? People don't know how to take care no chilren," Mrs. Campbell mumbled. "Go on, he back now." Mrs. Campbell pushed Bianca towards the threshold and out of the door. Then she firmly shut the door behind her and sealed the deal by locking it. Bianca jumped a little when the latch clicked into place. She was sucking her right thumb. Her face was streaked with dirt and tears, and she kept wiping her eyes with the back of her left hand.

"We'll find your mommy, today," Charles said. She reached up and grabbed the cord of the cowboy lamp and stood there holding it while they waited for the elevator.

ROSETTA AND CHARLES

Rosetta knocked lightly on Charles Rivers' office door. She hadn't seen him at the beginning of the semester and assumed they were teaching on different days. But this evening, two weeks after the Towers went down, she decided to check to see how he had fared during the crisis.

"Who is it?" His voice sounded tense.

"Rosetta."

"Come in."

She pushed open the door. Charles was putting a stack of papers into his briefcase and there was a little girl about Ryan's age sitting in the sagging chair at his desk with only her uncombed head and neck visible behind it. Once she stepped into the room Rosetta saw that the child was wearing a red tartan dress a size too small. A big box of new crayons lay open in front of her, scattered like thick colorful pick up sticks, giving off that distinct crayon odor Rosetta knew so well from her boys. The little girl held a bright yellow one in her right hand and was painstakingly transferring the waxy color from crayon to page in a fat coloring book, and when she looked closer Rosetta saw that the little Black girl was coloring a picture of Goldilocks.

"My new little friend," Charles said with a gruff laugh.

"What?" Rosetta shot him a quizzical look.

"Really, don't ask."

"Are you okay? I mean after the attack."

"Oh, yeah. I'm okay. How about you?"

"My husband actually had, had a job interview there that morning. He likes to be early for everything, but he got coffee. I usually make him coffee, but I guess it was good I was a bad wife that day." She laughed a little. "But he saw it. He came home with the ashes all over him. The kids were terrified."

Bad wife. Those words reverberated in Charles' head, and he didn't reply to her right away. There was a silence that was more than awkward.

"Okay, well, I gotta go to class. Have a good one." Rosetta turned to leave.

"Wait," Charles said. "What would you do if you knew someone, a, a, former student was abusing her child and then they left the child with you and disappeared."

"What?" Her curiosity and concern aroused, Rosetta spun around and fixed her gaze on Bianca. Charles turned and looked at Bianca, too. The little girl continued to color, her jaw tightened in concentration, aware, but pretending not to be, that they were talking about and staring at her.

"How long have you had her?"

"Two weeks."

"Did you, like, call the authorities?" Charles slowly shook his head. "Two weeks, was her mother in the towers?"

"No, they were with me when it happened."

"What are you going to do?" Charles winced.

"I don't know. Wait for her mother to come get her?" Bianca suddenly looked up at Charles, her eyes large with fear.

"What if she doesn't come back?"

"She went out for a smoke."

"Went out?"

"It's a long story, but she ended up at my apartment on September 10."

"Ended up? Were you, like, *involved* with her?" Rosetta's eyes narrowed and her expression hardened. It was nothing she would put past him given his eagerness to sweet talk *her*. God! What was wrong with her, she thought. Why did she even come by to speak to him? It was so obvious that he was a player.

"Of course not! I would never…" Rosetta shot him a look of skeptical reproach. "No, not at all, not like that."

For her own reasons, Rosetta wanted to believe him, so she turned her gaze back on Bianca.

"I can see she's attached to you." And then quickly feeling that it was somehow wrong to keep talking about the child in the third person, Rosetta addressed her.

"What's your name, sweetheart?" Bianca did not answer. Rosetta reached out and lightly touched her head. Bianca stared at Charles. Her gaze was like an anesthetic that suddenly paralyzed his limbs.

"Bianca. Her name is Bianca. I don't know what to do."

"Shouldn't you call the police?"

"Then what happens?"

"They'll find her mother?"

"What if they don't?"

"They'll put her in a foster home?"

"Her mother was in foster homes. They had been staying in a shelter."

"It's kind of 19th century. Baby on the doorstep and all that."

"This is not English literature, Mrs. Ocean," Charles said sounding peeved and excessively professorial. Rosetta was shocked and then hurt by the sudden shift in his attitude and register, and she stepped back towards the door.

"It's Ms. Ocean. Not Mrs. My husband's last name is Sheridan." Charles raised an eyebrow. "I didn't take his last name." The word "husband," like the words "bad wife" had a kind of kryptonite effect on him and he quickly backed down.

"I'm sorry. That was rude," he said. Rosetta nodded, acknowledging his apology but thinking he was a kind of strange volatile guy.

"Well, I guess I'd better get to class."

"Yes, me too."

"What about Bianca? Is she going to be alright in here?" Bianca looked up from the coloring she had resumed, and when she did, Rosetta observed the answer to her question in the almost ancient stillness behind the little girl's eyes. She was reminded of something very old—the primordial gaze of a sea turtle, perhaps, or some other creature that had been on this earth a long time. At once she understood Charles' dilemma because in that moment, it seemed she caught a glimpse, as corny as it sounded, of the child's soul.

"You could say she is your grandchild."

"What?"

"I mean, say that's why you have her."

"Keep her?" Charles asked, a little ticked off that Rosetta saw him as someone's grandfather, in spite of his age and his earlier talk about retirement.

"You know how the students are always writing that everything happens for a reason?"

"That's because they're ignorant and believe a big man in the sky is moving the chess pieces around." What do *you* believe in? Rosetta thought but answered instead,

"You don't have to believe in God to think that." She took another look at Bianca, thinking that someone needed to comb her hair, and then she backed out of the door.

After she left, Bianca asked in a soft voice, "What's her name?"

"What?" Charles was deep in thought and the child's small voice had startled him. "Her name is Rosetta. Miss Rosetta."

"It sounds like a rose," Bianca whispered.

"Yes, it means little rose," Charles said. Bianca leafed through the coloring book and when she found what she was looking for she showed it to Charles.

"This is a rose," she said. Charles looked at the page. It was a picture of Sleeping Beauty with a rose in her hand. "I'm gonna color it red for Miss Rosetta."

ROSETTA

It was a clear night and the full moon shone through their 25th floor window like a klieg light illuminating the bad movie that was becoming their life. Will was snoring beside her, but Rosetta could not sleep. Not because of the snoring. She was used to it. But tonight, her mind kept returning to that little girl with the uncombed hair and too tight dress sitting at Charles Rivers' desk. Generally, she was a good sleeper. Sleep was her refuge and now that the boys were older, she was getting more of it, but the vortex of feelings that churned inside her when she thought about Charles Rivers disrupted more than her sleep. Why was she so preoccupied with him? He was old, at least fifty, kind of an asshole, and she could tell he was completely old school in the classroom. He seemed to be obsessed with grammar and speaking and teaching his students standard English. He was always talking about "correcting" papers and anyone who knew anything about current trends in the teaching of writing knew that it was about more than that. But there was something that drew her to him. He actually seemed to take an interest in her. To most people in the department, except some of the ones she had studied with, she was nothing more than another invisible adjunct drone, whose own aspirations to write had through necessity been repurposed into teaching what the university called basic writing to the neediest students with a minimum amount of support and zero recognition.

Chatting with Charles on occasion had made her feel less isolated and that's why she didn't want to believe he was like some of the other professors who viewed sexual access to female students and colleagues as one of the perks of the profession. She knew she was probably kidding herself because of the way he looked at her and the flirtatious things he said. It was a bit galling but also flattering, and if she had to admit it, kind of titillating, too.

Maybe he was a stand-in for the father she never knew. And come to think of it, her father might have actually looked something like him. He was almost as tall as Will, but wiry and trim in a kind of well-preserved old guy way. She smiled to herself thinking that he kind of looked like Nat King Cole on the cover of that vintage Christmas Album her Aunt Essie had loved to play during the holidays, but he had a neatly trimmed mustache and shaved head instead of a 1950s conk. His skin was smooth, except when a disturbing thought or comment wrinkled his forehead, and he was even darker than she was, a shade of deep coffee brown that put him in a category of black that even Black folks viewed as a curiosity.

She lay beside Will with Charles on her mind, and a line from a Nuyorican poem she used with her students came to her: "Black when I walked/and some of them said I was white when I talked." Charles moved with the fluid gait and proud carriage of a brother, despite a slight limp on his left side. But his diction was intentionally crisp and a little bit affected, as if he had to compensate for being so black by cultivating a white way of talking. Still, there was something about the baritone timbre of his voice that made her heart quiver like timpani whenever she heard it.

The more she thought about it now, the more she realized it wasn't *just* a daddy thing. And so what if he was old enough to be her father, he was a sexy guy. *Oh god*, was she allowed to admit that? And maybe, honestly, the attraction had something to do with him being a Black man. She hadn't been with a Black guy since high school. In college she had crazy crushes on all kinds of guys, but she hadn't really gone with anyone until Will came along.

Will was tall and white, a man of few words, a former football player at their college upstate. Theirs was an uncommon love story. He could have had his choice of any blue-eyed blonde on campus, and he went out with a bunch of them, but he and Rosetta became friends and bonded in Freshman English. Early in the semester they were paired up and had to do an exercise where they worked on interpreting a poem together, reading and then explaining the line they read. They were assigned "The Word" by Pablo Neruda. Every time Rosetta read her line and explained, Will, who seemed almost too big for the standard sized metal and plastic chair, fixed her with a sharp gaze and seemed to listen hard. Then he would say, "That is amazing. I would never have thought of that." By the end of the exercise, they were laughing helplessly and both saying, "That is amazing, I would never have thought of that."

Rosetta helped him keep up with work when he missed class for games and practice. And sophomore year when she started working in the campus writing center, he came to her to get help with his writing projects. At the time he seemed to be colorblind in the best sense of the word. Once a girl Rosetta knew on the cheerleading squad overheard a bunch of white guys on the team rating women. They went through their list of hotties and Will asked what they thought about Rosetta Ocean. "Who's that?" They asked.

"You know that girl who works in the writing center?"

"Which one?"

"Kathy Byrd's roommate."

"That Black girl? You're kidding, right?"

"Yeah, and no I'm not kidding. She was in my English class freshman year; she's really cute."

"That's an oxymoron, Will; She's BLACK! Black. Black is not cute."

It became a joke among the rest of the writing center staff that so many of Rosetta's sessions were with Will. Though neither one of them said it, they both knew it was a legit and safe way for them to spend time together and enjoy each other's company without risking the opprobrium of certain of their peers by publicly dating or hooking up. Rosetta loved that they were total opposites. She was city; he was country; she was Black; he was white; she was petite; he was large; she had the gift of gab and he struggled to find the right words; he played team sports, and she ran cross country.

In the middle of junior year, he suffered a bad concussion, and his mother convinced him to quit the football team. After missing several weeks of classes, he was behind in his work, and he brought Rosetta a history midterm paper for which he had gotten an extension. They were sitting across from each other at a worktable in the writing center. She was reading his paper and trying to explain the difference between eminent, the word he needed to describe an historian he was quoting and imminent, what was going to happen next, and he was staring at her the way he always did at these sessions with what looked like wonder in his pale blue gray eyes.

"My bad, I meant eminent, but I'll tell you what is imminent," he said.

"What?"

"This," and then he leaned across the table and kissed her, right there in the writing center.

After that they became a couple. And once Will made his choice, he seemed oblivious to the fact that some people saw their relationship as something unnatural. Maybe it was a function of white male privilege and physical strength; he could do whatever he wanted and more power to you if you tried to cross him. Although her close friends thought nothing of it, Rosetta endured hate stares from white girls and Black men and once, ironically, during a protest against apartheid, a group of Black girls got up and walked away when she and Will sat down on the lawn next to them. Will punched a white guy in the face after he whispered a lewd comment about black pussy one morning when they were leaving her dorm together.

Rosetta looked at Will now. He was a sleeping giant, like Gulliver without the tiny ropes and pinions tying him down, and he was as handsome as the drowned man in the story by Marquez, but in a Nordic way, except that he was alive and when he exhaled through his mouth his breathing made a whistling sound like the boys' toy train. She felt a pang of guilt because she could have lost him in the Towers and up until a couple of years ago, they had been happy. She had benefited, small, working-class Black woman that she was, from being married to

a white man with a commanding presence and a pros-
perous family, even if beneath his outward appearance
there lived a terrified child that cowered at the prospect
and doubted the possibility of ever making a success of
his adult life. Now that he had lost another job, he was
becoming distant in that way that he sometimes could,
and he was lashing out verbally at her and the kids when
he experienced them invading his space.

He was also spending more and more time in the
gym downstairs, going with the same kind of regularity
that others went to work, claiming it helped him de-
compress from the job search. But as the Schwartzeneg-
ger muscles increased in size, he became even more
taciturn and removed from everyday affairs. The boys
misbehaved and fought just to get his attention. And it
was ironic that she had gotten pregnant because they
rarely had sex anymore. Will started wagging his head
in his sleep and mumbling unintelligible words, as if
protesting her negative thoughts. She turned to him and
stroked the thick muscles of his arm and wondered what
it would be like to lie in bed with another man, to lie in
bed with Charles.

But then she thought about Charles' crazy story
of the student just leaving her child. What kind of bullshit was that—she just showed up on his doorstep? He
had to be fucking the girl. *Bastard.* Those guys in the
department were notorious, but it was usually with grad
students. Charles had practically *propositioned her* that
time in the mailroom. Talking about populating some

island, which was not only sexist but also some ridiculous colonizer bullshit coming from an educated Black
man who should know better. But then again trying to
get some almost always seemed to trump political ideol-
ogy. In his sleep Will choked out, "Not today." And then
he turned over, and his back was like a mountain range
between them. In any case, what was going to happen
with the kid? Rosetta's indignation morphed into feelings of concern for the girl who reminded her of so
many of the children she had grown up with, and more
poignantly, of herself when her mother died and she was
told her mommy went to live with God in heaven. She
never understood that because she thought her mother
was happy living with her.

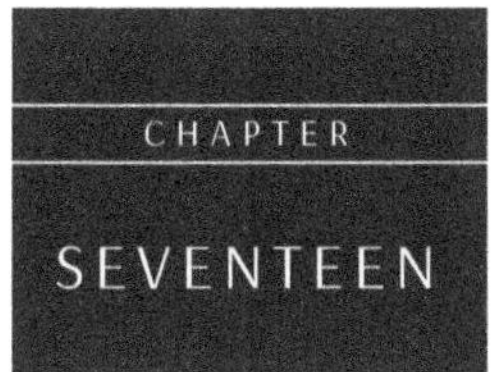

CHARLES

After she showed him the burns on her thigh, Bianca stopped asking for her mother. And although he knew he should, Charles did not call the police. He rationalized the decision by telling himself that they were overwhelmed with trying to find missing people since the towers had fallen and that just as mysteriously as she appeared the first time, Keisha would surely re-appear. In the meantime, he took care of Bianca the way he had taken care of Jason after his wife died, one meal, bath, and bedtime after another. And although he bris-tled when Rosetta suggested he pose as Bianca's *"grand-father,"* during the two weeks they had been together he gained a strange satisfaction and sense of contentment from caring for the little girl.

He took Bianca to school with him and left her in his office with coloring books and toys during his classes, checking on her between and sometimes during class when he assigned his students in-class writing. It wasn't so different from what he had sometimes done with Jason after Maddie died when he had a day off or was on break and Charles had to teach. Bianca was quiet and cooperative. She loved to color, and like Jason, she liked to draw. At the end of the first week, she drew a picture of two stick figures touching hands—one large with no hair and one small with squiggles on its head.

"Who's that?" Charles asked.

"The little one me and the big one you."

"Where's your mother?"

"She not in this picture."

His office was at the end of the hallway and the classrooms where he taught were just around the corner. Mostly Charles managed to avoid other faculty and staff, but a couple of times he ran into people and explained her presence with one word and no explanation: "Baby-sitting."

When he went to get Bianca the evening after Rosetta came to his office, he asked what she wanted for dinner. She said "pizza." He took her to a place a couple of blocks from the college that was crowded with com-muting students. While they sat at a small Formica table in the narrow restaurant that reeked of garlic and cheap mozzarella cheese, a young man came in and greeted Charles.

"Professor Rivers, hey!" It was Carlos Mejia from the previous semester.

"Hi, Carlos." Carlos looked from Charles to Bianca.

"Hey, ain't that Keisha's little girl?" Bianca started shaking her head vigorously.

"Have you been in touch with Keisha?"

"Huh, no, I mean she was in the class. Your class. And she brought her kid a couple of times. Your class was one of my favorites." He grinned. "Good to see you, professor. Gotta get me a slice." Carlos got on line, paid for his slice, scarfed it down near the counter, and left as a crush of other customers entered the crowded space. Bianca ate slowly, picking strings of cheese off with her fingers and eating them separately.

"Why did you shake your head when he asked if you were Keisha's daughter."

"I don't like Keisha."

"Keisha is your mother."

She shook her head again. "I like you," she said after dropping a string of cheese into her mouth. It occurred to him to say something about not talking with your mouth full or about the proper way to eat a slice of pizza, but he thought better of it. It scared him a little to see how attached Bianca had grown to him in such a short amount of time, and he was surprised by her seeming indifference towards her mother because he knew that even when abused, children defended their parents and sought their love. But then he asked himself what he would have done if someone like him stepped in and tried to father him kindly after his father beat or berated him, and he decided that he too might prefer a stranger's kindness to parental abuse.

They took the number one train to 96th Street and the number two back uptown to 110th. Bianca trudged up the crumbling steps of his stoop like a veteran, having adapted quickly to their routine.

"What should I read to you tonight?" Charles asked once she had brushed her teeth with her new *Sesame Street* toothbrush and climbed into Jason's bed. There was a shelf of worn children's books that had belonged to Jason in his room. Bianca was especially fond of *Clifford, the Big Red Dog.* Charles noticed that she cringed when they passed dogs on the street, and when he asked if she was afraid, she shook her head no, while grabbing his leg and pulling herself as far away from an approaching canine as she could get.

"Clifford."

"Oh no, not him again!" Charles laughed at their little joke and sitting awkwardly on the side of the sagging twin mattress, he read her the book. When he finished, she said, "The End." And they both giggled. Something in the now unguarded brightness of her laughter and the sheen of her wide eyes sparked a feeling of recognition that Charles could not explain. As he tucked her in, it came to him that somehow, he had always known her. That Keisha did not abandon her but had actually brought her back home. She was the flower that emerges from the earth after the forest burns, and he was beginning to feel that it was his mission to protect her. He felt guilty when he went out for his run in the morning, but he instructed her to stay in bed if she woke up before he got back. And for the past few days she had been sound asleep when he came back at 7:30. He had sometimes left Jason for an hour or two as well. It probably wasn't entirely safe, but when you were the only parent, sometimes you had to take risks.

ROSETTA

"I was hoping you'd be in today." Rosetta looked up from the student paper she was reading in the small drab office she shared on alternate days with other adjuncts and saw Charles Rivers, dressed in the knife creased black slacks and one of the pastel oxford shirts he seemed to favor, standing in the doorway poised to enter the small space. As soon as she recognized him blood rushed to her face, her nipples tingled, and she was immediately embarrassed by her body's involuntary response. "Bianca needs some clothes, and I don't know where to shop for them. I mean, it's been a while since my son was little and you have kids, so I thought you might..." His delivery was quiet and somewhat self-conscious as if he'd asked about some private female matter like menstruation. That caused Rosetta to pause before she spoke and to scrutinize him as her vision adjusted from the closeness of the page to the distance of his face.

"So, you decided to keep her?"

"Well, until her mother comes back. She left her with me, so she'll know where to find her."

"Are you sure you shouldn't, like, file a missing person's report or something? Get some help looking for her?"

"Wouldn't they just take Bianca, then?"

"You really want her? I thought you were getting ready to retire to some desert island." Rosetta tried to smile at her reference to what he said that time in the mailroom, but Charles didn't acknowledge it. Instead he frowned in that signature way of his.

"She needs some stability." Rosetta thought about that. No doubt it was true, but how was living with a stranger after your mother disappeared a stable situation?

"Are you sure you don't know where her mother is? Are you the father?" The snarl of suspicion in her own voice as she posed the question that had become popular on a cheesy daytime TV show took Rosetta by surprise. Charles stepped back.

"What are you accusing me of?" Rosetta began tapping the pencil she was using to mark the papers on the desk. She had so little time to get through all of the essays and she was in the middle of reading one that was very painful by a Muslim student who wrote about her brother being beaten up after the WTC attack, and now this. She took a deep breath.

"Nothing. I don't know. This is weird. I know I said you could pretend to be her grandfather, but that was silly. You should go to the police," Rosetta said, at once flustered by this intrusion on her time, strangely flattered that he was asking for her help, and angry that he might be concealing some sort of wrongdoing. "You're involving me in something—"

"I understand. I'm sorry. It's not fair for me to get anybody else mixed up in this. It's just that I, I, trust you."

"I'm just an adjunct here."

"It has nothing to do with your job title. I can tell that you're a good person, and I don't trust a lot of people."

Why is that? Because you fuck undergraduates and make them disappear? the cynic in Rosetta silently retorted.

"Look, this is not some weird come on, is it? Because it's having the opposite effect," Rosetta declared looking back down at the papers on her desk. But that wasn't true; even as she denied being moved, she felt she was taking a step closer to him in her heart. "Where is she now?"

"She's at home in my apartment."

"By herself?"

"Well, I had a meeting."

"That's really not okay, you know. I would never leave my boys alone like that. Who says you're even fit to parent?" She blurted out.

"You do speak your mind," Charles sputtered. Again, his forehead erupted into that riverbed of deeply etched grooves, and he looked as aghast and hurt as her children did when Rosetta spoke sharply.

"I'm sorry. I just..." She instantly felt bad about what she'd said. Despite his composed appearance, he clearly was not someone who could easily hide hurt feelings.

"I told you they were homeless. I'm sure she's been in far more dangerous circumstances than this one."

"I'm just confused about the whole situation, and I have to read these papers before class," Rosetta said, picking up the stack and leaning back in the sagging worn office chair that was probably older than she was. She looked up at Charles and then back at the papers on her desk because the hurt look on his face was more than she could bear. "There's a store. It's a chain," she said. "Fabway on 34th. They have cute clothes for kids. Pretty cheap."

"What size would she be?"

"Usually the size pretty much matches their age, but she's kind of chubby. How old is she exactly?"

"She will be six on October 25."

"How do you know her birthday?"

"That's what it says on her birth certificate."

"Maybe a seven. Wait. Why do you have her birth certificate?"

"It was in the stuff her mother left." Rosetta found herself suspicious and frowning again, which felt good, actually, because it instantly killed the troubling feelings of desire that had overtaken her the moment before.

"She brought a big bag of stuff the night she came to my door."

"What are you going to do about school? Shouldn't she be in school if she's six?"

"I guess, but I think she was bullied in school." Rosetta waited for Charles to say more, but he seemed to get lost in his thoughts, and he did not continue speaking.

"Are you ok?"

"Yes, yes. Sorry," Charles said. "I'm really imposing. Thanks for the information about the store." He turned to leave.

"Wait. Let me get this straight. You are going to keep this little girl, and you will need some help and, and a kind of confidante, and you want me to be it?"

"No, I simply," he began, but he corrected himself. "In a way, yes, I guess that's it."

"Why would I do that? Who would do that? I have my own kids to worry about. I have a husband." She took a deep breath, but as she exhaled the logical answers to her own questions evaporated. There was no good reason to do what he was asking her to do, but she knew she was going to do it because she wanted to get close to him.

She tore a little piece of paper off the bottom of the cover sheet of one of her student papers. Charles looked alarmed. "I always tell them that they don't need a cover sheet, but some of them insist. Too well trained for their own good." She wrote her address and phone number on the tiny, ragged triangle of paper and handed it to him. She was quivering inside.

"Ok, maybe you can bring her by my place about 6pm on Halloween and she can trick-or-treat with my boys. We live in a big safe building and there's always tons of candy."

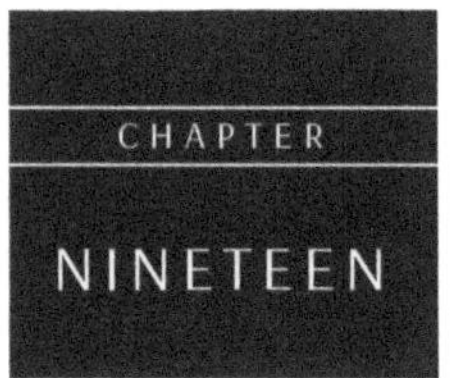

CHARLES

She lived on the 25th floor of a large red brick high-rise building that was part of a complex on 3rd Avenue. The floors of the spacious high-ceilinged lobby were highly polished and glass sliding doors at either end opened onto landscaped courtyards. The doorman's desk was a circular affair set in the center and staffed by a sixtyish uniformed brown-skinned and white haired South Asian man who kept the building's inner access doors buzzing continually as kids in costumes, some chaperoned, some not, went in and out. Charles approached the desk with Bianca, who dressed in a Snow-White costume and carrying an orange Ronald McDonald Trick-or-Treat bucket, clutched his hand. The doorman gave them the once over before he raised the handset to his ear and called the apartment. Charles thought he detected a little sneer of disdain as he said their names. He could hear a man's deep voice over the intercom, "Let them in."

There was no one on the express elevator that the doorman instructed them to take when they first entered it, but before the door closed a gaggle of mostly white elementary school boys laden with shopping bags full of candy and dressed as the usual superheroes and pirates and such, dashed between the closing doors and stabbed at the buttons.

"We should go to thirty and walk down," said a ghoul with a bloody rubber dagger stuck in his neck.

"Duh," said another kid in a cape who was wielding a light saber. A boy with thick dark hair and tan skin in a peaked Batman mask looked up at Charles and politely asked,

"Which floor?"

"It's already pressed." Bianca stood like a Disney figurine observing the restless and sugar crazed boys who, as the elevator ascended dipped into their bags, loudly comparing, trading, and chomping on their loot.

"Who likes Nerds?"

"I'll trade you this Snickers for some Starbursts."

"Yuck. Mary-janes are gross."

"Dum Dums are so dumb."

Charles and Bianca got off the elevator and walked down a long corridor. At the end there was a window framing an impressive view of the West Side of

Manhattan including a panorama of Central Park, the lake at the center reflecting the orange glow of the sun that was just about to set. They rang 25D and the door was opened by a muscular fair-haired white man who was so tall, his head was higher than the door frame.

"Hi, I'm Will. You must be Charles and Bianca. Please come in."

Will shook Charles' hand as if he were gripping a barbell. Charles flinched a little.

"The boys are in the living room," Will said to Bianca, who looked up at him from the corner of her eye and took a step back to hide behind Charles.

"Shy," Charles said. Will nodded. "They're here, Rosetta."

Rosetta came into the foyer dressed in tight black jeans and a long-sleeved black shirt wearing a black cat mask over her eyes with little ears sprouting out on either side of her head.

"I'm Catwoman," she announced with a cheery somewhat self-deprecating grin. Charles tried to keep a neutral expression and to tell himself that this visit was to give Bianca a chance to trick- or- treat in a safe building with other kids and that Rosetta's husband could mash him like a flea if he ever suspected he was lusting after his woman, but *Damn, Catwoman was fine*!

"Hi Bianca, how pretty you look! Let me guess who you are. Snow White!" Bianca nodded vigorously and smiled almost imperceptibly. "Who did your hair?" Rosetta glanced at Charles.

"A lady at my barbershop is a braider. Who knew?" Charles chuckled softly. Bianca's hair was braided in cornrows that curved prettily around the circumference of her head and ended in a thick French braid at the back that grazed the middle of her neck. When Charles went to his barber on 116th to have his head shaved, a Senegalese woman who rented a chair in the shop, noticed Bianca waiting for him by the door, and she offered to braid her hair. Bianca flinched and cried softly as the woman pulled the puffy strands into tight braids, encouraging Bianca by saying, "You want to look pretty, right? I make you look pretty."

"Boys, they're here." Rosetta led Bianca and Charles into a living room with picture windows of the same view they had observed in the hallway, but the sun had set and all one could see now was a dark field that seemed to extend past the horizon like a black ocean stippled with starlight. The boys were sitting on the floor frantically manipulating video game controllers and staring at the action of a virtual soccer game on a large Sony TV encased in a dark wooden entertainment unit and bookcase.

"They're addicts. Already," Rosetta said. "What can you do?" She shrugged. Charles shuddered inwardly at the word addict. "It's time to go trick-or- treating guys. You know, candy!"

"Yay!" The smaller one abandoned his controller and jumped up in his cheap baggy Superman suit.

"Bianca, this is Superman, I mean, Ryan," Rosetta said tousling his hair. "And that's Evan, I mean, Batman."

The boys' faces were vanilla and butter-pecan versions of Rosetta's. Their bodies were tall, thin well-proportioned replicas of their father's. Evan, the older one, had pale skin, black poodle curls and slate-colored eyes. Ryan's skin was golden, his eyes dark amber, his hair straight and brown.

"Who are you?" Ryan asked.

"Snow White," she said in a whisper.

"Where's your mask?"

"It broke." Bianca looked up at Charles. The thin elastic of the cheap plastic mask depicting the Disney character's raven colored hair and paper white skin snapped as soon as she put it on, so they left it behind.

"We have a jack-o-lantern, Ryan said. Want to see it?" He grabbed Bianca's hand, but she pulled it away from him. Undaunted, he ran towards the dining area and pointed to a lopsided pumpkin with jagged geometric shapes forming its eyes, mouth and nose sitting on a platter in the middle of a cherry wood dining room table that was surrounded by six matching ladder-back chairs. The older boy was still trying to score a goal in the game.

"You play video games?" Evan called out to Bianca, all the while keeping his eyes on the screen and his fingers on the controller.

"Girls don't play video games," Ryan, the younger boy, responded.

"Yes, they do. That's sexist," Evan said.

"What's sexist, Mommy?"

"Are we going trick-or-treating or not," Rosetta dodged the question.

"Trick-or-treating, trick-or-treating." Ryan started jumping up and down. Evan finally dropped the controller and pulled a rubber mask over his head.

"Let's go."

Rosetta produced plastic shopping bags from the local supermarket for the boys.

"This is a budget operation," she joked.

"Where's Daddy?"

"Daddy's staying home for the trick-or-treaters. It's my turn to take you this year."

Charles looked over his shoulder and realized that Will had disappeared.

"Your bucket is cool," Ryan said to Bianca. "Mommy won't let us go to McDonald's."

Bianca's head swiveled in Rosetta's direction. She had been quietly taking in the surroundings, the piano in the corner of the room, the enlarged photographs of the family on every wall, the big inviting sectional couch, the bookcases, the rocking chair, the potted plants, the area rug with splashes of color that looked like the inside of a crayon box and was covered with all kinds of toys: cars, trucks, Legos, balls for different types of games. She had never seen anything like it. It looked like something from TV. She tugged on Charles' pants, and he bent down to hear her whisper.

"Miss Rosetta they mommy? I wish she was my mommy."

Rosetta had a list of all of the apartments that were welcoming trick-or-treaters, and like the boys Charles and Bianca encountered in the elevator when they first arrived, their party took the elevator to the 30th floor and walked down. Some tenants left the candy outside their doors in big bowls or baskets. Rosetta had to tell the boys not to grab handfuls. Sometimes they found themselves as part of a large group of kids and grown-ups from the building and when the door opened the children had to take turns lifting their bags to be filled. Some of the tenants dressed up or wore masks. One lady asked to take pictures of the kids in their costumes. There were only two incidents. One older white man on the 10th floor whose apartment was clearly listed and who had a paper skeleton taped to the door slammed it in right in their faces when he saw Charles, Catwoman and the children, announcing that he had no more candy, but on their way to the stairwell, they saw him open the door and generously fill the bags of the small white children who had come to the apartment with their father.

On the 5th floor a woman with badly dyed and cropped red hair whose tight tan sweater made her look like a lumpy sausage, and whose yipping peek-a-poo ran out to greet and lick Evan and Ryan and then ran back into the apartment, gave each of the boys a generous handful of M&M packs, Twizzlers and Tootsie Roll pops, while dropping a single lollipop into Bianca's bucket. The boys noticed.

"Hey, that's not fair. You gave us more than you gave her," Evan said.

"I know you, but I don't know huh," the woman said, smiling vaguely, her words tinged with remnants of another, possibly, Eastern European language. "Trick of treat," she said and closed the door. Ryan had already started moving towards the next destination. But Evan stood still as if trying to process what had just happened, as if the pieces of a puzzle he had been working on for a long time in his head, were slowly moving into place. He looked up at his mother; then he reached into his bag and took out a big fistful of candy and put it into Bianca's bucket. The children exchanged glances, but neither of them said a word.

Charles planned to leave once they were back on the ground floor. Rosetta and the boys accompanied them downstairs and when they all went through the buzzing doors separating the elevator bank from the main lobby, the boys ran over to friends who had congregated on wooden benches by one of the exits. Bianca stood by Charles' side gripping her bucket to her chest closely watching them from afar.

"This was fun. Thank you for coming," Rosetta said rather formally, possibly on her guard because of the presence of neighbors.

"Thank you for having us. Your boys are really something." Charles could see the doorman eyeing them suspiciously.

"They're great kids," she said. She pulled off her mask and the headband with the black pointed cat ears. There was a wishbone indentation across the bridge of her nose where the mask had bitten into it. "That's a relief," she said, looking up at him with a completely open and guileless expression. In that moment her naked face with its dark, dark eyes, cacao skin, and valentine cheekbones took him back to his origins, their shared origins, and it seemed to embody all of life and all of the things he had wanted from life but had not been able to obtain or hold on to. He turned away from her and glanced at the doors behind them because the feelings were too much. He was becoming undone. When he turned back, she was still looking at him. Still revealing herself, seeing him, allowing him to see a new version of himself in her image.

"Do you still run?" Charles asked trying to mask his emotions, delay goodbye, and figure out when and how he could see her again.

"Almost every day after I drop them off at school."

"What time is that?"

"8:30."

"I go earlier."

"I can't go earlier."

"I can go later."

"You can?"

Rosetta glanced anxiously towards her children who were busily and loudly trading candy with their friends. "So maybe I'll see you out there," she said. But now she seemed nervous, back in mom mode, and she glanced around the lobby to see if anyone was looking at them. "Did you do anything about school for her?"

"I got some workbooks." Rosetta looked doubtful.

"She needs to be around other children. Are you still leaving her alone?"

"Where do your boys go to school?"

"They go to a private school near here. My in-laws pay for it. They don't completely approve of me, but they love their grandchildren, and they have the money."

"Jason went to one on the West Side, but then he got kicked out," Charles said, his voice trailing off.

Rosetta took a deep breath and moved closer to Charles so that Bianca could not hear them. Bianca's eyes were glued on the other children who were shouting and gesticulating wildly like clowns in a pint-sized circus show.

"Look, I have to be honest with you. I know I invited you to bring Bianca and everything, but I don't think you're doing the right thing. How do you know that something bad didn't happen to Keisha? You can't just take in somebody's child, no questions asked."

"It happens all the time in the Black community. But maybe you wouldn't know that." The words rushed out and then hung awkward and abashed in the space between them, like outside children waiting to be disowned.

"What?"

"Maybe you're not so familiar—"

"I'm not familiar with the Black community?" Rosetta's voice rose in anger.

"You—"

"You don't know anything about me, Charles Rivers. And how dare you presume to," Rosetta abruptly turned away from Charles and Bianca and hurried over to the group of costumed children. She shooed her boys towards the door leading to the elevator bank. "Boys, boys, we're going upstairs." As an afterthought, she turned around and called out, "Bianca, I hope you had a nice time." Another mother came towards the doors and when Rosetta recognized her, she hugged her and seemed to be expressing words of condolence.

Charles stood where Rosetta had left him until he realized the doorman was staring at him and Bianca as if willing them to disappear. Charles took Bianca's hand. They walked through the building's automatic doors. She looked up at him in amazement the same way she did when they had entered, and the doors magically opened for them. The bus stop was right outside the building and Charles walked numbly towards the lighted bus shelter, his young ward in tow. Kids were still out trick-or-treating. And there was a steady stream of mostly white pedestrians weaving between them on the street, as well as a ceaseless current of cars and taxis flowing along Third Avenue, their headlights flooding the dark streets. Charles berated himself inwardly for saying the wrong thing to Rosetta. How could his words so completely contradict what he was feeling? He was totally in love with the woman. She was probably sensitive about the whole black/white thing though and then he had to go and put his foot in his mouth. But truth be told, he still felt uncomfortable some-times when he was in a majority white environment. And sometimes he did not know how to talk to people without sounding pedantic on one hand or completely at a loss for words on the other. He tried too hard, and he knew it was probably because of where he came from and from feeling intellectually and educationally inferior to his wife who had been a Ph.D.

"I'm cold," Bianca said. Charles looked down and saw that she was shivering in her thin costume. He hadn't thought to bring a coat or sweater for her. He was wear-ing a navy windbreaker, and he took it off and wrapped it around her.

"Did you have fun," he asked.

"I got a lot of candy. A lot!" She grinned.

"Did you like Evan and Ryan?"

"They nice. They got a lot of toys. Are they white?"

"They are mixed."

"What's mixed?"

"One parent is white, and one is Black."

"I think they white."

ROSETTA AND CHARLES

The day after Halloween, Rosetta dropped the boys off at their private school on 91st Street between Park and Madison Avenues. She was wearing a powder blue running suit that her in-laws had given her for Christmas, with her hair twisted into a tight bun at the top of her head. She engaged in a few pleasantries with Jimmy, the young, Black security guard who most likely went home to a very different neighborhood somewhere uptown, in the Bronx or Brooklyn. Every school day he stood outside in a gray and white uniform protecting the precious progeny of the solidly rich and upper middle class, along with those chosen few of different classes or races, like her sons, who were allowed a place in classrooms designed to reproduce the privilege of the powerful. Rosetta was on speaking terms with a couple of the other parents, more like nodding terms, and some of them magnanimously tolerated her presence at birthday parties and playdates, but for the most part, she was invisible to the other mothers who recognized nothing of themselves and nothing of interest in her. They were pleasant enough to the boys, who in different ways clearly bore their father's imprint, and whom they accepted as that touch of diversity that gave their own children a richer educational experience, but Rosetta was not a part of their social milieu or their children's development, and they felt no obligation to acknowledge her existence.

She crossed the street and walked to Fifth Avenue past another private school, where mostly white girls of various sizes wearing blue and green tartan jumpers and quilted fall jackets had gathered outside and were waiting to enter, monogrammed backpacks bulging on their backs. Rosetta went into the park at 90th Street and once inside, she found an empty bench to hold onto as she stretched her calf and thigh muscles. She would run, go home, shower, straighten up the apartment, read a few papers and then pick up Ryan who was in Kindergarten and only went to school for half a day. Will had started a new job the week before, selling insurance in downtown Brooklyn. It hadn't helped his mood yet, and he was still shaken from his experience at the towers. But it had gotten him out of the apartment, which Rosetta considered her sanctuary during the day.

She had a hard time sleeping the night before because she couldn't stop thinking about how Charles looked at her after she took off her mask in the lobby before he accused her of being out of touch with the Black community. She wanted to feel angrier with him than she actually did, anger being her protection against feelings of attraction and desire. She felt ashamed to admit this to herself. Even under the circumstances. Especially under the circumstances. Was she that unhappy? Was she that neglected and dissatisfied with Will and his kin that she would allow herself to be taken in by the arrogant womanizer Charles Rivers surely must be? Aunt Essie had warned her and her cousins time and time again about the trifling nature of Black men, based on her own experience with her ex-husband and the lovers and spouses of family and friends. When Rosetta was in high school and she steeped herself in African American history and learned about the societal forces that drove the dysfunction between Black women and Black men, she resisted this message. But her personal history seemed to support Aunt Essie's point of view. Where was her father when her twenty-year-old mother gave birth to her? Where was he when her mother died of an asthma attack in the emergency room at Metropolitan Hospital when Rosetta was only five years old? Where was he now? She had no idea. And even though she understood the sociological causes, there was still a big hole in her heart and in her life where her father was supposed to be.

She adjusted the Walkman she carried in the black fanny pack she wore around her waist, the pouch resting on her right hip. Soon Latin music blared in her ears; she liked to listen to it while she ran because she loved the rhythms even though she only understood a few words like amor and ojos and cabeza. She jogged up to the cinder track that encircled the reservoir and then she took off, carried away by the beat, and entranced by the trees and their medley of fall colors.

She usually ran around the track three times. That was about four and a half miles. At first, she was relieved when she had been running for a while and there was no sign of Charles, but after the first lap she wasn't feeling angry anymore and she hoped he would show.

When she reached the stone pump house at the north end the second time around, Mark Anthony was crooning "Make it with You" in English. No one was around and high on endorphins she began singing along to the chorus, "I wanna make it with you." Soon someone was running close behind her. She moved over to let them pass and realized it was Charles.

"Good morning!" he said smiling and looking pleased with himself for pulling off a stealth approach.

"You're here," she said, ripping out her headphones. His face was covered in a thin sheen of sweat that made him look bright and youthful.

"What are you listening to?"

"Mark Anthony."

"Who's that?"

"Latin singer."

"But you were singing in English."

"You heard me singing?"

"That Bread song."

"Bread?"

"The group that made the original recording. In the seventies. Before your time."

"Oh."

"I wanna make it with you…" He sang and his voice was mellow and in tune, as if he really was Nat King Cole. She blushed.

"Okay, okay. Stop." She slapped his arm playfully and felt a rush. They were running parallel to Central Park North now, and other runners were entering the track from the roadway that looped around the park. Rosetta shoved her earphones into her fanny pack, and they ran in silence for a while. Surprisingly, it was not awkward because of their matching strides. The sound of their feet striking the packed earth and gravel at the same time put them into a rhythm that eschewed further conversation. It felt good to be running beside someone at the same pace. When she tried running with Will he always left her behind. Even when they walked together, they were out of sync. He was always slightly ahead and always looking forward seeming not to be aware of her existence by his side.

"You're in really good shape. How long have you been running?" she asked.

"Good shape for an old man, you mean?" He smiled. "Since I was in junior high school, officially. I wasn't much of a fighter, so I had to learn how to run," he laughed. "I got injured, shrapnel in my leg, when I was in the army, but it wasn't bad enough to keep me from running."

"Were you in Vietnam?"

"Yes."

"Why the army? Weren't those guys like cannon fodder?"

"You could say that."

"And you're okay now?"

"Okay?" He laughed a little and stuck out his left hand with the missing finger. "That depends on what you mean by okay."

"So why do you want to run with me?" Rosetta asked.

"I enjoy your company."

"And...?"

"As I said, I like running."

"What do you hope will happen?"

"I can't answer that," Charles said.

"I think you can."

"Why did you invite me to your house?"

"For Bianca."

"Only for Bianca?"

"So, it doesn't matter that I have a husband?"

"Does it matter to you?"

"It--" Rosetta did not finish. They continued running in sync. She pondered the question. Of course, it mattered. It had to matter, but a space had grown between her and Will in which the seeds of flirtation with Charles had taken root and now there was the potential for the seedlings to grow.

"He is not the man I married. It's such a stupid cliché and I shouldn't even be telling you this, but it seems like I can't hold back things from you. We've been together since college. We're very different, not just the obvious things, but that used to be what made being together so much fun. He's not intellectual at all; I'm not saying he's not smart, just that ideas and things don't really interest him, and he doesn't talk much. And he's just like a really white guy who by some strange quirk of fate ended up with a Black woman."

"A very beautiful Black woman," Charles said. Rosetta turned her head and looked at Charles and frowned, annoyed that he was macking as she was trying to explain.

"Yeah, okay. The prettiest girl on the island thing. He's had trouble keeping a job. He has depression but he won't take medication. He gets headaches that are overwhelming. He has to go to bed. For days. I think it has something to do with concussions in high school and college. He played football, you know. And he drinks. Not hard stuff, but beer 24/7."

Charles was not prepared for all of this information. But he was learning that she didn't hold back when there was something on her mind. He wondered what she would think about the glass of scotch he drank every night. And he felt a bit chastened and exasperated because once again she had injected a shot of gravitas into the situation that forced him to see her from her perspective instead of his. He forgot how much women liked to talk about their relationships when given the chance.

"His family lives upstate," She was on a roll. "His brother was the golden boy. He was this big football star and then he went to Harvard Law School and he's a partner in a Wall Street firm now. He lives in Westchester. And boy is he a piece of work. I remember when I first met him he tried to relate to me by talking about how much he liked *Family Matters*, you know, the TV show with Steve Urkel, when he was growing up. I don't think Will ever felt like he could measure up, which is so ironic because he's so big, physically, you know, and handsome. I sometimes wonder if handsome guys aren't at a disadvantage. Everybody is threatened by them and expects them to be as competent as they are good looking."

Charles couldn't help wondering how competent the big guy was in bed. He figured they must be having sex since she had gotten pregnant the previous semester.

"I feel committed to him, and of course to the boys, but it doesn't feel like there's very much for me in the relationship anymore. My job is to make sure everyone gets fed and gets to school and work and has clean socks and goes to the dentist. It feels like that's all marriage is. Just a set up to get everyone where they're supposed to be on time. I can't say we really enjoy spending time together anymore, and like I said there's like zero communication."

Charles glanced at her face and saw a tear rolling down her cheek. She wiped it away with the back of her hand. Seeing her cry scared him. He realized that each word of her exposition was a brick she was laying down on a path that led to his door. He might really get what he was wishing for. Could he handle it? Because if she was willing to open up to him this way, she would surely expect him to do the same. He thought for a while. He didn't want to blow it. But he decided to go for it.

"That reminds me of something I read about W.E.B. Dubois. You know W.E.B. Dubois?"

"No, of course not, I'm not Black enough."

"I'm sorry about what I said last night. I didn't mean it like that."

"Don't make assumptions. I hate that Black people do that to each other. I mean it's not our fault. It's whitey's fault, but why are we always judging who is blacker or whiter based on that phony field nigger/house nigger yardstick?"

"Believe me, I don't want to make assumptions about you. I want to know everything there is to know about you." Charles surprised himself by saying this. And his words made Rosetta shiver inside because she wanted to be known more than anything, but at the same time they registered on her bullshit meter.

"Dubois had a marriage, had a wife who wasn't his intellectual peer, and he took care of her, but he also had a companion."

"Companions, you mean. The brother was a genius who elevated the race, and he told the truth about this country. But he was a total player. That's what men do. They think it's their right. It doesn't always work so well for women. We get called Jezebels and loose women and shit for having lovers."

"Now you sound like somebody from my block."

"What? You mean ghetto? Cause I said, "and shit?" They were rounding the curve of the track and running back towards the East side. "First, I don't understand the Black community. Now I'm ghetto? I am somebody from your block, or I was. Just cause I married a white man don't mean I ain't Black." Her use of the vernacular rattled Charles.

"My wife was very light skinned. And she used to get upset with people who thought she was white. But we know the whole idea of race is a fiction. Look at the Human Genome project, what they found is that we are 99.9 percent the same."

"Biologically, not socially, not culturally, not in the house that white supremacy built." Charles was surprised by the militancy of her tone.

"What about your kids?"

"What about my kids?"

"Are they Black?"

"Of course!"

"And you're okay with that?"

"Why wouldn't I be? I want them to accept themselves and be aware of all their ancestry, and it will be up to them to decide how to identify. But it's also about how they will be perceived. As not white. And to be honest, I would hate for them to think of themselves as white or to be able to pass. That would be a terrible thing—because whiteness has a way of blotting out everything that's not white. Like a snowstorm. I don't want them to be white, but I want them to be treated right. I don't want them to have to second guess every little simple thing like going into a store or going on vacation or into a restaurant or even a library to become complicated because they are Black or mixed. The worse thing is not knowing how you will be treated, you know? You could be going along okay, just living your life like any other human being and then bam—you are a victim of some racist act or remark. It could be a small thing like you are waiting in line and some white person comes up and whoever is in charge ignores you and calls them first. It's a kind of terrorism, even when it's unwitting. A lot of white people, and I'm talking educated white people, now, speak about us as though we are essentially different from them. Another order of beings. The blacks. I hate it when people say the blacks. I had this so-called liberal professor who was always talking about the blacks. It's white *people* and the blacks, as if we aren't people and as if we are all the same." Charles saw that he had hit a nerve.

"The year I graduated from the program I invited that professor; he was visiting and not on the regular faculty and the whole class came to my house to have the final party. And this guy, who is from Vermont, but a Jew who grew up in New York and should know better, comes into my apartment and starts looking around like he's shocked. He looks in the kitchen at all the appliances and at the French casserole pot that the food is cooking in, and he says, "I have one of those." Then he goes into the living room and looks at all the furniture and bookshelves and pictures on the walls and he says like completely flabbergasted, "*I* could live here." It was like he assumed because I was Black that I would live in a slum. In his mind, and granted it was an old mind, I fit into "the blacks" category so I wasn't supposed to be living like that, white husband not-withstanding. He probably imagined something out of some old Life magazine photo essay by Gordon Parks back in the day."

"That's how I grew up."

"Me, too, but this was like 50 years later on the Upper East Side!"

"Your kids are being raised white, though. White schools and everything. Jason, my son Jason started getting confused in that school and he didn't even have to deal with the being mixed thing, except when he was little. They thought he was mixed because his hair was red like Maddie's. But then she opened her mouth and set everybody straight. 'I'm Black. His father's Black and he's Black.' End of story." Charles laughed.

"Yeah, it's probably going to be a problem at some point. But everybody deserves the privileges that come with whiteness, right? Why should my boys and their white peers get a better education than Bianca? But they probably will. Why should they be valued more? When I think about this stuff it just makes me sick."

"Will says shit like, 'I don't see you or the boys as black or white. We're all just people' and I wish it could be that easy. When we're with him and at home we're not walking around thinking about what color we are. And when we go out with him, we have a kind of honorary status because of his whiteness. And there are times, I have to admit, when white people disrespect or talk down to me, like in a store, I'm thinking, you think I'm just another ordinary nigger, don't you, I'm probably way more educated than you are; I have a passport, and French cookware," She chuckled. "And my husband is white. It's kind of messed up the way I sometimes lean on his whiteness for my own self-esteem. It's like I need it to prove that I'm human and that's pretty fucked up."

"I don't want you to be from my block," Charles blurted out after a brief silence, surprising even himself with his spontaneous admission. "That's not how I picture you."

"Are you serious, Professor Rivers? You are joking, right? I'm not a picture! That's some sexist shit, Charles, racist and *self-loathing* too."

"Why do you keep saying shit?"

"That should be my question. Why does it bother you?"

"It feeds into the stereotype."

"Which one? Angry, foul-mouthed Black woman? Oh, that's not who you thought I was? We have many identities, Charles. I was actually born in Harlem Hospital."

"I thought you were born in Ohio."

"Ohio?"

"You wrote that story. You know the one for the Roth prize?"

"What? You read that?"

"I was on the prize committee."

"That was fiction."

"You carry yourself with too much dignity."

"For what? To use four letter words? You don't want me to curse, but you want me to commit adultery?"

"I never said that. Maybe you're projecting."

"Oh, come on," she laughed. It was mirthless and mocking. "Now you're going to get all Freudian on me? We both know you want to fuck me, Charles. Fuck, fuck, fuck," she said, the words punctuated by the thump of their feet pounding the track. Charles looked around to see if anyone else was in earshot. "How dignified is that?" She was looking ahead focused on the ropey muscled legs of a skinny white guy with an odd gait and limp running shorts who had passed and now was several yards ahead of them. "But I'm not interested in being another link in your chain."

"What chain?"

"The chain of fools. You know, chain, chain, chain, originally recorded by Aretha Franklin."

"What...?"

"Come on. You can't expect me to believe your Keisha story. I mean, I know how you guys in the department roll. You are not the first one to approach me..." *What?* Charles thought. Who else had approached her? A stitch of jealousy needled his side.

"Everything I told you about Keisha is true. She just showed up at my place with her child."

"And you didn't, like, take advantage of the situation?"

"No!" Charles said. The vehemence of his denial was meant to establish his innocence as well as cover up the sexual feelings he had somehow telegraphed to Quintasia and had briefly felt for Keisha when he found her in his bed.

"What about your wife?"

"She's dead. You know my wife is dead."

"Was she your student?" He shot her a pained look.

"No, no, just the opposite, she was," he stumbled, "She was my professor."

"Oh!" Rosetta let that sink in as they ran past the water station at the south end.

"Okay, I guess I shouldn't be making assumptions about you either then," she said in between heavy breaths as they neared the end of the last lap. "But I'm quite sure it's a fact and not just an assumption that you want to fuck me, right? Either that or you got some lyin eyes, and I'm not talking about the Eagles."

She looked over at Charles and grinned. Even though he was in motion, he felt like a mouse in a glue trap. He hadn't expected her to curse so much, and to be so crass and blunt. "You don't have to answer. We both know what the answer is. And that's okay with me. I have to be honest; I've been struggling with this. But I want to fuck you, too, even though you seem totally clueless about how you are objectifying me."

She was huffing and puffing now, and her arms were pumping her through the last stretch, but she looked over at him and smiled the smile that slayed him every time. Again, he was shocked to the point of being shaken by her honesty. "But you have to promise, we have to promise each other that running together will be fucking for us, okay. We can do this almost every day during the week, if you want to, but I can't ruin my marriage."

Charles stopped dead in his tracks; that is his mind did; his legs were on automatic, and they kept running. He recovered himself after a bit and said, "You do speak your mind."

"Well, so do you. Even the part that's not conscious," she laughed. Charles inhaled deeply. His muscles were starting to ache, a spur in his left heel announcing its presence. He had come out early because he didn't want to miss her, and he ended up doing double his usual run.

"True dat," as my mother used to say."

"What? Wow! I never thought I'd hear that from you, Professor Standard English. Is your mother alive?"

"She's in a nursing home not far from where I live."

"Do you go see her?"

"Once a week. She has dementia. She doesn't recognize me. She tells me she has a son who favors me, her words, but that he's in the merchant marine and doesn't visit her. My father was in the merchant marine before they met but he died when I was a kid."

"Oh, that's very sad. Sorry. Do you have brothers and sisters?"

"No."

"Me either. I have older cousins, but no siblings. My mother died when I was seven. My aunt raised me. She lives in Brooklyn and she's the one who warned me about men like you." She smiled again.

"So that's why you married a white guy?"

"Probably."

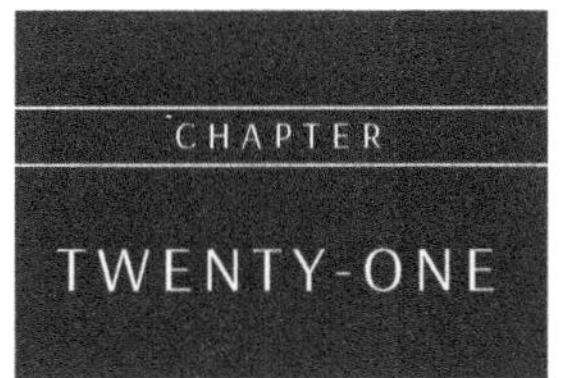

CHARLES

Running together became a regular thing in the mornings after dropping the children off at school. At Rosetta's insistence, Charles managed to enroll Bianca in a small Catholic school in East Harlem. He was able to pull it off with the papers Keisha left behind in the woven bag. Inside one of the composition notebooks was Bianca Theodore Brown's birth certificate, with no information about the father, and a little booklet documenting her immunizations with her Social Security card tucked inside it. Surprisingly, Keisha had been good about taking her for well-baby visits at a downtown clinic. Charles passed Bianca off as his granddaughter. He told them her mother went missing after the Twin Towers went down, which was true, and that he had assumed responsibility for her, also true, and the school did not question it.

For weeks both Charles and Rosetta seemed to accept that they could have their cake—the other's company—as long as they were not foolish enough to try to eat it too. But one chilly gray day in late November at the north end of the track at the spot where Charles usually headed home, after their customary neutral wave, he grabbed Rosetta's hand and pulled her along as he ran down the slope of the hill towards a path that led to Harlem through the North Woods.

At first, she resisted, but then she was running beside him. They giggled as they bumped into and almost tripped each other on the crumbling stairs that led to the roadway bordering the north end of the park. At the bottom of the steps, at the bend in the road, under a dome of gray sky and surrounded by nearly leafless old trees, Charles pulled Rosetta close, cupped his hands around her face, bent down to her height, and kissed her. Their mouths parted at the same time, and it was as if an underwater lock had opened and each of them began flowing into the channel of the other.

Everything was a blur after that. He had no idea how they managed to run the last few blocks, get upstairs, and into his bedroom, or how, clutching and kissing and undressing all at once, they made it to his bed. He couldn't get enough of her—the apples and coffee tang of her mouth, the moist, salty softness of her skin, her musky but flowery scent, like that of an actual rose, enveloping him. She moaned when he brushed his lips across her nipples and buried his face in her slightly pendulous mother's breasts. He felt, almost literally, that he could die there, and he started murmuring that she was a goddess, an African goddess. She responded by finding his mouth and kissing all the clichés out of it. He had fantasized so many times about what he would do to her if the opportunity ever presented itself, but somehow, he did not fully imagine what *she* might do to him.

She reached down and caressed him, and he experienced a frisson of nearly unbearable pleasure. When was the last time someone else had touched him there? He had to hold it together. He tried to slow himself down by focusing on her face. It was flushed and glowing, her eyes half closed, her features softened by desire, the anticipation of pleasure concentrated in the succulent fullness of her lips. She looked like the younger woman that she was, and she seemed so adept that he doubted himself for a moment.

"It's been a long time," he said.

"It's like riding a bicycle," she whispered into his ear.

"Little known secret about me," he whispered back, "I don't know how to ride a bike."

"Time to learn."

ROSETTA

Rosetta borrowed money from Charles and took a gypsy cab straight back to the school to pick up Ryan. As the taxi headed east and then south, in a matter of blocks they traveled from East Harlem to the Upper East Side—neighborhoods that were worlds apart yet right next door to each other. Her body was loose, relaxed and thoroughly sated, but her mind was racing. She felt like a different person from the one she was when she left the apartment that morning, but also like she had never been more herself.

Charles came as soon as he was inside her, but she was so close that she was able to catch and ride that first wave with him. There was something desperate in the way he held on to her afterwards.

"Relax," she said. "I'm not going anywhere."

Despite the danger inherent in the situation, Rosetta felt happy and secure lying in Charles' arms on his dingy white disheveled sheets, running her fingers across the patchy salt and pepper hairs on his chest. They laughed about the hurry they had been in and then they made love again at a connoisseur's pace.

Rosetta leaned her head against the cracked leather seat of the aging Crown Victoria sedan. The driver was trying to catch her eye in the rearview mirror. She ignored him. She was full of Charles. And she was full of herself with Charles. It delighted her that he was as handsomely built as she imagined, with well-defined but not bulky pecs and abs. He reminded her of a chocolate Ken doll, only he was endowed in a way that Ken was not. She was glad she'd had the IUD inserted after the pregnancy was terminated. But her panties were damp with her fluids and his, and she was thinking about how she needed to wash away the evidence. She should have made him use a condom, but it was so sudden, and she was pretty sure he wasn't lying about not being involved with other women, especially after his brief riding a bike freak out.

It was amazing and frightening to think about how close they actually lived to each other. Now that they had crossed the boundary, whenever they were apart the distance would seem great, and when she was at home with Will the distance between the two of *them* would be greater still. Realizing this, Rosetta felt afraid for a moment, but she was still too physically satisfied to feel remorse. She got out of the car, and Jimmy, the school security guard greeted her as she joined the group of mothers waiting for their children outside the elegant brick townhouse that was home to the school. She wondered if he could tell what she had just done. She was embarrassed to be wearing the same running gear that was limp and sweaty now. And her hair was all over the place.

When she realized how late it was and jumped up to leave Charles' apartment, she couldn't find the elastic that had slipped off her ponytail while they were in bed. Her hair had returned to its natural fullness and now it stood out in a thick bush. One of the mothers she didn't know looked at her and said, "Wow, you must have done one hell of a workout."

CHARLES, 1957-1968

When they were eight years old Carol Jones declared that she and Charles Rivers would get married someday. They lived next door to each other in apartments 3A and 3B respectively in a run-down building on St. Nicholas Terrace between 126th and 127th Streets in Harlem. It was also home to a considerable population of cockroaches and rodents. They grew up in each other's decrepit but rambling railroad apartments. Miss Brenda, Carol's mother, kept Charles when his parents were at work before he was allowed to stay at home alone. And almost every day of their young lives Charles, Carol and her brothers, Skylar and Aubrey, who were a couple of years older, and her sister Pam who was two years younger watched TV and played together. They played tag, house, church, hide and seek, cars and cards, punch and dodge ball. They played with the cheap toys they received for Christmas and broke shortly after and the ones they created for themselves like clothespin slingshots and go-carts made of roller skates. In their shabby surroundings, they performed skits and shows, perfected dance moves, sang along with the radio and records and presented themselves as a unified posse when threatened by other kids on the block.

As they got older and Charles spent more time with school friends and other boys in the neighborhood, it started to bother him that Carol acted like she owned him because he was starting to realize that besides proximity they actually had very little in common. He would be playing basketball in St. Nicholas Park and she and her friends would come by giggling and pointing in their short shorts and cropped tops laying claim to the guys they liked as they watched them play. Charles didn't dare look at another girl because Carol made it clear to everyone that he belonged to her.

She was slightly plump with a butterscotch complexion, a dimpled smile, and hot comb straightened hair she was always trying to grow longer. When they were in high school, she wore it in a Gidget-like flip hairdo. She was the eldest girl of the five siblings, and she helped her mother and blind grandmother care for her brothers and sisters and the neighbor children they often babysat. Carol's father was in prison in upstate New York for an armed robbery that everyone insisted he did not commit, and once a month at 5am on Saturday morning her mother took a bus to visit him. Carol's grandmother taught her how to cook. And sometimes to raise money the family sold plates of food to their neighbors—fried porgies and banana pudding and a magical dish made from elbow macaroni and welfare cheese. Carol spent most of Saturday cooking and all-day Sunday at the Tabernacle For All People on Eighth Avenue where she got saved at the age of eleven. She had a terrible voice, but no one had the heart to tell her, so she sang enthusiastically in the small church choir. She was good with hair and could braid and cornrow like a professional, and in the summertime, she often sat outside and did the younger children's hair.

Carol liked to brag about how smart Charles was and how he loved to read when she and her friends hung out on the stoop or in the park. But Charles wanted more than admiration. He wanted someone who also read and thought about life and the ideas in books and movies and the way people were living all around them.

She wasn't that someone; she was satisfied with the world, however limited, as it presented itself to her day by day. She was surrounded by family and girlfriends and church people, and she had not been brought up to ask questions. Charles grew up to be a loner who inherited, without fully comprehending it until he was older, unmediated pain from the deep racial wounds and disappointments in life suffered by his parents, who migrated north only to find that prejudice and privation followed them there. What made it even worse for them is that they didn't have a happy family life.

His parents had lost touch with the religious traditions and community connections that sustained other Black people, so there was very little of a social or spiritual nature to salve their wounds. When he was small, they sent Charles to church with the Jones family, but neither of them went; his mother often worked on Sundays. They kept to themselves and did not socialize or band together with others to improve their situation. Religion, hope for the future, or in their absence, thick keloids of resignation helped other Black families strive or at the very least survive the indignities of poverty and racial injustice, but the scar tissue covering the wounds of Charles, Sr. and Delores Rivers was thin and the stresses of daily life continually ripped it open.

When Charles was small he learned to shrink and flatten himself inside like the Gumby toy he received one year for Christmas so he wouldn't provoke his parents' anger or feel the heat when it exploded. There were the usual tongue lashings or getting slapped upside the head after spilling milk or refusing to eat the grits and sardines on his plate or contradicting his parents. But there were also times when the "whippins" he got from his father unleashed a fury that went way beyond appropriate punishment for his childhood misdeeds. One time his father beat him bloody with a leather belt, yelling that he would "teach him a lesson" because Charles went home with a friend after school and didn't come back until after dark. His mother tried to explain that his father's rage was fueled by fear for his safety, but Charles couldn't understand how hurting him was supposed to protect him from getting hurt.

Charles' father and mother lived at odds with each other until he died, trading insults and evil looks and disagreeing on just about everything from taking out the trash to how to properly cook pork. They got married after World War II when both of them moved up north—him from South Carolina, her from Alabama, where they met one night at the Savoy Ballroom. They were each with a cousin who had come to New York before them and wanted to show them the sights. Delores was already thirty, and she had never been married. She spent her youth caring for her widowed mother and five sisters and brothers; Charles, Sr. was over forty with an ex-wife and grown kids who wanted nothing to do with him. They got married at City Hall a week after they met, thinking it would be easier to pool their resources so they could make it in the big city. Their first "apartment" was an 8x8 foot room with a shared toilet at the end of the communal hallway in a rooming house on 135th St. It was hard making ends meet, especially since Charles, Sr. liked to drink. And after that first time at the Savoy, they never went out dancing again.

Dolores Rivers was disappointed to discover that the tenderness she sought from a husband was not forthcoming from Charles, Sr. whose heart had been incarcerated by hardship and mistreatment and pickled by alcohol. She was devastated to find out that with her spotty sixth grade education the only work open to her was the same type available in the south: running herself ragged to make life more comfortable for white folks. She wanted to have a baby more than anything, but they were married for three years and she had three miscarriages before she was able to carry Charles, Jr. to term.

Charles, Sr. worked as a longshoreman on the Brooklyn docks. He was used to heavy labor on farms and in factories and he had delivered cargo during the war. He was "John Henry" strong and locomotive black, the kind of powerful looking Black man that whites feared and used as a screen for their racial animus. Their apprehension reduced him to the status of a brute and the dehumanization deeply wounded Charles, Sr. His wounds became pellets of rage that he sprayed all over his wife and child. He told Charles stories about trying to get work at the docks. The men had to "shape up," meaning arrange themselves in a semi-circle to wait for a boss to look them up and down before deciding to hire them. He told him about how the Irish and Italian guys complained that the Negros were taking their jobs and how they turned their noses up when the cargo was dirty or difficult to unload and left those jobs to the colored men and Puerto Ricans. Even though he was in a union, he said, they still treated him like a nigger, and he felt like a nigger standing around and waiting to be chosen for work that could kill him. "What was the difference between that and an auction block?" he asked.

Charles was ten when his father got injured and had to have his left leg amputated when a hoist gave out and a shipping container nearly crushed him. He got some compensation from the union for a few months but after that he couldn't work anymore. His day at home began with him demanding that Delores make him bacon and eggs and grits before she left the house at 7 o'clock in the morning. He spent the rest of it listening to John Gambling on the radio, then drinking one particular brand of Dutch beer all afternoon and playing his collection of old blues and race records on an RCA Victor HiFi he had bought on an installment plan when they first moved into the apartment on 127th Street. Sometimes Charles, Jr. would come home from school and the needle would be stuck in a defective groove and the same musical phrase by Howlin Wolf or Sister Rosetta Tharpe would play again and again--"Little bitty boy we, Little bitty boy we, Little bitty boy we" until his father angrily ordered him to lift and reposition the needle as if it were somehow his fault that it was stuck in the first place.

The catalog of names ending in bitch or cunt that Charles, Sr. called his wife Dolores seemed endless. He criticized her no matter how she looked, what she wore or didn't wear, what she said or didn't say, what she cooked or didn't cook. And he monopolized her time during the few hours when she was home from work and not asleep by constantly ordering her to bring him one thing or another declaring, "If you can wait on them white folks, you can wait on me."

If he saw Charles with a book in his hand, he told him he was wasting his time with nonsense. And if Charles and his mother wanted to watch a different TV show when *Gunsmoke* and *McHale's Navy* came on they were out of luck. Charles, Sr. loved mocking Black performers like Sammy Davis, Jr. when they appeared on TV, "Look at that nigger actin' like he got a right to be out there on the stage." And there were times when Charles or his mother came into or happened to be sitting in the living room, when Charles, Sr. would suddenly banish them to the kitchen or their bedrooms by yelling, "Get outta my sight."

When Charles was twelve, his father died of a heart attack in the tattered living room armchair from which he ruled their raggedy roost. Delores rose at five, as she usually did, to find him sitting up in the once overstuffed chair, whose cushions had been cruelly com-pressed by his bulk, looking startled and about to rise, his crutches at his feet, his lips twisted in a final and ironic smile of agony, a bottle of beer knocked on its side on the table next to him. Once he was gone and the heat of his anger was a cool ghost, Charles, Jr. began to slowly understand where it had come from. The year he turned fourteen he saw boys and girls who were his own age and younger on TV marching against segregation in the streets of Birmingham, Alabama, the state where his mother was born.

He had never been to Alabama; although every summer before he died, his mother begged his father to let him go down and meet his cousins and experience life in the country. "I ain't sending no boy of mine down there," his father bellowed and that would be the end of it. As Charles watched people who looked like him being pounced on by snarling dogs, beaten by baton wielding cops, and catapulted and felled by powerful jets of water, he was glad his father never let him go.

Why do they hate us? What is wrong with us? What is wrong with them? he thought. The faces of the police and the blood-thirsty, acrimonious crowd looked like his father's face looked when Charles knew he was about to get a whipping. Then came the epiphany. It was those hate-filled white people acting *through* his father who had burst his eardrums with racial epithets, smashed their fists against his flesh, demanded he get out of their sight, and threatened to destroy his body if he did not obey.

A few months later in August, Charles, sweaty and overheated, came home to an empty apartment after playing basketball in the park. Inside it was hot and dark; his mother always kept the curtains drawn against the sun, though she was rarely at home during the day. He went to the bathroom where paint curled off the wall in thick layers around the tub and sink. Above the toilet a basketball-sized chunk of ceiling had fallen down. He peed into a bowl whose permanent rust stains always made it look dirty, no matter how much his mother scrubbed, and he rinsed the salty sweat off his face at a cracked and pockmarked porcelain sink that listed dangerously away from the wall, the handle of the faucet on the hot side broken and made operable by a pair of pliers lashed to the cartridge.

Charles had grown so tall that the top of his head was no longer visible in the small, low hung medicine cabinet mirror. He wiped the sweat off his body with a stiff thin towel, left the bathroom and headed to the kitchen to find something to eat. He heard kids shouting outside and behind their childish voices the crescendo-ing woof and whine of a police siren. The sound was indistinguishable from the fear it triggered in him ever since he and Claude Greene had been chased by cops on 125th Street earlier that summer after some other teen-agers cursed and threw bottles when an officer tried to force Mr. James, the local Italian icy man, to move his cart to another location. Hearing the sirens made Charles feel apprehensive even though he was safe at home.

Charles went to the kitchen and turned on the light, which made the roaches scavenging for food in the dark scurry back to their hiding places. He took the remains of a quarter pound of spiced ham, wrapped in greasy white paper from the corner bodega on Eighth avenue, and made himself a sandwich from the ends of a loaf of Wonder Bread. To make up for the stale bread and skimpy portion of meat, Charles slathered on an extra-large dollop of mayonnaise. Then he poured himself a jelly glass full of grape Kool Aid and took his lunch into the living room to watch TV.

The small oblong screen of the Motorola television that his parents purchased the year he was born was soon filled with news coverage of the March on Washington. He saw endless throngs of people Black and white walking in the sunlight of the Washington Mall with signs demanding equal rights, jobs and freedom. They sang "We shall overcome," "We shall not be moved" and shouted, "Freedom now." As he watched, Charles was filled with a kind of wonder and then exhilaration that intensified as he chewed his sandwich and watched the people marching and chanting. "Freedom! Freedom Now!" He saw a phalanx of dignified, intelligent-looking Black men surrounded by dignitaries, police and reporters and National Park Rangers in funny hats standing at the podium beneath the Lincoln memorial. "Freedom!"

The Black men seemed as angry beneath the surface as his father had been. But unlike his father, whom he suddenly began to yearn for in his heart, these men were educated and they joined together with others to demand a better way of life. Something came alive in Charles, call it race pride, as he watched the coverage of the March and saw those men standing up so erect and proud as they spoke out for the rights that had been denied them and their people, his people. For as he continued to watch Charles began to understand in a way he never had before how gaining the freedom they were talking about applied to him. It meant finding his own path in a wider world instead of walking in the crippled circular footsteps of his parents.

Charles was riveted by the speech of a young man, John Lewis, who seemed to be only a few years older than he was and who favored Carol's brother, Aubrey. When Lewis, who spoke with a cadence and country accent similar to Charles' mother, mentioned sharecroppers, Charles remembered his father's stories about picking cotton and tobacco; when he referred to maids making five dollars a week, Charles thought of his mother working for the white people on Park Avenue, and he wondered how much money they actually paid her. When Lewis brought up the police, Charles saw the anger and loathing on the faces of the cops who had chased him and Claude. "We want to be free now," Lewis said, and he listed all the places where people were tired of waiting, including Harlem, and it felt like John Lewis had looked across the screen and into the very depths of his soul and spoken his name.

The next day Charles went to the library. He took out books about slavery and Abraham Lincoln and a volume of poems by Langston Hughes. The poems brought tears to his eyes which made him think there was maybe something wrong with him since words could affect him so strongly. Carol came over later to ask if he wanted to go with her to the store. She had her baby sister Mimi on her hip.

"I'm reading," he said.

"You always be reading. What's so special in all those books?" He opened the book of Langston Hughes poems.

"Listen to this poem." He began with, "I, too, sing America" and when he read the last line, "Besides they'll see how beautiful I am and be ashamed," he waited for Carol to react. Mimi batted at the book.

"If it's supposed to be a poem how come it don't rhyme?"

"It kind of does. But do you know what it means?"

"I guess it's something about eating." She seemed impatient.

"How come there are no white kids in our school?"

"White kids? I don't know. There's that one girl in my home economics class, but I think she Spanish."

"There are no white kids because we go to a segregated school, but segregation was ruled illegal in Brown vs. the Board of Education almost ten years ago. A Supreme Court case. You know what the Supreme Court is, right?"

"Uh huh," she said unconvincingly. "I gotta get some Milk of Magnesia for Nana."

"White kids have better schools than us," Charles continued. "They have everything better than us. We have to sit in the kitchen because we are second-class citizens. That's what civil rights is all about. That's what the poem is saying. We are not welcome at America's table because we're Black."

"I'm not black. I'm lighter than you."

"Colored. Colored is Black."

"Oh."

He wanted to share with Carol what he thought of as his awakening after having seen coverage of the March— his realization that he wasn't just himself, his mother's son, his father's survivor, a resident of New York, a 9th grader in Miss Thompson's homeroom, a Yankees fan, and a boy who liked to run—he *was* the darker brother. He was Black. They were all Black. That's why they lived where they lived. That's why none of the main characters looked like them in movies and on TV. That's why his mother worked for white people on Park Avenue who were allowed to call her out of her name. That's why Carol's mother was on welfare and her father was in jail.

When Charles was younger his mother sometimes took him with her to her job as a housekeeper in the home of a prominent New York banker. They rode up to the twelve-room two-story apartment on the freight elevator, and the Black elevator operator, Chester, exchanged friendly greetings with Charles. Sometimes Charles hung out with Chester in the basement in between elevator calls and he talked to him about baseball, his brother Ben who was a short stop in one of the Negro leagues, and about growing up down south in a town called Blackville, South Carolina. "Up here, ain't really no better. No sir, ain't no better."

Once they were inside the apartment it was like another world. The banker's wife, Mrs. Price, sometimes came into the kitchen to make some demand of his mother. When she saw Charles sitting on a small stool by the dumb waiter reading a book she would exclaim to his mother Dolores, whom she insisted on calling Elsie, the name of her childhood nanny, how amazing it was that a little colored boy like him loved to read while her own son never picked up a book when he was growing up.

"Best schools in the city, but Beau wasn't interested." At first Charles did not know how to react to these comments. They sounded like compliments, but they also made him feel like there was something wrong with him, especially when his mother would answer by saying something like,

"More to life than a book. Mr. Beau a big man now. Didn't let that stop him." When Charles asked his mother why she answered that way, she said,

"White folks always need to think they better than you."

When the Price family wasn't around Charles sometimes peeked into rooms that looked like museum exhibits. There were more sofas and chairs and settees than anyone could ever imagine sitting on. Ornate mirrors and oil paintings took up whole walls and thick patterned rugs lay upon the polished wood floors like continents on the globe. Once when he was six or seven, he watched while his mother stood on a ladder and took down for cleaning one by one the crystal prisms of a chandelier in the dining room. He wanted to steal one so he could make rainbows on the wall at home. His mother seemed to read his mind, and she gave him a look that said, "Do, and I'll whip the black off you."

In the Prices' apartment and in the neighborhood where they lived, he came to see with his own eyes that the "one nation under god" that he pledged allegiance to everyday in school was one place for rich white people and another place entirely for people who looked like him, and that white people like Mrs. Price wanted to keep it that way, even when they pretended to be nice to you.

Later on, he would read W.E.B. Dubois and acquire a term--double-consciousness-- that named what he had been experiencing but couldn't quite express about being an American and also being Black, and how your Blackness made white people blind to any other qualities you might possess.

Carol didn't seem to be conscious of doubleness. Charles both envied her and regarded her with disdain for not seeming to notice that they were not free. Even as she and her girlfriends would look at magazines and watch TV shows and say of white models and actors, "I'm her," and even though they were obsessed over the length and texture of their hair and the relative darkness or lightness of their skin, Carol seemed satisfied living in a circumscribed Black world and did not experience the crisis of identity or ambition that Charles could not fully articulate but felt so keenly.

Maybe it was because of her family that white people were irrelevant to her—there was always enough company, food, activity and drama to keep her occupied without having to worry about what could or should be. And there was love. Despite their troubles the Jones family cared for one another and expressed their affection. In order for Carol to be as aggrieved by the supremacy of whiteness as Charles was, or at least recognize it as the cause of her inferior living conditions and her father's incarceration, she would have to believe there was something wrong with the way she was living, and she didn't; furthermore, white people and a white world would have to actually exist, and although there were images of them everywhere, in her material reality they were the stuff of fantasy, no more real than animated characters in a Disney cartoon.

One day in the middle of their senior year, they were in Charles' room after school. His mother was working. She was always working. They were listening to the radio and the Temptations were singing "You're My Everything." Charles sat at the head of his bed studying for his history test and Carol, who was on a vocational track and didn't usually have homework, pestered him to pay attention to her.

"Am I your everything?" Carol asked.

"Everything annoying."

"You so mean and so serious. Why all of a sudden you have to study so much? There's no way you ain't gonna pass that test." But it was important to Charles that he do well. He had a crush on his history teacher, Miss Darling, who was young and white, new to the school that year, and who looked like the actress in *I Dream of Jeannie* but without the harem pants. Miss Darling wore short skirts and long boots and when she wrote on the board Charles couldn't stop looking at the way her skirt hiked up and her backside jiggled. She was different from a lot of the girls and women he knew, not just because she was white but because she looked open and happy, as if the world were a benign and friendly place and she was safe in it even while she was teaching Black kids in one of the worst schools in Harlem. He couldn't have expressed it verbally, but something inside him noticed and he wanted to be like that. He wanted to feel safe and be happy anywhere he went. He wanted some of the easy confidence that came with being white, and not just the projected swagger, which he was afraid he lacked, or the rigid body armor of toughness that was necessary for protection if you were Black. He knew she liked him and thought he was smart; after his first essay exam, she had called him to her desk and asked him why he was in that school, but this was something he couldn't tell Carol. Carol started tickling him and he grabbed her by the wrists and pinned her down and before you knew it, his mouth was on her mouth, and they were rolling around on his bed making out.

No matter how serious he was about studying, eventually, Carol could get him to stop because the pleasure they found in their bodies made everything else, school, the room, loneliness and worries about the future, disappear. Compared to other young men in the neighborhood, Charles came late to full carnal knowledge since there was always a point when they had to stop because she was a Christian. That day Satan got the better of her. She helped Charles pull off her panties and wrapped her legs around him and afterwards neither one of them could technically claim to be a virgin anymore.

He went to history class the next day feeling like a real man, and he wondered if Miss Darling, whom he was also thinking about when he and Carol were doing it, had noticed. After that he and Carol would cut school during lunch, sneak into his apartment and get it on. That lasted for a couple of months. Then she got pregnant, and everything changed. She was buoyant when she told him the news.

"We can get married after graduation," she said. Graduation was only two months away. The anticipation in her voice and the hope in her eyes were like twin torpedoes poised to annihilate his future.

"We can't get married! We're way too young."

"Mama was younger than me when she had Skylar."

"And did she marry Skylar's daddy?"

"She..."

"That's my point."

"She married *my* daddy."

"And where is your daddy now?" Carol flinched.

"What that got to do with us getting married? I only did it with you because we were getting married."

"Who said?"

"Everybody."

"*I* never said anything about getting married."

"But now we have to! I always thought you and me were going to have a family someday."

"You have too much family already."

"What you mean by that? I'm talking about your family. This your baby. You don't care about that?"

"I don't see how we can get married, Carol."

"Ain't it what people sposed to do?"

"You already said your mama didn't do it."

"So, I'm supposed to just have the baby by myself?" She glared at him, and he watched her rich brown eyes grow enormous like those of a big-eyed waif in a discount store painting. They were sitting on the side of his unmade twin bed thrust together by the deep sag in the middle, in the room he had lived in ever since he could remember. A thick paisley comforter, a hand me down from the Prices, was bunched up at the foot of the bed. He turned away from her and looked around the room as if trying to locate a secret means of escape. But the nondescript walls seemed to close in on him. He noticed a ragged semi-circular hole in the ceiling near the door revealing wooden slats and dark recesses exposed behind the missing plaster that only vermin and insects and odd bursts of air could pass through. His eyes passed over his battered dresser, covered with track trophies and the few toiletries he used every day, Royal Crown Hair Dressing, Right Guard Deodorant and Vaseline, the stocking cap he used to make waves in his hair. Next to the dresser there was a soot-coated window facing a dark air shaft, and across the space, a neighbor's blind window edged by a crumbling wooden sash and covered with a dark blanket. Charles looked down at his feet. They were big like his father's and his white athletic socks had holes at the big toe and heels.

"Why you lookin at everything except me?" Carol demanded. Charles looked at her then quickly looked away again. Her face was so familiar he realized he hardly even saw it. It was too painful to really look at her now and acknowledge that he had never truly seen her. He passed his hands over his eyes and face and leaned forward resting his elbows on his thighs and he stared at the floor trying to discern the pattern on the linoleum that had been worn away from years of wear. It was really stupid, but it had never occurred to him that she could or would get pregnant. It just seemed natural for them to be fooling around because they had always been together, and it just felt good. He wasn't thinking about the future. He wasn't thinking about marriage. He wasn't even thinking about her. She reached out and put her arm around his back. He felt like shrugging it off, but he didn't.

"Did you tell your mother?"

"No, I was waiting till I tole you. I thought you would be happy." *Happy?* He didn't really know what happy was, but he knew it wasn't having a baby with Carol. He also knew this was not the reaction she was expecting and that there was something wrong with him feeling this way. It would have been different maybe if he loved her in another way, a romantic way, but he wasn't sure what that would feel like, and she was Carol. She was home. She was everything he hoped to escape one day.

The next evening, a Wednesday, and his mother's day off as a domestic, he came home from a track event at school to find Carol, his mother, her mother, her grandmother and her little sister Mimi in his kitchen. Mimi ran up to him clutching a tiny troll doll with green hair, and as he stood in the doorway she said in a pretty clear bell of a voice, "I'm gonna be the flower girl!" Then she said it again to her troll, "I'm gonna be the flower girl!"

"We hear you have some good news," Brenda Jones, Carol's mother said. She was sitting at their oil clothed covered kitchen table with her blind mother, Nana, whose cane was leaning on the edge of it. Brenda was a heavy-set, brown-skinned woman with pert features like a baby doll's. Her brow was always wet with sweat no matter how cold or hot it was in the room and her massive arms always reminded Charles of giant hams. At the far end of the narrow room Charles' mother was at the stove frying something. He hoped it was chicken, but he quickly realized it was liver. Miss Brenda looked at him with a tight somewhat weary smile.

"Come over here, Charlie," She reached out her hand to him. He came and stood next to her at the table.

"We hear Carol is expecting." At the sound of the words, Nana touched his hand and flashed a huge grin that exposed the food caught in her dentures and made her milky eyes crinkle at the edges. Charles glanced at Carol who was leaning against the refrigerator with her arms crossed in front of her chest, a self-satisfied look on her face.

"Good news," Charles repeated as if he had no idea what either of the words meant. "Good news for who?" He pulled his hand away and as he did so, he knocked down Nana's cane, which clattered to the floor. Carol burst into tears. Mimi ran over to her and pushed the troll into her hand.

"I don't want no troll," Carol sobbed and threw the troll at Charles' head. Mimi shrieked. Charles bent down, picked up the doll, handed it to Mimi and then went to his room..

The next day, when he came home from school, Carol's brother Aubrey confronted him in the empty vestibule.

"What's wrong with you, man, disrespecting my sister?" Aubrey did not spend all day Sunday in the Tabernacle For All People. Lately, Aubrey had been spending most of his time hustling near the bodega on the corner and chugging malt liquor in the park or somebody's stoop in between. "She a good girl."

"Nobody said she wasn't. And look, I didn't do anything."

"She ain't knock herself up. You did something, bro."

"How many girls have you gotten pregnant? I don't see you wearing a wedding ring."

The blows to his stomach and shoulder did not surprise Charles. The one that ruptured the blood vessels in his nose did. It did not keep him from butting Aubrey with his knee and sending him flying down the four long marble steps that led to the building's entrance. Aubrey was startled to find himself lying on the floor with Charles' blood splattered on his clothes and his own head banged up against the iron filigree and plate glass of the front door. While Aubrey was down, Charles galloped upstairs and locked himself in the apartment leaving an ascending trail of blood on the steps.

When Dolores Rivers returned home at 11 o'clock that night from her second job cleaning offices, she was alarmed by the red smear on the vestibule floor and the drops of blood that led up the stairs, and her trepidation rose when she realized they led to her own door. She unlocked it, and she found Charles sitting in front of the television squinting at a textbook with two black eyes and a bruised nose. She asked what had happened. She suggested that they go to the emergency room after he told her, but he refused. "At least put some ice on your face," she said, pulling off the light beige textured wool coat that was a cast off from her employer and hanging it on a wire hanger in the closet by the front door. Now fifty, Dolores Rivers was a slight woman with steel wool colored and textured hair that she wore in a twisted braid on the top of her head. The fingertips on her right hand were yellow with nicotine and smoking had given a grayish cast to her rust brown skin. She gave the lie to that familiar chestnut, "Black don't crack." Life had used her up early as she served her white employers, her disabled husband, and her impoverished relatives back in Alabama, and she looked like it. She went into the kitchen, inspected the freezer compartment of the ancient refrigerator and found that the one metal ice tray, prickly with frost, had already been emptied. "Let me go next door and get some ice."

"From who, Miss Brenda?" Dolores sighed.

"What you gonna do? You act like a man; you get a man's responsibilities. I didn't raise you to be no coward."

"But I don't want to be with her, Mama."

"You been with her. That's the point. She a nice girl. You ain't gonna find a nicer girl than Carol. She sweet. Always in church. Cook like nobody's business. You been with her your whole life, Charlie. Why you gone act like this now?"

"I don't want to get married."

"Why you ain't think about that before?"

He understood why she was singing Carol's praises, but he also knew what she thought about marriage. Her own marriage had been a living hell. She used to mutter as much in the kitchen as she waited on his father and bore his insults. He sometimes heard her talking on the phone to her sisters and nieces warning them, "Watch out now. All kinds of traps out there. All kinds of ways people be trying to take your freedom." He had seen how his parents' marriage was a kind of prison. It was like they were locked together in a cell and the only way they would get out was if one of them died. Charles had never seen them hug or kiss or express any type of affection. There were few family photos and none of them showed the three of them smiling or looking happy. His atheist mother was an anomaly among her religious neighbors and kin. He didn't know why she was praising Carol for going to church because though superstitious, she had no use for formal religion.

When she was a teenager, she had prayed to Jesus to have the minister of the Calvary Baptist Church and the husband of the white woman whose floors she scrubbed keep their hands off of her; when they didn't, she had stopped believing. The only time Charles heard her praise Jesus' name was in the cemetery in Queens when his father's coffin was lowered into the ground and she began whispering, "Thank you, Jesus," and shaking her head up and down as if she had suddenly become possessed by the holy spirit.

"But I can't get married, Mama. Miss Darling says I should go to college."

"How you gonna pay for college? I thought you was gonna take the test for the Post office. She in the family way now. I didn't raise you to be no coward, boy."

Charles did not want to be a coward, but he also didn't want to fall into his Daddy's grave. Miss Darling had shown the class slides of her trip to Yellowstone National Park. Some smart aleck had called out, "Ain't that where Yogi Bear lives?" But according to Miss Darling it was a real destination and not just a cartoon set up for Yogi Bear. She and her boyfriend—she had a doggone boyfriend—posed in front of Old Faithful, and water-falls, the Grand Canyon and a neon blue lake that she called the Grand Prismatic Spring. There was a picture of her riding a horse and of the two of them paddling a boat on a river. His father had told him about Big Ben, the Eiffel tower, Paris cafes and the white cliffs of Dover. He doubted that he would have the chance to see any of those things if he married Carol.

The next day instead of going to school he took a long walk on Fifth Avenue, watching the neighborhoods and the complexions of the people change along the way. He ended up in Washington Square Park, now an official gathering place for young people who were disillusioned with the status quo, with its white arch modeled after the one his father had told him about in Paris, this one dedicated to the so-called father of the country, George Washington. The arch was covered with graffiti. "Make Love, Not War" was a popular motif. Charles could not get over how ironic that phrase was for him. There was a war going on inside him now that he had been making so-called love. Kids his age, mostly white but some Black and Spanish, were hanging out in the park behaving as though it was their living room, bedroom or even stage, many of them appearing to be high. It was still just early spring, but some of the white girls were roaming around without coats in long skirts and peasant blouses, their scraggly hair blowing around in the wind. Other kids sported mushrooming afros, Indian style head-bands, and frayed bell bottoms with soiled cuffs, some of them even walking on the cold pavement with dirty feet and no shoes. Charles didn't understand their embrace of slovenliness; to him dressing as neatly as you could, trousers creased, shoes polished was a badge of pride, but he envied their freedom and their desire to question and transgress the boundaries society had set up to contain them. One of them came up to him and asked, "Got any dope, man?" Charles shook his head and hurried away.

He found a bench. Someone was playing bongos near the fountain and a couple was making out on a blanket in the grass behind him. He could not marry Carol. He could not marry anybody at this point. And even if he could marry her, he could not protect her from the misery that seemed to be the lot of so many of the people in the neighborhood where he was born. His father had not been able to protect his mother, and he had spent his life punishing her for his inability to do so. Why should it be any different for him? What would happen when the reality of their status in society struck like the hit and run driver that had catapulted Carol's little sister Pam into the air as she ran across the street to catch a pink rubber Spaldeen? After Pam plummeted back to the ground her light brown body became a red rubbery balloon swelling with blood on the hot black skillet of the street. She died of internal injuries two days later. He couldn't marry Carol, he thought, because if he did, he might turn into his father.

He sat facing the beautifully maintained red brick row houses on Washington Square North with their black wrought iron fences and white columned entryways. But in his mind, he was back in Harlem, in the heart of the graffiti-emblazoned ghetto, the frozen inferno that had been starved and gutted by red-lining and neglect, left for dead by the rest of the city and abandoned by many former inhabitants who had mustered up the means to move to the Bronx or Queens.

In the sixth grade, his best friend, Paul and his family had moved out of the neighborhood to projects in Astoria, Queens. They were one of only three Black families out of a thousand living in the development. When Charles went to visit him there, he was astonished by how clean everything was. Sanitation trucks picked up the garbage, the sidewalks were smooth and level. There were no broken windows in Paul's school and the books they gave him were new. What Charles learned from this was that even poor white people in the projects were better off than he was.

A couple of years later parts of the neighborhood were further smashed by crowds of angry people reacting to the shooting by a white cop of a Black junior high school student on the Upper East side. Charles knew he could have been the boy who got shot. Any one of them in his neighborhood and neighborhoods like it could have been that boy and knowing that had caused a little part of his hope for the future to die. His mother was shaken and one night he saw her rifling around in a box of old photographs and papers. She pulled out a copy of Jet Magazine dated September 15, 1955.

"Time you know about this, if you don't already." In the magazine were the graphic images of Emmett Till before and after he was kidnapped by two white men in Mississippi, then beaten, shot and dumped into the Tallahatchie River, a metal fan wrapped around his neck with barbed wire.

"Best be careful. Don't give em no sass. Do, and they can take your life."

By the time Charles was a freshman in high school, the place that was his home and the beating heart of Black people everywhere had become a war zone, with blocks of grimy streets, empty rubble and garbage-strewn lots, windowless abandoned buildings, and swaying junkies who dealt with the pain of existence by injecting oblivion into their veins. Residents who could afford it installed two or three locks on their apartment doors to protect their homes from robbery and some carried box cutters, knives and even guns in case they needed to fight off muggers, gang members, and drug addicts desperate for their next fix. There were pockets of prosperity and order, but they were as foreign to Charles as the white, affluent suburbs that lay no more than twelve miles north. What he saw were the listless young men on many stoops and nearly every street corner, some hustling, some haranguing, some vacant, staring off into space, all doppelgangers who might mirror back his own face and fate if he were to look into their eyes. Around this time his friends began disappearing from school.

Unlike the kids who had more involved parents or better guidance counselors, Charles had not applied to any of the specialty high schools in other neighborhoods that would have provided him with a better education in an integrated environment. He ended up in one of the worst neighborhood high schools in the city. The supplies and facilities were poor, the teachers and administrators turned a blind eye to the daily fights, gang battles, drugs and sex in the hallways, and many of the students were so distracted by fear, disrespect, despair and poverty that they hardly applied themselves to the second-rate academic programs they were offered.

By sophomore year, half the kids who had started with him dropped out. Girls got pregnant, boys started selling drugs and going to jail. His friend Claude joined the Nation of Islam and could be seen on occasion selling *Muhammad Speaks* on the corner of Lenox and 125th wearing a dark suit, a white shirt and a bowtie, and other kids he knew joined gangs.

A Black nanny pushed a baby carriage past the bench on which he was sitting in the park while a white new mother walked slowly beside her. Charles felt a stony resentment at this reminder of the racial hierarchy. And then as the invisible white infant morphed in his mind into the unborn Black child he had unintentionally brought into being with Carol, a new wave of fear overtook him. How could he be a father? His father was an example of what no father should be like. And his mother was caring for white people when he and Carol and the kids in the neighborhood were running up and down the streets playing with sticks and balls and rocks and cans and reveling in the freedom of a childhood that would prove to be too short. How could he bring another child into this world when he had barely grown up himself? How could he be a father when he might never get the chance to really be a man?

He stood up abruptly, and with a strong sense of urgency he walked towards West 4th St. He felt around in his pocket to make sure he had two dimes for a subway token, picturing in his mind the army recruiter's office on 125th St.

"Boy, what you say?"

"I enlisted, ma."

"How you gonna enlist when that mean you going straight to Vietnam?"

"I'm not afraid."

"What you talkin about, you ain't afraid. You done loss your cotton pickin mind. You afraid of marrying Carol, but you ain't afraid of gettin blowed up in the jungle? I ain't give birth to you and raised you on my own all these years to give you up to fight in no white man's war. This just another trap. Can't you see it? Another plan they got to kill colored people. Them folks over there in Vietnam ain't done nothing to us, point of fact, they niggers just like us."

"I'm not a nigger."

"Ok, true dat, but why you gone let them treat you like one?"

Delores had just come through the door, and Charles had blurted out his news before she could even take off her coat. She was so stunned that she left it on and sat down on the worn overstuffed sofa, covered in quilts to hide the ripped upholstery, and fished a pack of cigarettes out of her bag. The portable TV set that rested on top of the old, busted Magnavox was on. Charles had been watching *Star Trek*.

"You don't know what you're talking about. And why do you always talk like you're still down south? You sound so ignorant."

Charles had become ashamed of the language patterns he inherited from his parents and neighbors when a white teacher in fourth grade asked him what Southern state he came from. He had wanted to disappear into the floor as his classmates tittered and he explained that he was born in New York. He vowed from that day on that his English would be as correct as a news anchor's. He also avoided four letter words because his father's speech had been laced with them. Carol and his friends teased him for shunning Black English and painstakingly enunciating every word.

Every time his mother opened her mouth it rankled him, no matter what she had to say, but he was especially critical when they were at odds. But Dolores' speech was a form of resistance. It was her way of holding on to who she was despite having to humiliate herself and sacrifice so much of her dignity to keep them alive. She had to serve white people, but she didn't have to try to be like them. "I can send money home to Carol. Daddy was in the military, right? He went to war."

"Put on the news. See what's going on over there where you say you wanna go. You should be out there protestin steada enlistin." She lit her cigarette.

"Why do you smoke so much? It's not healthy." Dolores took a long drag and then a long look at her son.

"Neither is goin to war. I don't want to lose you, baby. Why you wanna choose death over life?" She flicked the ash into a little cracked saucer with a pattern of wheat sheaves on the border that many years in the past had came inside a box of soap powder. Now it was full of cigarette butts that threatened to spill over onto the battered coffee table in front of her where there was a TV Guide, some dirty glasses and papers, and brochures from the army recruiters.

"We done this to you. Me and your daddy did." She looked around the drab living room, fixing on a fake Hummel figurine of a little white girl with an umbrella that rested in a frilled plastic doily on a spindly side table next to the TV. On the screen Captain Kirk said something about things only being temporarily hidden and temporarily not understood.

"I been working so hard all these years and for what? He dead. We still ain't got a pot to piss in and you willin to put yourself in harm's way to avoid opening up your heart." Dolores shook her head. "We ain't teach you right. We ain't teach you how to love and love yourself because if you did love you, you would love Carol after all these years and as much time as you spent with her. You don't love you, so you can't love her because loving her would be loving me, and you can't love me because I can't love my own self." She took another drag on her cigarette. Her words found their way into a deep part of Charles' psyche, circling around like the smoke she had just exhaled. She sighed. Then she sighed again. She rubbed what was left of the cigarette into the saucer and covered her face with her hands. She didn't make a sound, but Charles saw her shoulders heaving and he realized she was crying and that despite everything she put up with in her life he had never seen her cry.

"Mama," he started, but he didn't know how to continue.

"Mama," He picked up one of the army brochures and touched her hand with it, but she did not look up. He placed it back on the table and said, "They pay for college. When I get out."

He was in basic training at Fort Dix, New Jersey when the letter came from Carol saying that she lost the baby and that she didn't know what his plans were when he came back, if he came back, but that she wasn't going to be part of them. Charles suspected that her mother, who was a lot sharper than Carol, had written the letter. So it was ironic or maybe it wasn't that he found comfort thinking about Carol, lying on her bosom, pressing his nose against her warm flower-soap scented skin and being encircled in her plump arms, when his escape from home morphed into the wetness and terror, the stink and fear, sci-fi insects, monster rats, murderous snakes, relentless rain, boredom, explosions, marijuana haze, and the casual and intentional racism among his fellow soldiers in the primordial soup of the Southeast Asian jungle. All his images of the jungle were from TV and movies of Tarzan, king of the jungle, an improbable white man swinging like a brachiator through the trees and flaunting his dominance over the natives and nature. This was not the African jungle, but it didn't take him long to realize that he and his fellow soldiers were just so much ammo in the white man's quest for domination and that the money they were spending on this war against "communists" could have been used to improve the very streets and conditions he had fled.

He started calling the Hueys and the F4 phantoms Tarzan when he was stoned and laughing insanely at his little inside joke to the point where his buddies just shook their heads. When he was sleeping fitfully and lying with his lady, his rifle, the innocuous harmonies of "Stoned Soul Picnic" by the Fifth Dimension, a song he hated that Carol loved, played constantly on the turntable in his brain, filling the ominous silence or silencing the pop pop pop of gunfire. Along with that song, he heard his mother's words over and over again: *You don't love you, so you can't love her because loving her would be loving me, and you can't love me because I can't love my own self.* He missed his mother and the way she talked, and he wanted to tell her that maybe she was right about him not loving himself and Carol but she was definitely wrong about him not loving her.

He was in the Mekong Delta for nine months. Long enough for half his unit to be blown to kingdom come. He saw his buddy Franklin, a quiet farm boy from rural Mississippi, who couldn't wait to get back home to the pregnant wife he loved, explode in a display of corporeal fireworks when he stepped on a land mine on his way to warn Charles about a sniper. Charles' injuries were minor compared to what happened to Franklin and many of the others: there was shrapnel in his leg, the ring finger of his left hand had been blown off, but those were the only physical wounds. He spent the rest of his tour in an army hospital and when he got back home, he learned that Carol's father had been released from prison and that the whole family had moved to the Bronx.

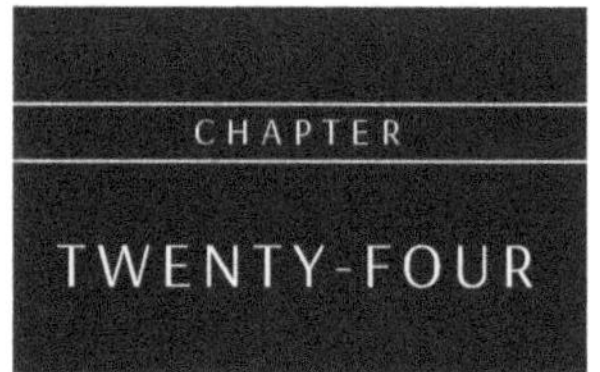

CHARLES AND ROSETTA, FEBRUARY 2002

After the first time at Charles' apartment there was one night on campus when they couldn't keep their hands off each other and they ended up on the big desk in Charles' office. It wasn't like in the movies. They got tangled up in their clothes, bumped into the file cabinet and sent stacks of books and papers flying, and their climaxes were anti-climactic. They never did the deed at work again, but knowing they had made them feel closer and was their inside joke whenever they were at work together around other people.

They settled into a ritual of running together three mornings a week and going back to Charles' place when he didn't have an early class. When they were together, little by little, Charles became comfortable talking about his past and Rosetta loved asking him about it.

"What happened when you got home from the war?" she asked as they lay in his bed together one morning, still naked after making love, talking quietly in the darkened room as daylight seeped between the gaps of the heavy curtains

She kissed and caressed his four-fingered hand and traced the brown grooves in its leathered palm as if they held the answer to her question.

"I don't know. I was in a daze. I laid on the couch and watched TV all day. The worse thing about the war was that you went there to kill people but as soon as you got there it wasn't as clear as it should have been which people you were supposed to be killing. I smoked a lot of pot over there—it was the only way to calm down after the amphetamines. They gave us speed to keep us going and when you came down it made you crazy and the marijuana mellowed you out. It was better than the Thorazine that was part of our drug kit because it didn't give you headaches. They banned marijuana after I got out and soldiers started using heroin. At least I wasn't hooked on the needle, but I became one of those people I hated, a lazy, shiftless pothead.

"My mother wasn't working as a maid anymore. To her credit she got into a training program, and she became a nurse's aide. And when she left early in the morning I would be lying on the couch and when she came back from her second job cleaning offices, I would still be there.

She brought home newspapers that had been thrown away in the offices. That's how I started reading the New York Times. Martin Luther King was assassinated when I was in Vietnam. I was still there when the riots happened but there were a lot of protests and rallies still going on when I got back. One day I was looking for one of my contacts to get more weed, as they call it these days, and he wasn't in the usual spot, so I ended up just walking, and I heard all these people shouting and I was in the middle of this rally at the college, which was not too far from where I lived. I was really high, and I bumped into this guy at the rally, and I was wearing an army fatigue jacket, and he started yelling at me about being a traitor to the people. Various activists were giving speeches and that was the first time I saw Madeline. She was on the podium, and she saw what was going on and she stopped in the middle of the speech and said, 'Leave the brother alone. He's a victim, not the problem.' I didn't know she was a professor at the time, and I couldn't tell if she was Black or white. She was tall and rangy and very light-skinned and freckled, and she had this crazy long, wavy, red hair."

Charles tipped Rosetta's chin towards him and kissed her to reassure her that she was the person who mattered to him now.

"It's ok. You can talk about her. I asked you what happened. I'm married. Remember?" she said making a comical "duh" face.

"And she's dead," Charles said, feeling a sudden pang of grief not because Maddie was dead but because Rosetta would be leaving soon.

"I know and you loved her."

"I couldn't love you if it hadn't been for her, baby. I couldn't have met you if it hadn't been for her."

"I'm happy you loved her, Charles," Rosetta said putting her arms around him and nuzzling his chest. "Love is good." Except when it's not, her inner voice scolded.

"I don't think I actually loved anyone before I met her. I should've loved Carol, but I didn't. I don't think I believed in love or even knew what it was."

"What is it?" Rosetta teased.

"Being here with you. Black and naked."

"Nekkid," is how we used to say it when we were kids, "Black and nekkid." Rosetta whipped off the sheet covering them, stood up on the bed and began to do a wobbly, gyrating dance over Charles as she chanted, "Black and nekkid." Charles leaned forward and tried to grab her hands, which she moved with Kali-like fluidity to avoid his grasp.

"You know who you look like? You look like Josephine Baker dancing like that."

"*Who?* Josephine who? Baker, 1920s? Oolala! You old, Charles, You really old!"

They burst out laughing and Charles pulled her back into his arms where after their laughter subsided, they lay quiet and content.

"You are so beautiful," he said. With a reverence reminiscent of prayer, he brought his lips close and gently brushed hers, moving on to touch her cheeks, her eyes, her ears, her neck, her breasts, and onto the mound of her belly, finally paying his obeisance at the altar between her thighs. Rosetta was both taken out of and fully delivered to herself by his voracious though patient attentions there. And afterwards, the intensity of her feelings for Charles became equal to the intensity of the pleasure he had given her.

"I just think it was hiding," Rosetta said as they curled up together again.

"What?"

"The love. The feelings. Fear drove them down. All the fighting, your parents, war. Love was there but it had to hide. When you wear your heart on your sleeve, you're vulnerable and that's scary."

"Like now?"

"Are you scared?" Charles cupped his palm around the lower portion of Rosetta's skull. The weight of his hand on the most vulnerable part of her body was his answer.

"I am terrified of going back to my old life. I am terrified of losing you."

Rosetta tightened her arms around him, almost as if she were cradling one of her sons. She loved this man. This human being who had become a part of her, whom she had invited inside her, who treated their lovemaking as a sacrament, who belonged to a different time, who had seen and felt things she would never see, who was a strange amalgam of intelligence, pride, arrogance, fear, stability, fragility and loneliness, who found a little girl and loved her, and found another man's wife and made her his own.

When they started out, she had been wary, fearful that he wanted to take advantage of her. But now she believed that awkward flirting was the only way he knew how to ask for love.

"So, what happened after the rally?"

"What rally?"

"Where you first saw Madeline."

"Oh, I ran into her again. She was coming out of the subway on 135th St. and St. Nicholas Avenue about a week later, and I was sitting on a bench with the newspaper, ostensibly looking at the want ads. My mother told me she was going to put me out if I didn't get serious about getting work, so I made an effort to leave the apartment, but I never went very far. Maddie saw me and she came and sat next to me, and she said, 'How you doin, brother, I recognize you from the rally.' And she started asking me what I was reading about in the paper and where I went to school and where I lived and how it was for me in the war and basically, I told her my story; I'm wasted and she tells me about what's happening with the college and open admissions and that she can help me apply, and the rest is history."

"History? But how did you end up getting married? How old was she?"

"She was an assistant professor in the sociology department at the time, but she was young. She was intellectually precocious, impatient, really." He chuckled a little. "But awkward socially, like me. She graduated from high school when she was seventeen, and she finished college in three years. I had just turned twenty when we met. She was twenty-four, working on her dissertation on urban minority students and educational achievement, which she finished the next year. She grew up in the South and she came up North to go to school and she found conditions shocking here. She thought it would be better because there was no legal segregation, but she saw that it didn't mean there was opportunity for all. She was a serious devotee of Malcolm X and she believed Black people would be better off trying to develop themselves and their own institutions rather than just trying to be with and like white people. I don't know how she ever finished and published her dissertation because she was always going to demonstrations and meetings. It just started out with her being my mentor. And I was her personal case study and project. She was actually the first person to really believe in my academic potential, except maybe this one teacher I had in high school when I was a senior."

"Miss Darling?"

"Yes. She used to tell me, 'You somebody, Charles.' You know that line Jesse Jackson made famous--"I *am* somebody." He didn't invent it. A minister in Atlanta wrote a poem in the fifties and she said her father used to recite it to her every day. She sometimes got discouraged because her professors and colleagues were not always that supportive. They didn't understand her. They couldn't find the niche to put her in her place. She was so smart, and she was Black, but she looked white, and they couldn't fathom why she was so angry. I think I helped keep her going in spite of that. So, it was mutual."

"Did she ever write another book?"

"She wrote a lot of articles. She was brilliant."

"Hmmm," Rosetta said. "I gotta go to the bathroom." She got out of bed, and he quickly switched on his bedside lamp to indulge in the pleasure of seeing her walk naked from the bed to the door. "Damn, it's cold in your apartment," she said.

"Sorry it's not the Upper East Side, Madam. Come back quickly and I'll make you warm again." Rosetta came back after a few minutes and snuggled in beside him. She had checked the clock and realized she would have to leave in about twenty minutes. Since that first time, she always went home and made herself look respectable before picking up Ryan.

"But how did you end up marrying her? Were you guys like fucking the whole time?"

"There you go! No, but we did get high together in the early days. She didn't have a lot of friends. She knew a lot of people. She had comrades and fellow activists. But it was hard for her to get close to people. Darker skinned folks didn't trust her sometimes. Other women were jealous; men were always hitting on her. She almost got raped one time by a friend of a friend she let stay in her apartment. I had a key and I happened to come in the morning when this guy was pinning her down. It's a good thing I came because she would have killed the motherfucker—"

"Oh my god, Charles, you said, mofo! Congratulations! You get points!"

"I don't like people messing with my women," he grinned.

"Too good to be true. You just lost the points—your women!"

"We became best friends. I was always in her apartment. She tutored me. She took pleasure in introducing me to new things. She cooked for me. Her specialty was this kind of gumbo. She said it was an old family recipe, but I think she actually made it up. There was all sorts of seafood in it, shrimp and blue crabs and a lot of Old Bay Seasoning." He laughed. "We got married right after I graduated. She proposed. I was in awe of her. I would never have asked her because in a way, she was kind of my Pygmalion. She created me." Charles grew pensive, wondering in the moment if that was a good or a bad thing. "We went to Cuba and Haiti for our honeymoon."

"Cuba? They let you go to Cuba?"

"It was an educational trip. There were ways to go there if you were an academic. When we went and we met those beautiful people, I realized that Americans had been told so many lies and that you should never believe everything you hear on the news. Like now, with this war on terror. Why are we attacking Iraq when most of the hijackers came from Saudi Arabia? I think it's just another excuse for them to get in there and get the oil. I'm afraid it's going to lead to another decade of war. But that's another story.

"The Cubans had chosen a different way to organize their society, but we vilified them because of their ties to

Russia. It was amazing how they were so poor, but everyone was literate, and art and music was like air and food. They got punished for not wanting their destiny controlled by U.S. corporations. Maddie wasn't a communist, but she was sympathetic and she was invited to speak there. A lot of Black people joined the founding of the Communist party in Cuba and throughout the 30s, 40s and 50s a lot of them were leaders in the party and a lot of Black people supported Castro in 1959. This really influenced their ideas about racial identity. There was race and color prejudice to be sure, left over from the colonial days and slavery, but they aspired to a national identity that transcended race. Maddie found that fascinating. Racial heritage got expressed through cultural traditions like dance and music."

"Cool," Rosetta said.

"We traveled a lot before Jason was born. We did it on a shoestring, and mostly we went to conferences and meetings of the groups she was part of, but I was finally able to see all those places my father told me about and many more."

"And many more," Rosetta laughed. "You sound like a student. Be specific! What about Africa?"

"We went to Mali one summer with the American Friends Service committee and worked on a project to combat the drought. Maddie helped to train local women to serve as social workers."

"What was it like? How did you feel in Mother Africa?"

"Like an American," Charles laughed. "No, but they were very generous and welcomed us. They were a bit confused by Maddie at first. The people were physically very beautiful and most of them were coal black. But she got along well because she spoke fluent French. That was another place, like Vietnam, where there were giant rats. They don't just live in Harlem," Charles laughed. "The settlement village was trying to build up their agriculture and these rats came in from the desert and ate the seeds and chewed everything up. It was really bad. We were just overrun. It was like it was their country and we were invading; we had to beat them away with clubs. And when they finally returned to the desert everybody had lice. I will never forget being deloused. We went to Timbuktu, and we saw the mosques made of mud and we rode camels. They stink."

"Wow!" Rosetta said, "I've always wanted to go to Africa. I guess I have to wait until the boys grow up. And now I need to go, babe." Rosetta got up and started putting on her underclothes and sweatpants. Charles leaned against the headboard watching her dress. This was the sad part. She always left.

"Are you going in today?"

"What day is it?"

"Tuesday, man, I've turned you into a slacker."

"You've given me something to live for besides grading papers."

"There *is* more to life. Although sometimes it doesn't feel like it. I'm dreading the next batch that I have coming in."

"What are they?"

"Textual analysis papers."

"Oh, you mean summaries? "

"Exactly! It's so hard to teach them the difference. And I can't run tomorrow," Rosetta sighed. "We have a meeting with Ryan's teacher. They're saying he's hyperactive."

"Ryan?"

"Yeah, it's bullshit. The Black boy thing. He does the same thing the other kids do, but in him it's pathological. I hope I don't run into your neighbor, that old lady on the first floor. She seems to wait by the door. The look she gives me."

"Screw her!"

"She probably could use it. I see you're really coming along with the expletives. Must be because I'm such a good teacher," Rosetta laughed.

"Come here." He reached out to her.

"I gotta go now." Charles got out of bed and pulled Rosetta to him.

"Let's meet someplace else. Let's go out. On a date."

"We--what we can do is limited. You know that, Charles. We can't be seen— "

"Come away with me on my boat!"

"You haven't built it yet," Rosetta said chuckling and wiggling out of his embrace. "Thursday, okay? And put on some clothes. You're Black and nekkid!"

PART 2

CHARLES, OCTOBER 2002

"She has a high fever," the secretary at the St. Joseph's school, a middle-aged Irish woman with skin approaching the color of Ivory soap and hair the color of coal, worriedly informed Charles as he strode into the school office. Bianca was slumped in a chair beside the secretary's desk taking tiny sips of water from a paper cup. The white blouse under her maroon plaid jumper was damp with sweat. "You best take her to the emergency room. Miss Davis says she spent the whole morning with her head down on the table. But she's not coughing or nothing. It don't seem to be a cold."

"How are you feeling, BB?" It was a dumb question because the answer was obvious. Bianca reached out a hand. He took it. It was hot. Charles frowned. She had been listless all week. It started at the beginning of the school year and Charles had attributed it to being exhausted from the summer and long hot days of playing outside in the park and in the city pools where he signed her up to learn to swim.

"Get a cab and take her, Mr. Rivers."

"Yes, of course, I will." Charles said. But the thought of taking her to a hospital emergency room where questions would be asked made him nervous. He pulled her up; she was as floppy as a rag doll.

"I'll put her sweater in the backpack," the secretary said. He lifted Bianca over his shoulder. She had grown taller in the year since her mother had disappeared and she had lived with him, but she had also slimmed down, and he was used to carrying her now, so her weight was not a burden to him. The nurse handed him her backpack, and with it slung across his arm and Bianca nestled against his neck he carried her out of the small brownstone school building and flagged down a black livery cab. He did not take her to the hospital, but back home to the apartment where he laid her down on Jason's bed, now her bed, in the room he had painted yellow and mint green at her request. She was too ravaged by fever to protest. He put a washcloth with cold water on her head and then he dialed Rosetta's number. He let it ring. Then he hung up. That was the signal, admittedly a primitive one, to be used only in the case of an emergency. Otherwise, it was pay phones and e-mail and meetings on the track and at work. They had not run together today because Rosetta's knee had been bothering her and she had a physical therapy appointment. She called him back almost immediately.

"Hey!"

"Any chance you can come over here now? I had to get BB from school. She has a fever. She's really sick."

"I'm on my way out the door for my appointment."

"They told me to take her to the emergency room."

"You should."

"You don't see a problem with that?"

"If she's sick, Charles..."

"I am not her legal guardian. They will ask for her insurance. She actually has a Medicaid card. It was in Keisha's stuff, but..."

"Maybe you can take her to the boys' pediatrician, but you probably can't just walk in. And it's pretty fancy. I doubt they take Medicaid. Just take her, Charles. Take her to the ER. If they find out, maybe they can help you find Keisha."

"I don't want...I could probably get arrested for this." There was silence on her end. "Are you there?"

"Yes, I was just putting my shoes on."

"Okay. I'll just take her and whatever happens happens. I just don't want to lose you."

"This is not about that."

"Everything is about that." Bianca called weakly from her room, "Papa Charlie."

"She's calling me."

"Go. Take her and let me know what happens later."

"I love you."

"I know."

"You know?"

"Yes, and you know how I feel. Do what you have to do, Charles. There's a time and place for everything."

"I'm thirsty," Bianca said in a soft raspy voice, "and I'm tired." Charles was alarmed by her almost lifeless torpor.

"I'll get you some water," he said. "And we're going to go to the hospital so you can feel better."

"I don't want to go. I'm tired."

"How tired?" She didn't answer, and all at once the potential seriousness of her condition struck Charles. He went to the kitchen to get the water, but he ended up grabbing the wall phone instead and dialing 911.

The ride to the hospital in the back of the ambulance was dizzying and disorienting. It was only blocks away but sitting sideways in the back of the cab strapped into a narrow padded bench against the wall made it difficult to get his bearings. His legs kept banging up against the gurney where Bianca lay with a clear oxygen mask over her nose and mouth.

One of the paramedics, a husky baby-faced Latino, had filled out the paperwork while his partner attended to Bianca. He asked what Charles' relationship was to her.

"Guardian."

"Legal guardian?"

"No, yes." The young man looked up from his clipboard with raised eyebrows. "I'm her, uh, grandfather."

"Oh, okay."

The ambulance stopped and the baby-faced EMT warned Charles to watch his head as he climbed out the back doors. The guys lowered the gurney and rolled Bianca from the ambulance into the back doors of the emergency department. As soon as the automatic doors opened Charles was flooded with panic and images of Madeline dying and Jason almost dying from an overdose flashed into his mind. The two men lifted Bianca from their gurney to one provided by the hospital and reported her vitals and information to the triage nurse who sat at a desk in a small room near the ambulance entrance. He waited by Bianca's side, and the nurse began interviewing him and entering information into a computer.

"Fever and lethargy?"

"Yes."

"A rash and bruises on her arm."

"Yes, I don't know how she got the bruises."

"When did the symptoms begin?"

"Well, the fever, they called me from school this morning, but she seemed very tired all week, and hasn't been eating much. No cough or cold though."

"Primary care physician?"

"I don't know."

"You don't know who her primary care physician is?" The nurse, a heavy-set middle-aged West Indian woman with shiny slicked back hair and a uniform shirt bright with cartoon characters, eased her glasses off her face and let them dangle around her neck on their pearl chain. She looked up at Charles with narrowed eyes.

"And you are her…"

"Uh, grandfather."

"Do you have authorization to seek medical care on her behalf?"

"I, ah…"

"Where are her parents?"

"I don't know."

"Do they, either of them, live with you?"

"No."

"You are the legal guardian?"

"That's right."

"Do you have proof?"

"Proof?"

"Because if you don't we have to contact her parents before we can treat her."

"Do you have her insurance card?" With a sinking feeling, Charles handed over the Medicaid card he'd found in the bag of Keisha's belongings. He knew it had expired because the EMT had told him so.

"This is no good. This card is expired."

"We need a number to call to speak to her parents."

"There is no number. Her mother just left her with me, and she didn't come back."

"When?"

"About a year ago."

"Your daughter."

"No."

"Your daughter-in-law?"

"No. Yes."

"Your son?"

"My son?"

"Where is your son?"

"I don't know where my son is," Charles said, irritably. He was beginning to feel like he had left his body and was watching himself acting in an absurdist drama. "Look, this is a long story, but the important thing is this child is very sick and she needs care, and this is a hospital, and you need to help her."

"Did you harm the child?"

"What do you mean?" The woman must have pressed a buzzer of some sort because two hospital police officers appeared in the doorway.

"Something's fishy here. He says he's the child's guardian, but he doesn't have any information or authorization. He says he doesn't know where the parents are."

"Do you mind stepping outside with us for a moment, sir?" Of course, I mind, Charles thought. But he knew the drill when someone like him was confronted by a police officer.

"Can we see some ID?" Charles reached into his pocket and pulled out a worn black leather wallet. He handed over his driver's license.

"This is expired." He handed him his work ID card. "Ok, so you're a professor?"

"This is a long story. One of my students…"

"Where are the girl's parents?"

"I don't know."

"Do you know the parents?"

"The mother. I knew the mother. She was my student."

"Where is she?"

"I don't know."

"When was the last time you saw her?"

"September 11, 2001."

"Over a year ago?"

"What happened to her?"

"I don't know."

"Did you try to find her?"

"I looked for her, but she just disappeared."

"Disappeared," is that what you said? As Charles answered the questions, two other officers appeared and unlike the hospital peace officers, they had guns and batons bulging out of the leather holsters on their hips like cyborg body parts, and one of them produced handcuffs.

"We're going to have to take you down to the station to answer some questions."

"What?"

"You're under arrest."

"Arrest? Why?"

"You are not legally authorized to have custody of that child."

"But I tried to explain."

"Are you resisting arrest?"

"No, no. Not resisting."

It was every Black man's nightmare. He, Charles Rivers, who had somehow defied the odds and never had a serious run in with the law, was handcuffed in the back seat of a police car and was soon back in that same New York City traffic he had experienced when he was strapped onto the narrow, padded bench of the ambulance. The policemen did not like the answers he gave about Bianca in the hospital. When they announced that he was under arrest he knew better than to open his mouth to say anything more. The police car smelled like a combination of a deli, a gym, and a broom closet. He was not strapped in and the handcuffs rammed the small of his back with every stop and pothole as he slipped around on the slick faux leather backseat. He should have felt afraid or angry, or as if his body were about to explode like a cache of TNT. Instead he was numb with shock and he began to watch himself from an out of body distance, something he had learned to do when he was a little boy and his parents were fighting.

At the precinct they asked the body of Charles Rivers for his name, address, and social security number. They searched it, relieved it of its keys, wallet, watch and the navy-blue backpack that contained a marbled composition book, a little girl's white sweater, a Disney princess coloring book, a dented box of apple juice, a pink clip-on hair bow, Barbie panties, a pair of elastic waist denim pants size 7, a yellow My Little Pony tee-shirt, and a small red stuffed dog toy. Charles had thrown the assorted items into the backpack before the ambulance took them to the hospital not knowing what she would need for the trip. The body of Charles Rivers was positioned so that cameras could capture its face from three angles. Electronic prints were made of its thumbs.

The body of Charles Rivers made three phone calls:

1. To Rosetta Ocean:

"Hello?"

"Sorry about calling."

"It's okay, he's not here."

"I got arrested. I'm at the 23rd Precinct."

"Arrested, oh my god!"

"Apparently, I was not authorized to seek care on her behalf."

"How is she?"

"I don't know. They arrested me when I was trying to get her admitted."

"For what?"

"I'm not sure."

"Do you have a lawyer?"

"My cousin's a lawyer."

"Well, call your cousin."

"I don't have his number. Can you look up the number? His name is Stanley Davis. His office is in the Bronx."

"I don't have a Bronx phone book. They must have a phone book."

"Will you go see her?"

"At Mt. Sinai? I will try to get over there. But what's going to happen to you? And what's her last name, again?"

2. To Stanley Davis:

"You have reached the law office of Stanley Davis. Please leave a message clearly stating your name and number after the beep."

"Hey, cousin, it's Charles. I'm at the 23rd Precinct. I think I might need your help."

3. To the English Department Office:

"Yolanda, something has come up and I have to cancel my afternoon classes."

After these calls the body of Charles Rivers was led into a holding cell. Two other bodies occupied it. A young man about Jason's age who was sitting on the slatted wooden bench attached to the wall, wearing spotless tan Timberlands, baggy jeans and a Chicago Bulls Jersey that looked like it had just come off the rack, and a scruffy older guy in grimy work pants and a ripped waffle weave underwear shirt who stood in the corner of the cell near the feces-splattered toilet scratching himself all over.

"Hey, ain't you Professor Rivers? What you doing in here, prof?" Charles came to himself when he heard the young man say his name. He recognized him immediately.

"DeVaughn?"

"Yeah, it's me! Sit down, professor." Charles remembered the student's name even though it had been several years since he'd taught him. DeVaughn had an infectious smile and the gift of gab that he tried to rely on instead of handing in papers. He was absent for a long stretch during the semester. When Charles asked where he had been he told him, "jail."

"What you doing here professor? This the last place I expected to see *you*! This here my English professor," he told the scruffy guy. The guy looked Charles up and down taking in his button-down shirt, cotton knit pullover sweater, dark khaki pants and running shoes.

"Word? To Sir with Love?"

Charles sat down next to DeVaughn on the hard bench, the sharp knobs of his knees jutting up at an awkward angle since the bench was so low. DeVaughn talked non-stop, trying to school him about what to expect, but the words held no meaning for Charles. After acknowledging DeVaughn, he became numb again. A thick Hispanic kid wearing a red hoodie was put into the cell, his expression as inscrutable as an Aztec death mask. He crossed his arms in front of him and leaned against the wall across from where Charles sat with DeVaughn. Later a tall thin black man in his late twenties with what looked like permanently blackened eyes, cornrows, and dragon tattoos circling his neck was put in there as well.

"How y'all doin?" He actually said to the other detainees in a raspy but almost high-pitched smoker's voice. He smiled a smile that was more a warning than a greeting and revealed a mouthful of blackened teeth.

"You know what it's like to be a gravedigger?" he asked them. "You heard of Potter's field? Where they bury people who don't have no family? Well, the last time this happened to me, they made me a gravedigger there. In Potter's field, and you know what was the worst? Burying little babies." Charles' head twisted away involuntarily. An image of bloody dismembered body parts came into his mind.

"You listening to me?"

"Yeah, man," somebody said.

Two officers came in and began handcuffing him and his fellow detainees to each other.

"You're all going downtown." Charles' four-fingered hand was coupled with DeVaughn's. The scruffy guy in work pants was handcuffed to the gravedigger who said irritably, "You ain't gotta make it so tight," to which the cop replied, "Telling me how to do my job?" And then he tightened it even more. The Hispanic kid was cuffed to himself.

The cellular memory of being chained to other human beings was triggered deep in Charles' hippocampus. He heard the officers' voices, sneering and unnecessarily gruff as they herded them out of the cell along a dank corridor and into the back of a police van. Their voices got remixed in his head with other voices yelling commands. The blue of the officers' uniforms and black of their belts, guns and nightsticks blurred together as they pushed him and the others onto the bare metal floor of the van. His body, attached by metal to the body of his former student sat itself as upright as it could. There was a jerk as the van accelerated into drive and their captive bodies tumbled against each other eliciting groans and curses but no apologies. Charles was probably the only one for whom this trip in a police vehicle down to the Halls of Justice, otherwise known as the Tombs, was a first-time occurrence. When the van made its final stop after lurching forward and careening around what seemed like every corner in Manhattan, Charles and the others were let out and steered into the basement holding area of the jail cum courthouse, where they were un-cuffed from each other, singly handcuffed and made to take their place on a long processing line. Just ahead of them, there was a group of Asian women in high heels, short skirts and garish makeup, their breasts popping out of low-cut blouses because of the way their shackled hands were pulled behind their backs. Three young guys all with the same tattoo and a knowing air were behind him. It had to be the worst queue he had ever been on, the atmosphere around him buzzing with curses, moans, farts, taunts--people calling out that they were sick, hungry, that their handcuffs were tight and that they weren't going to Riker's.

Once it had been processed, the body of Charles Rivers was prodded towards a stainless-steel counter surrounded by holding cells. It was told to disrobe. Corrections Officers whose faces were masks of boredom and irritation examined its orifices. A cursory medical examination was also done to determine whether it was a carrier of infectious disease. Soon his body was sent to take its place with about a dozen other bodies, all of them black or brown, some of them with angry expressions, some of them with cuts and bruises on their arms and faces. The 20x30 cell consisted of two steel benches on either side of a wall, a metal toilet behind an L shaped partition, and a pay phone attached to the back wall. Those who could not fit on the benches leaned against the bars or walls or laid down on the concrete floor. Charles' Black body found its back against the wall close to the bars on the right side of the cell. After a while the physical sensation of the hard wall against his shoulder and back pulled him back inside his body and triggered a surge of feeling that he was afraid might bring him to tears. It was hot and the air inside the cell was thick and fetid. He imagined Bianca's fear when she realized he was no longer there. Guilt and dread crawled up from the inside of his belly like the insects he imagined skittering along the floor. He knew it had been wrong to keep her without going to the authorities. But those authorities were the ones who were humiliating and manhandling him and his fellow captives here, treating them as less than human, as if they were guilty of whatever they were charged with just by virtue of having been born. Nobody really cared that Bianca had been born. No alerts were sent out to signal that she was missing. And what an irony that in attempting to protect her the triage nurse tore her away from the only stability she had ever known. Something his mother used to say, "You can't win for losing," came into his mind and he guffawed aloud.

"You laughing at something?" He looked up and saw a burly guy dressed in layers of tattered clothes with a face and hands smeared with soot glaring at him.

"No, no." Charles answered, recognizing the paranoia in his stare.

"You got a cigarette, then, brother?"

"No, no, don't smoke," Charles said, realizing that it was too much information and that he sounded like some elitist dweeb instead of the boy from the hood being here clearly proved that he was. He looked around him and took in his fellow inmates. Two were actually engaging in small talk about their local haunts and favorite sports teams. But most looked stonily ahead or were slumped over with their eyes closed. One young man sat across from him on the floor with his arms wrapped around his knees. This was probably his first time too. His boyish face with its coffee black skin and finely carved features was tight with anger and shame. It made Charles think about Jason's first run in with the police when he was twelve. He had to retrieve him from a police station after Jason was caught jumping the turnstile and spray painting a subway station during a sleepover with a classmate after the boy's mother fell asleep.

What could that young boy in the cell have done to end up behind bars instead of in the principal's office? But age was no protection. It was a liability. He thought of the hasty apprehension and what he was sure was the wrongful conviction of those young men charged with raping the jogger in the area of the park where he ran every day and of how ordinary false accusations were against Black men.

DeVaughn had been put in a different cell. Charles was glad because it was hard to disguise his humiliation and shame in the presence of his former student. But the grave-digger, clearly mentally ill or seriously high, was there and he seemed to be arguing with another guy in a navy-blue hoodie about Riker's. It was the red clad kid's turn to use the phone, and he was speaking in very fast Spanish with his left hand cupped over the receiver. An older man kept moaning, "I need my medication. I got diabeatus." Another stood with his face between the bars haranguing the corrections officers about getting something to eat and not them shits they call baloney sandwiches.

Could he really be surprised that he had ended up here? Something bad was bound to happen because he had been happy, and everything in his life experience had taught him that happiness was fleeting, especially when it was stolen. Bianca was not his child, and Rosetta was not his wife, but he had felt joy caring for Bianca and watching her slowly open up to life. She was, as it turned out, very bright. She learned how to read just by being read to and had graduated from coloring books to elaborate and colorful drawings of her own. In many ways it was as if Jason had come back into his life, and Madeline, too, because there was something about Bianca's spirit and the way she repeated what he said and then turned it into little tunes that reminded him of the way Maddie used to make up songs about their daily activities for Jason. Her favorite color was yellow, and that had been Maddie's too.

When he allowed himself to think of Rosetta, his whole body ached as if he'd suddenly come down with the flu. The thought of calling her from the pay phone in the holding pen crossed his mind, but it was way too late; he couldn't hang up and wait for her to call back, and he didn't want to call attention to himself or sully her by bringing her into the jail, even by way of the telephone. The way he missed her and longed for her when they were apart was like an illness. An addiction. And the prospect of losing her was tantamount to death. And yet he knew he could never really have her even if she were someone who could be possessed, which she wasn't. He didn't know anyone else like her, and he didn't *know* anyone else like he knew her, not even Maddie, because of they way she had been so generous with herself. Even her bluntness and honesty were a kind of gift because most people didn't say what they were really thinking. Their time together was always limited, but when she was with him, she held nothing back, not her thoughts, not her body, not her pleasure, or her pain. "This moment is all we have. And so, in the immortal words of Ram Dass," she'd joke, "Let's be here now."

To say that their time together was like a dream was no exaggeration because as if in a dream, they were able to cast off their daily personae and return to an elemental state of being outside of linear time. When he was with her, he was relieved of the taxing burden of having to construct, moment to moment, a distinct and unassailable ego out of all the fragments of his shattered self. She made him feel whole. He experienced a kind of religious ecstasy in coupling with her that had nothing to do with divine beings and everything to do with the sacred nature of life itself. It wasn't just sex; though that had been a gateway to a kind of openness, acceptance, comfort, laughter and play he had never experienced with anyone else.

He felt a guilty pleasure and a satisfying sense of revenge knowing that he was taking her back from a white man. He knew she would object to the ownership trope, insisting that she was neither his nor her husband's property, but he also knew she would agree that in coming together they had both come home to Harlem, so to speak, and that they found in each other an affirmation of Blackness that had sweetened and deepened their bond.

ROSETTA

Rosetta busied herself with dinner preparations, periodically shouting at the boys to start their homework when they became boisterous while playing their favorite computer game. Will would be home any minute with a depressing report from his office and complaints about the commute home, no doubt, malaise encircling him like the the rings of the saturnine planet. In the year since she and Charles had been meeting, Rosetta was able to ignore or at least patiently tolerate Will's alternating cycles of depression and manic excursions to the gym, as well as his drinking. She was even able sometimes to cheerfully encourage and comfort him when he was down. She found she could be quite pleasant going through the motions of being a wife because being with

Charles buoyed her spirit. She no longer feared drowning every time Will's ship took on water; she had found a life preserver in Charles.

But she knew it could not last. She tried not to dwell on what might or might not happen. It took a tremendous amount of effort to live what was essentially a double life. She was lucky that she did not have to lie that much, but sometimes the logistics got wearyingly complicated, especially if she or Will or the boys got sick or there was a holiday or out of town guests. Charles had come to rely on her in a way that was a little scary. It worried her that she and Bianca were everything to him now because he did not have a legitimate claim to either one of them. She loved when they were together, but the feeling of being an imposter in her real life and numbly going through her checklist of daily tasks only to become fully alive and engaged when she was with Charles disturbed her at times.

She was generally there for the boys, but occasionally she would be playing with them or reading a bedtime story and her mind would drift to Charles and it felt like she was cheating on them. She taught her four classes a week, and her students seemed to be satisfied with her course, but she was always distracted at work because Charles might be close by, and she wasn't writing at all, except in her journal, and most of her entries were about him.

Now she was on autopilot, tearing the leaves of the lettuce, slicing tomatoes, prodding the meatballs that sizzled in the skillet with a fork, trying to process Charles' arrest and Bianca's illness. Her first thoughts after he called her from the police station were completely selfish. Was this how it would end? Then she tried to wrap her mind around the word arrested—*Arrested*! She could not imagine Charles with his hard-earned professorial demeanor and awkward gentleness behind bars. He had grown up in Harlem with parents who continually fought, and he had been to war, but those experiences had rendered him the least hardened, least bellicose person she knew. It was odd, really. She was worried for his safety, and she couldn't help but feel guilty because she had aided and abetted him in the subterfuge; in fact, he probably wouldn't have been able to pull it off if it hadn't been for her and he probably wouldn't have gone through with it if she had objected more strongly. The more she thought about it, the more she had to accept that she had willfully denied that something like this was bound to happen. She had gone along because she wanted him. Bianca became the excuse for their relationship. They used her to get what they wanted from each other and justified it by telling themselves that they were improving her life. Now she was a kind of collateral damage. Feelings of remorse began to grow in Rosetta as she slid linguine from the box into a red enamel pot full of boiling water. Just then the apartment door opened and Will stepped into the foyer that opened onto the kitchen where she was cooking.

"What a day," he sighed, letting the door slam and dropping his briefcase just inside it. "And wouldn't you know there was some problem with the train, so it went local after 14 St. That's why I'm so late. What's that I smell?"

"Meatballs."

"You're a good wife," Will said, hanging his suit jacket in the hallway closet and stepping into the kitchen to peck her on the cheek. "I don't deserve you." He put a piece of the torn lettuce in his mouth then opened the refrigerator, bent down and took out the first of the numerous beers he would likely consume that evening.

"You're right," she answered, reciting her part in the marital script just as the first opener ring popped. Despite the fact that she was the one having an affair, Rosetta could usually agree that he didn't deserve her, but today, given what had happened, there was a hint of doubt in her voice. Will did not pick up on the change in her tone. He took a long sip from his beer.

"The insurance business sucks. Where are the boys?"

"Playing a game on the computer." Will nodded and strode towards the bedroom to change out of his work clothes.

"I'm going to need you to help them with their homework tonight. A friend is in the hospital, and I said I'd go visit."

"Who?"

"Somebody from work."

On the corner of East 91st Street and Lexington Avenue across the street from the looming brick edifice of the 92nd Street YMHA, Rosetta stabbed the silver buttons on the payphone she sometimes used to call Charles, entering instead her best friend Tracy's number. While the phone rang, she shifted impatiently from foot to foot. A neighbor whose son her sons sometimes played with in the building playground emerged from the supermarket on the north side of the street and waved and with a half-smile, Rosetta waved back at the woman, whom she thought was probably wondering why she was using a pay phone so close to home, or maybe why she didn't yet own a cellphone. It was around 7:15 pm, past rush hour, but the street was fairly busy with shoppers and other pedestrians and patrons en route to the fitness center or concert hall at the Y.

"Hello?"

"Tracy?"

"Hey girl, what's up?" Tracy answered.

"Charles got arrested!"

"What? Why?"

"He took Bianca to the hospital, and he didn't have the right ID for her, and I guess they thought he abducted her or something."

"That's crazy! Where are you? You sound funny. All breathless."

"I'm on my way to the hospital to see her."

"What about Charles?"

"He was taken to the police station near the hospital. He called me and I told him to call a lawyer."

Rosetta had confided in Tracy about her relationship with Charles. They had been friends since kindergarten and there weren't many things that they kept from each other. Tracy's family of five, including her parents, grandmother, older sister, and younger brother, was like a real-life working-class version of the Huxtables. Rosetta had fancied herself a fourth child to Tracy's parents Marvin, who worked for the Metropolitan Transit Authority and Ruth, who was a teacher's aide. Tracy's parents were her model for what a happy marriage looked like, and their love and mutual respect contradicted the bitter warnings issued by Aunt Essie. Tracy, who was a nurse-midwife, had followed in their footsteps and was happily married to her high school sweetheart Gregory, who was a math brain and worked as an actuary for an insurance company. They lived in a gentrifying section of Bedford Stuyvesant, Brooklyn not far from where they had all grown up.

Tracy advised her to be careful but said she realized she could not tell Rosetta how to live her life. Tracy had never been that fond of Will, even though she had been the maid of honor at their wedding and had to walk down the aisle with his successful older brother, who in the pictures appeared to be uncomfortable with a petite chocolate bridesmaid on his arm. Tracy had listened eagerly to all the juicy details about Charles while at the same time telling Rosetta, "I just don't want you to get hurt. Somebody is bound to, and I don't want it to be you."

"What are you going to do?"

"I don't know."

"What's wrong with Bianca?"

"She had a very high fever and a rash. I hope they let me see her."

"Hold on for a minute," Tracy said and then called out to her husband, "Honey, can you check on Kenya in the bathtub? I'm back. Is it even legal?"

"What?"

"For you to visit her?"

"Why wouldn't it be?"

"I don't know. If she's like a kidnap victim, wouldn't there be police protection or something?"

"I doubt it. It's not a like a high profile case or anything." But after she hung up, Tracy's question troubled Rosetta. *Would they let her in to see Bianca? Who should she say she was? Was Bianca still in the emergency room or had she been admitted to the hospital?* The black tailored jacket she had pulled over her tee shirt and jeans to lend an air of respectability to her appearance was decidedly too hot as she hurried down Lexington Avenue past a florist, a bakery, a plumbing fixture store, and blocks of ritzy brownstones and solid pre-war apartment buildings along the intersecting streets. At 96th she crossed over to Park Avenue, turning over in her mind with every step the actions that had led to this moment, berating herself for going along with this fool's errand that in retrospect seemed a very bad idea.

The lobby and waiting room of the pediatric emergency room was familiar to Rosetta. She had been there before with Ryan for a really bad ear infection when he was two and with Evan when he was four and fell off the monkey bars in the playground in Central Park and 97th Street and needed five stitches in his head. There were only a few children waiting to be seen, a girl about twelve whose ankle was wrapped and propped up on a chair, a toddler with a thick honking cough who was playing with a truck at his mother's feet, and an infant in a stroller wrapped in many layers of blankets screaming at the top of its tiny lungs. "I'm here to visit Bianca Theodore Brown" Rosetta said to the receptionist, a middle-aged Latina with a shock of white hair falling over tired dark eyes, who typed the name into the computer and stared at the screen.

"When was she brought in?"

"Earlier today."

"Where?"

"She was brought to the emergency room. A little girl."

"Bianca. B-I-A"

"I know how to spell it. But she's not here. You sure you have the right hospital? Wait."

"Bianca Theodore?"

"Theodore Brown. The last name is Brown." The woman seemed tired, and the computer terminal out- dated.

"Oh, wait, I see it. I was looking under T. She was admitted earlier today. She's in the children's hospital. Room 508."

Rosetta followed the receptionist's directions to the main hospital entrance and was waved through the security checkpoint once she gave the name and room number. She thought about Ryan and Evan as she stepped into the elevator, wondering if Will had followed her instructions and was properly supervising their homework and showers. A young female doctor in a white coat with the signature stethoscope draped around her neck stepped into the elevator and nodded towards Rosetta, and as the doors were closing, another visitor ran towards them and Rosetta stabbed at the door open button, but she was too late, and the doors closed before the man could enter. Her children had never been admitted to a hospital, and as the elevator rose and she anticipated seeing Bianca in a hospital bed, Rosetta was thankful for that and suddenly her heart filled with a love for Evan and Ryan that felt stronger than any force she had ever known.

With some trepidation Rosetta exited the elevator and walked down a corridor with glossy photographs of exotic locales on the walls. She passed through a door to the children's pavilion and suddenly came upon the cir- cular beehive of the nurses' station filled with monitors and keyboards and binders and staffed by nurses wearing white pants and brightly patterned tunics. She wondered if she should stop there, but everyone looked busy. She walked past, but someone called out, "Can I help you," and she turned back and stammered Bianca's name. The nurse motioned her down the hall.

Rosetta entered the room. Bianca was asleep in the bed closest to the door. She was hooked up to an IV and there was an oxygen tube in her nose. The curtains were drawn around the bed near the window and Rosetta could hear a family visiting with their child. She stood awkwardly by the side of the bed gazing down at Bianca, listening to the family members surrounding the other bed laugh and joke while watching *The Fear Factor*. Even with the nasal cannula looped across plump cheeks that were smudged with traces of tears, Bianca looked angelic, peaceful, and almost untroubled as she slept. Long black eyelashes fringed her almond shaped eyes and curled prettily against her light brown skin and her perfectly proportioned tripartite nose and dark pink bow like lips. Her beauty and the poignancy of her innocence in the face of the suffering she had undergone and had yet to undergo brought tears to Rosetta's eyes. No wonder Charles had fallen in love with her. How could you not want to protect and nurture a beautiful young life that held so much promise if only it could be given a chance to flourish? A pang of grief and then guilt gripped Rosetta as she thought about the child she had not birthed almost two years before. She did penance in her heart and tortured herself for a moment with thoughts of what might have been, but then she pictured the animated faces of her boisterous little boys and the moment passed.

Bianca had played at Rosetta's at least one afternoon a week and she and her younger boy Ryan had become close friends. On Wednesdays when Charles had an afternoon class and Evan went to an after school program, Rosetta picked up Ryan and then walked with him over to Bianca's school on Lexington Avenue and took the children to the park or brought them back to her apartment. Charles paid her, and she was able to justify it as a babysitting job to Will. When Charles came to fetch Bianca, they tried hard not to look at each other or betray any connection beyond a collegial one, and usually by that time in the evening Will was either at the gym or passed out in the bedroom depending on what bipolar phase he was in, so he rarely came in contact with Charles. One time though, Will was in the kitchen when Charles came to the door and Rosetta was in Ryan's room with the children. She was shocked when she came out and saw Charles and Will having a heated yet friendly conversation about football and by the way they cordially shook hands when Charles left with Bianca.

"Are you her mom?" A nurse's aide, an older West Indian woman whose name tag read R. Robinson, came into the room.

"No, I'm just a friend," Rosetta said.

"Sweet little girl. I've been checking on her since they brought her upstairs. She wore herself out crying for her "Papa Charlie." Bianca's eyes opened, as if she'd heard what the woman said.

"Papa Charlie?"

"No, honey, it's Rosetta."

"I'll be back," Ms. Robinson said.

"Miss Rose, I want Papa Charlie."

"How are you feeling, sweetheart?"

"I want to go home."

"You're here in the hospital so you can get all better."

"But where is Papa Charlie?"

"He can't be here right now, but he asked me to come see you."

"Is Ryan here?"

"No."

"Where's Ryan."

"At my house."

"Is Papa Charlie at your house?"

"No, he—" Rosetta didn't know how to answer. She sat on the side of the bed and took Bianca's small hand in hers. "Would you like me to tell you a story?

"Tell me a story you tell Ryan."

"Ryan likes scary stories."

"I like scary stories too. Tell me one."

"Once upon a time there was a ghost," Rosetta started and then she shouted, "Boo!" Bianca laughed.

"That's not a real story, Miss Rose. You tricked me."

"Tell me a story about a girl."

"What kind of girl?"

"Tell me the story about Bianca."

"You?"

"No, the one Papa Charlie tells me."

"Which one is that?"

"The Shake Pear story."

"Shake Pear, oh!"

"Maybe you should tell me the story."

"Once upon a time there was a girl named Bianca and she had a sister, and her name was Kate. Bianca was a good girl, but Kate was a bad girl. She was mean and she didn't listen, and she liked to say bad words. Nobody wanted to marry her, but a prince wanted to marry Bianca because she was nice. The End."

"Wow! What a story." Rosetta said and smiled. Bianca rolled her head against the pillow. "I'm tired. They took blood out of my arm. Did you know that? Did they ever take blood out of your arm?"

"Yes, they do that to see why you don't feel well."

"And they put this needle here. You know what it's called? A I.V. And it goes into my veins with medicine."

Bianca's eyes grew wide and serious as she pointed to the I.V. port and explained.

"Did you ever go in a ambulance? Papa Charlie took me in the ambulance and then we came here, and I was lying on the bed with wheels, and he went away. And then police came, one was a man, and one was a lady and they said did Papa Charlie hurt me and how did my arm get hurt, and I said my arm was not hurt and that Papa Charlie does not hurt me at all, he took care of me and played with me and bought me toys and took me to school after Keisha went away. And they said is Keisha your mother and I said yes, and they said where is Keisha and I said I don't know she didn't come back."

Rosetta stroked Bianca's hand as she spoke, partially to calm her own nerves as she tried to imagine the scenario Bianca described and what it might mean in terms of what was happening with Charles.

"Everything is going to be okay, honey," Rosetta said wishing her words would prove true. A middle-aged Filipina nurse with a kind smile, short dyed red bob and an efficient but gentle manner came into the room.

"How are you doing, Miss Bianca?" I came to check your temperature and your I.V. Do you need to go to the bathroom?"

"No," Bianca said. The nurse whose name tag read "Monserrat Berger" nodded towards Rosetta. "Is this your friend?" Bianca shook her head in the affirmative.

"Ryan's mommy."

"Very nice of her to come to see you."

"I'm the mother of one of her playmates," Rosetta said. The nurse sized Rosetta up as if to discern how much she knew about the situation. "Pretty scary for her, but we are trying to make her comfortable." The nurse slipped a disposable plastic sleeve over the thermometer and slipped it into Bianca's mouth. It beeped a few seconds later. She looked down at the display. "Good," she said, patting Bianca's hand. She checked the level of fluid in the IV bag and left the room.

"Do you know Papa Charlie sings to me?"

"He sings to you?" Bianca nodded her head. "What does he sing?"

"He sings, "I got sunshine on a cloudy day.""

"My Girl?"

"You know that song? Can you sing me that song?"

"I got sunshine…" Rosetta began singing softly. Bianca smiled and her face brightened, but Rosetta became overwhelmed with sadness, and she croaked out the words instead of carrying a tune. Bianca chimed in at the "I guess you say part" that ended with my girl.

"You know what?"

"What?"

"Papa Charlie sings it better than you," Bianca said grinning mischievously under the cannula.

"I hope so," Rosetta said, trying to smile although her eyes were welling with tears. "I need to give you a hug now and go home, sweetheart. The nurses and doctors will take good care of you, and I will come see you soon." Rosetta gently embraced Bianca, being careful not to disturb the medical equipment protruding from her body. She turned from her and hurried out before Bianca could ask any more questions.

Tears streamed from her eyes as she headed towards the elevator, and then she heard a deep male voice say, "I'm Detective Nichols from the NYPD, can I ask you a few questions?" Rosetta spun around and froze when she saw she was face-to-face with a solid thirty-something man with a piercing gaze, red brown skin, and a buzz cut. He was wearing a suit jacket and a dark tie, and he was flashing a silver badge and looked more like a computer geek than a cop. She realized he was the man the elevator door had closed on. "You were here to visit Bianca Brown?" Rosetta's heart was pounding. She wasn't sure whether she should answer or not, but she found herself saying yes, feeling like maybe she could trust him a little more than she would an older white police officer.

"How do you know her?"

"I babysit for her sometimes. She plays with my son."

"So, you know her parents?"

"No." Detective Nichols cocked his head as if to say, *that's curious.*

"How did you know she was in the hospital?"

"The person who brought her here told me."

"Would that be Charles Rivers?"

"Yes."

"And your name is?"

"Rosetta Ocean."

"He called you after he was arrested?" Rosetta frowned and nodded her head, feeling like she might throw up the spaghetti dinner she had scarfed down before leaving for the hospital. "Why would he call you?" The elevator stopped on the floor. When the doors opened, nobody emerged, and then they closed again with a slight rumble and a beeping sound commenced as Rosetta and the detective continued to stand in front of the elevator bank.

"We're colleagues and friends. We teach at the same university." He cocked his head again.

"How long have you known him?"

"About five years."

"Do you live with him?"

"No, I live with my husband and children."

"Were you aware that he had no legal relationship with Bianca Brown and was lying about being her grandfather?"

"It wasn't like that. Her mother abandoned her."

"So, you were aware? What did he tell you about Keisha Brown's disappearance?"

"He said she left Bianca with him on the morning of September 11, 2001, and never came back."

"How close are you with Mr. Rivers?" Suddenly Rosetta's cheeks grew warm and then hot until she felt like her face might burst into flames.

"I don't feel comfortable answering these questions. I think I need to talk to a lawyer. I have to get home to my family."

"Why do you need a lawyer? You're not under any suspicion. But you do seem to know a lot about the suspect's relationship with Bianca Brown." A man in a white coat holding a clipboard came along and pressed the button for the elevator.

"Suspect? What is he suspected of? What kind of crime is it to take care of an abandoned child?" Detective Nichols looked displeased by Rosetta's response and the not-so-subtle reproach of his authority it implied. As a warning, he bared his teeth in a kind of canine smile.

"Why would a single man who lives alone want to have access to a six-year old child? Hmmm? Did you ever think about that? To your knowledge did he ever get physical with Bianca Brown. You know, anything violent or sexual?" Rosetta groaned involuntarily as if the detective had kneed her in the kidney.

"No! He would never do anything like that. He's a kind man. He's a good Samaritan. He wanted to help her. He loves that little girl. You should have seen her a year ago. She was totally unkempt, covered with rashes and scabs. She didn't smile."

"So, you bought his story, huh? The mother just disappeared. And he somehow has this child on his hands. That's what they do. They convince people that they have some kind of legitimate claim to the child or that they are helping them out. There's a lot of men out there like your friend. Men who want access to and prey on vulnerable children and use them and hurt them to fulfill their sick fantasies."

Rosetta wanted to protest but at that moment everything she was certain of, everything she thought she knew was called into question. It was strange that Keisha had just disappeared. And could she actually vouch for everything Charles had told her? She wasn't there. She did not know what happened between Charles and Bianca when they were alone. And as far as she knew, she was the only person at work who knew that Bianca was actually living with him. Those times he had brought her to his office the Department office had been closed and few members of the full-time faculty taught late evening classes. Since then he had changed his schedule so that he taught when she was in school. But if Charles had harmed Bianca, why would she cry for him and tell Rosetta sweet stories about their time together? And how could he have been so open and loving and passionate with Rosetta if he were that kind of person? As quickly as the doubts had formed, they dissipated. She knew Charles. And she knew she knew him. His spirit had flowed over her and through her like the body of water that was his name; she had become a vessel for his authenticity, for his truth, and she knew as surely as she knew her own name that he could not have hurt or abused Bianca.

"Apparently, he wasn't so kind to her mother."

"I don't follow you." Rosetta said, wary of what he might say next, feeling that she herself had probably said too much, impatient for the interrogation to end so she could leave. She was sure Will was losing it by now because she had been gone for so long, and she was afraid of what she would face when she got home.

"Keisha Brown is dead."

"What do you mean dead?"

"Is there more than one meaning for the word dead?" As the implications dawned on her, Rosetta blurted out,

"And you think Charles killed her? Charles Rivers? Really? That's ridiculous. That's just crazy. He's not a killer."

"Vietnam? Sometimes we don't know people as well as we think we do," Detective Nichols said. He bared his teeth again in that ominous non-smile. "Thank you, Mrs..."

"Ms."

"Ms. Ocean."

The hall lights were off, and everyone appeared to be asleep when Rosetta returned home. She could hear Evan snoring faintly in his room which was the first one off the long hallway in their three-bedroom high rise apartment. The door to Ryan's room was slightly ajar. She peeked in and saw him lying on his side, clutching the Elmo doll he'd slept with since he was an infant, illuminated by the dim glow of his Batman nightlight. The door to her bedroom at the end of the hall was shut, but a ribbon of golden light was visible under it. Rosetta quietly opened the door, expecting to see Will sleeping on his back on the left side of the bed and snoring in the manner that his older son had inherited. But he was sitting up fully dressed in a collared polo shirt and jeans, his large masculine form completely incongruous against the bedroom décor of framed botanical prints, a pastel-colored flowered bed comforter, and round night tables covered with frilled skirts and temple jar table lamps. When Rosetta saw the look of fury on Will's face, she went numb. She clutched the doorknob and hesitated before taking another step.

"I see you finally decided to come home, you lying black bitch. Look what I found." He held up the red leather-bound notebook she used as a journal and usually kept in the zippered front section of the backpack she used to carry student papers and materials for class.

"Where did you get that?" Rosetta asked weakly.

"Ryan was looking for a red pen for his homework and I thought you might have one in your backpack."

"You had no right to go into my stuff."

"I had no right? I had no right?" He sprang from the bed with the agility of a big cat and grabbed her by the twist of hair on the top of her head, "You come back here after fucking and sucking the cock of that black bastard and tell me about my rights?"

"Please let me go."

"Oh, I'll let you go all right." He shoved her against the dresser, and she fell into the lotions and perfumes arrayed on a mirrored tray that had belonged to her mother. One of the tiny perfume bottles skidded onto the parquet wood floor and broke at the same time Rosetta fell back against the foot of the bed. She struggled to get up, the improbable scent of jasmine from the broken perfume bottle overwhelming her nostrils.

"Will, I--" She pulled herself up to a sitting position on the bed. She was not going to say she was sorry because she wasn't. She regretted causing him pain, and her pleasure in the affair had always been tempered by that. But saying she was sorry she had come to know Charles in the way she did would be like saying she was sorry she was born when she found out that she would die one day. Before she could think of what to say, Will took the journal and smacked it hard across her face. The pain was searing and her tears instantaneous. She fell back onto the bed.

Rosetta rolled onto her side to protect her face.

"Now get out! Get out!" Will yelled. She heard Will's voice from a distance. It was a long moment before she could move or speak. Her consciousness, reflexes and strength were all concentrated at the site of the excruciating pain.

"I think you broke my nose," she finally mumbled, feeling her face and finding her hand covered in blood.

"Get out!"

"Where can I go now? The boys have to go to school in the morning. Are you prepared to get them ready and get them there?" She lay still. Hoping the physical assault was over. She could feel the blood from her nose soaking into the comforter. She sat up gingerly, glancing fearfully at Will as she reached into one of the dresser drawers and pulled out a tee shirt and held it to her bleeding face.

"Where can you go? Go to your fucking soul mate. Go to the black man who taught you all about love," Will said in a falsetto voice to mock what she had written in the journal. Saying the words seemed to rekindle his hurt and to anger him so much that he slapped her down again with his large open hand. It felt like a hot frying pan smashing into her face. She screamed in pain and slipped off the edge of the bed. Ryan came running into the room and when he saw Rosetta on the floor, he threw himself at her and began shouting, "Mommy, Mommy!"

"Go back to bed," Ryan," Will said, unsuccessfully trying to gain control of himself and bleach the anger out of his voice. But then Evan ran into the room and seeing his father's menacing stance, he made a projectile out of his body and hurled himself at Will's stomach screaming, "Stop hurting, Mommy. Stop hurting mommy right now!"

"Mommy's okay," Rosetta mumbled. "Go back to bed." Will grabbed the boys roughly and dragged them out of the room as they screamed for Rosetta. She curled into herself on the parquet floor staunching the blood flowing from her nose with the tee-shirt. What had she expected? It could not have gone on forever. But she had never pictured it ending with her lying on the floor with her face bashed in. The pain was so intense that it sucked all other thoughts and sensations into it, and as she lay on the floor, Will, Bianca, the detective, the nurses, Ryan, Evan, the faceless Keisha, and Charles disappeared into its vortex and left her alone.

JASON, OCTOBER 2002

Jason liked to watch *Jeopardy!* because he always knew the answers and the fact that Gracie Ellen and her mother, Donna, didn't know anything and were impressed by his knowledge made him feel better about himself. It proved he wasn't stupid despite what he had chosen to do with his life. It proved he was better than them even though he was Black, and they were white. But when it came on that night, and they were all so fucked up on pills to even see straight, a funny thing happened. Alex Trebek kept turning into his pops. He'd rouse himself from a nod and hear Trebek's voice, but when he opened his eyes and looked at the TV he'd see his dad the way he used to be when Jason visited his class, standing in the front of the room in a cable knit sweater and dark pants, a piece of chalk in his right hand. Eventually, Jason could no longer keep his eyes open, and he was pulled from the room and into his head and then out of his head to the place of the forgetting and floating and freedom from the pain that he had tried so hard to get to. But he woke up a few hours later hurting all over, feeling like he was going to piss himself. An infomercial about a knife that could cut through anything was blaring on the TV. Gracie Ellen was snoring on the other end of the couch with her mouth open, her knees and elbows stuck out in weird angles like a broken Tinker Toy creation. The massive Donna was reclining all the way back as if she were levitating in her stained beige La-Z-Boy, her head hanging to the side, and her mouth round and open and red inside like that of a big dead fish. Jason went to the bathroom and peed half in the toilet and half on the floor. He dragged himself up to the mirror and peeled open his eyes and jumped when he saw his own rust brown face, nappy brick curls, wide nose and the lips that Gracie Ellen said were just like Jay Z's. He always felt compelled to, but he really didn't like looking in the mirror because when he saw himself he saw his mother and father in him. And when he saw them in him, he was torn up inside by how profoundly he had let them down.

"Nigga, Nigga, what the hell are you doing here?" the face in the mirror said. He couldn't believe it was talking and he looked behind himself to see if there was maybe someone else in the bathroom. He went into the bedroom he shared with Gracie Ellen.

"Nigga, what the hell are you doing here?" He looked on top of the dresser, then in the drawer of the broken nightstand and then he started checking the pockets of the clothes piled on the floor near the foot of the bed looking for an Oxy or anything he could take to make his face stop talking. He grabbed the ashtray from the TV table searching for even the tiniest of roaches, and when cigarette butts and a mound of ash spilled onto the floor, he was surprised to see them there. He got down on his knees and ran his fingers through the ash still hoping to find something and then he stopped, and he started shaking because there was a message written in the ashes. It said, "*Nigga, you gotta get outta here.*" He found his sneakers and put them on and stuffed some clothes from the pile on the floor into the backpack he sometimes used to transport drugs.

He had a gun and he thought about taking it, but it was under the bed and somehow, he couldn't remember how to crawl under there. Gracie Ellen and Donna were still passed out when he squeezed his hands around the keys to their beat-up minivan that were lying on the kitchen counter. They were dead to the world and something inside was telling him he was dead as long as he stayed there with them. "*Nigga, you gotta get outta here.*" It was dark outside, and he slipped and fell on some loose gravel, skinning his forearm on his way to the parking lot. The air was so warm and thick with humidity that he felt like he was swimming through it. A dog barked and that made him jump. But then it barked again, and he could hear that the sound had traveled a distance. "*Nigga, you gotta get outta here.*" His right hand was shaking so much when he tried to put the key in the lock of the car door that he had to hold it with his left hand to steady it. The key wouldn't go all the way in and then he looked up and saw it was the wrong car. Their car was next to it and when he climbed in and switched on the ignition, it lurched forward like a rollercoaster cart because he had flattened the gas pedal without realizing it. "*Nigga, you gotta get outta here.*" He scraped the car next to him as he pulled out of the parking lot, circling around the inside road of the low-income apartment complex and then pulling onto the dark and deserted public road beyond it. "*Nigga, you gotta get outta here.*" He couldn't see anything, but he kept his foot on the gas pedal moving forward in his escape that felt like and might even be a dream. He drove in the dream for almost a mile, and then it occurred to him to switch on the headlights and a cone of light fanned yellow over the black road. He drove into the light, hunched over the steering wheel, gripping it to his chest like a lifebuoy and then he saw the round eyes staring into his, framed by the glow of the headlights. "*Nigga, you gotta get outta here.*" He jerked the wheel to the left and stomped on the brake. The tires screeched as the car bounced off the road, sliding along the shoulder and tumbling him over like a wave. His head slammed against something hard; his skull became a firmament of stars, and then there was silence and the dark.

CHARLES

It was impossible for Charles to find a comfortable position on the floor of the crowded holding pen. He was hot, overwhelmed by the smell of half-eaten food and perspiring bodies, and afraid that if he fell asleep he might be attacked. But at one point he nodded off and dreamed that he and Claude Greene were running from the police while eating ices from Mr. James's cart. Claude got away, but Charles bent down to lick his lemon ice and as soon as he tasted its sweet tartness he felt the crack of the cop's baton on his back. The blow took his breath away and then there was a deafening noise and lightning on the ground, and it was so hot that Franklin blew up right next to him and pieces of his flesh struck Charles in the face and fragments of his bone stuck in Charles' skin and Charles' rifle disintegrated into a pile of ash just as the gravedigger with the tattoos lunged for it.

Late the next morning Charles was brought up to a little cell behind the courtroom. His cousin Stanley Davis, attorney at law, was waiting for him in the cell with a sheaf of papers. Charles had finally been able to get in touch with him when he called from the pay phone in the holding pen. Stanley's skin was almost albino white; he had a broad nose and spongy pink lips and a once bald head that now was covered by a curly black afro hair implant. He was June's son, his mother's Northern cousin who helped her out when she first came to New York. Stanley was a solid middle-class family man, with a law degree from Fordham, a wife who was an administrator at the Board of Education, two sons who had graduated from college and a daughter who was a freshman in high school. He thumbed through the papers and squinted at Charles quizzically but kindly behind the heavy black frames of his glasses. Charles and Stanley did not have much contact over the years; he could count the number of times their families had gotten together, but there had always been a positive vibe between them.

"I'm sorry about all of this, cousin," Stanley said. "These are not the circumstances I had hoped we'd be seeing each other in."

Charles nodded. But his range of motion was limited because his head was heavy and his neck was stiff.

"So, first things first, I just gotta tell you that it's important that you don't discuss the case with anyone.

Not friends, family. The police, girlfriend, nobody. Are you in a relationship right now?"

"No, no, not really."

"Not really?"

"I need you to be honest with me about everything if I'm going to represent you. As your attorney everything you say stays between us."

"Well, I have been seeing someone. She's, uh, she's married."

"Okay, so no matter how close you are you can't discuss the case with her either. You feel me? You ever been arrested or had contact with law enforcement for any reason?"

"No, no."

"Have you ever been brought to court?"

"Brought? No, no, not for me. My son, you know, Jason. Jason has been in court; he's had some issues. But no, not me."

"I'm sorry," Stanley was taking notes. But he paused for a second, took off his glasses, wiped his brow and eyes with a handkerchief and then put his glasses back on. "Warm in here... So, do you know what you are being charged with?" Stanley looked down at the court documents.

"I really have no idea. They arrested me when I took, took my student's daughter to the hospital for treatment."

"Treatment for what?"

"She was listless. She had a fever and a rash. They called from the school and told me to take her to the emergency room."

"How did you come to have custody of her?"

"I don't have formal custody. That seems to be the problem. Her mother left her at my apartment on the morning of September 11 last year. She said she was going out to smoke a cigarette. I thought she was coming back, and when she didn't come back right away, I decided to take care of Bianca until she did."

"And in that year, you never saw," Stanley looked at the paper, "Keisha Brown?"

"She never came back."

"And you didn't go to the authorities?"

"No."

"Why?"

"Because I didn't want them to take Bianca." Stirred by the emotion in Charles' voice, Stanley looked at him over the frames of his glasses.

"Was she, by any chance, yours? Your child?"

"No."

"Were you aware that keeping the child and not reporting her mother's disappearance was illegal?"

"I wasn't sure."

"Did she go to school?"

"Yes, a Catholic school."

"How did you manage to enroll her?"

"I said I was her grandfather. Her mother left a bag of stuff with documents. I told them she disappeared on 9/11. Which was true. And they believed me."

"Did you harm the child? Or forgive me for asking, have any kind of sexual contact with her?"

"No!"

"Do you know why she had bruises on her arms?"

"When I picked her up from school, she had a rash and I noticed what looked like a bruise on her arm, but I don't know how she got it. She was in the school office when I got there. They called me to come get her because she was sick. She had scars from burns. Her mother burned her with cigarettes."

"How do you know that?"

"She told me and showed them to me."

"The mother?"

"No, Bianca." Stanley made a notation.

"What if I told you she was found dead?"

Charles' body ached from sleeping on the floor, and his brain was hazy and febrile, but the word "dead" shocked him into focus and a chilly current passed through him.

"Bianca is dead?"

"No, but Keisha Brown is. They ran the ID you brought to the hospital. It matched the information in the system. She was found dead about six months ago in an alley in Bushwick with multiple stab wounds. No sign of the killer."

"Why wasn't this in the news?"

"Indigent black women don't always make the news."

"How do they know it was her?"

"Fingerprints and a tattoo on her back."

"Oh, yes, Keisha, the tattoo said Keisha," Charles said, seeing her again in his mind's eye curled up like a fetus in his bed that morning, black curlicue letters on her lower back spelling out her name like a trademark. Stanley gave him a steely, "Don't fuck with me look." It contrasted sharply with the friendly facial expressions he'd exhibited earlier.

"How do you know that?"

"I saw it, but it's not what you think."

"You sure you're not hiding something, man? When's the last time you saw her?"

"I had no contact with her after she left that morning. And she stole twenty dollars from my wallet on the way out. They were homeless. I wanted the little girl, Bianca, to be safe."

"That morning? She spent the night with you?"

"I told you; she showed up saying she had no place to stay, and I let her spend the night in Jason's room."

"You gotta be honest with me, cousin. Were you in a relationship with this Keisha Brown?"

"No!"

"Does your, uh, current girlfriend know her?"

"We were not involved then."

"But does she know her?"

"No."

"Why didn't you report Keisha Brown missing?"

"I don't know. I wasn't thinking straight. I didn't think they would take it seriously with all the World Trade Center stuff going on. And I figured she'd come back. And when she didn't come back right away and Bianca seemed happy to be with me, I thought I'd just continue to take care of her. I wanted to protect her."

"Well, the charges against you are serious, cousin," Stanley said, shaking his head and frowning. "They are charging you with murder, kidnapping, and child abuse. If you are convicted, you'd be looking at life imprisonment or a minimum of 40 years."

Charles' muscles seized up and his mouth fell open, but no words or sounds came out. Finally, he said,

"How can that be? What evidence do they have to link me to a murder in Brooklyn?"

"You had her child, and you did not report her missing."

"How does that mean I killed her?"

A dreaded and familiar sense of vertigo overtook Charles, then the extreme heat, the acrid smoke, the rapid-fire booms and clicks of artillery blaring in his ears, and before he knew it, he had exploded into a million fleshy pieces that he frantically tried to put back together with bloody severed hands. He wanted to cry out, but instead he pulled against his handcuffs as hard as he could until the physical pain blotted out the other sensations and he was able to bring himself back into the present moment and reconstruct the semblance of physical and mental integrity he called a self.

"I didn't kill anyone. I didn't kidnap Bianca. Her mother abandoned her. I took care of her the way her mother should have. I can't believe this is happening. We have to fight this. Are you up for the fight or do I need to get another lawyer?"

"That's up to you if you want someone else. But I kind of feel like I have a special stake in this. You're my blood, cousin."

Charles was strangely touched by Stanley's words. He had been raised apart from most of his family members and had not experienced much family loyalty or affection. The fact that Stanley wanted to help him because they were kin and kind—Black men struggling to survive and somehow prosper in a society that had stamped them as inferior from the moment of their birth, raised a glimmer of hope in him.

"Do you have an alibi?"

"Alibi? You can't be serious. Do they even know when she was killed? My alibi is that I was with her daughter and have not been to that section of Brooklyn in years. And what would my motive be? To completely destroy my own life and career? To deprive a child of its mother? I saw that happen with my son when my wife died of cancer, which is probably why I did it in the first place."

"Did what?"

"Kept Bianca."

"With these charges it's pretty unlikely that the judge is going to grant you bail."

"What does that mean? Because I have money. I have savings."

"With Class A felonies the bail is either really high or they remand you. But I'm still going to request bail because of your work history and social standing."

"Remand?"

"You stay in jail until the trial. At the Manhattan House of Detention next door or at Rikers Island."

Charles jerked the handcuffs so that they delivered another shot of pain that killed his reaction to the thought of spending more time in jail. One night had practically sucked all the dignity, sanity and life out of him. And that was the intent. "All kinds of traps out there. All kinds of ways people be trying to take away your freedom," his mother's litany began repeating in his brain like one of his father's old, scratched blues records.

"This is just an incredible mistake," he said after a long pause. "I am a college professor, not a murderer. I am a father, not a kidnapper or a child abuser."

Stanley looked at Charles sympathetically, swabbed his brow again and said, "I believe you, cousin." Stanley's sympathy and the fact that the severity of the situation had elicited it, was almost too much for Charles to bear, and it was compounded by the realization that even with his legal expertise, Stanley's feelings and belief in his innocence might not be enough to halt the chain of events Charles' actions or lack of action had set into motion.

He thought about how Bianca trusted him and how through him she had begun to trust the world, how she was eager to pet dogs now instead of recoiling from them, how she would run and join groups of children in the playground, how according to her teacher, she would raise her hand in class. He was the father she never had. He had exposed her to things she'd never seen before. For one year he had given her a life her mother could not give her, and she had filled the void left by Jason. He had given her the love he once reserved for Jason. He had taught her to believe she deserved to be loved. So why was he sitting here in handcuffs? He was the good guy. It was a good thing. She had been happy. His thoughts came quickly like a fusillade of defensive fire. But then they slowed down and they circled around the truth he could not deny. The relationship he had developed with Bianca was built on a lie. He had led her to believe that she was safe with him and safe with Rosetta. That was his crime. Lying to a child. Betraying Bianca by allowing her to believe that he could protect her. He began to weep softly. He could not wipe his eyes. He did not care who saw him. She was sick; her mother had been murdered; he was facing a prison sentence, and now she had no one.

Later Charles was led into the courtroom by a female police officer whose abundant curves seemed almost cruelly disciplined into the girdle of her blue uniform and bullet-proof vest. With a bored expression, she motioned for him to take his place on the butt polished seat of a blond wooden bench populated by other denizens of the cells, among the alleged: thieves and drug dealers, muggers and wife batterers, gang bangers, prostitutes, check forgers, and others who happened to come into the crosshairs of law enforcement at the right time for the police and the wrong time for them. Charles heard the court officer call out a number, then "The People versus Charles Rivers." And as he was led up to the bench, the noun "people" and its definite article reverberated in his brain calling to mind the image of a fist and the phrase, "Power to the people." The fist of Black Power was a cruel joke in the face of his helplessness before the state now. And how could it be that the people were against him when all he was trying to do was help a child nobody else cared about?

The people in his case became its Orwellian opposite, and as far as he was concerned, it was just another alias for "the man." He looked across the courtroom at the arresting officer who had shown up to press charges against him. He was a paunchy guy in his forties with faded red hair and a faded red face, with a closed book sneer written all over it. He would have seemed like a crude stereotype if he hadn't been so real. And it was ironic to Charles that his mask, his obdurate expression, was the same one most of the accused wore. A Black guy in plainclothes who looked like Will Smith in *Men in Black* stood impatiently next to Officer O'Rourke, and the Assistant D.A. stood next to him.

Charles noted that Stanley looked more impressive in the courtroom than he had in the interviewing cubicle. Although he was on the short side and slightly pudgy, his gray suit was impeccable and his bearing professional, and for a moment Charles was able to step out of his situation and feel proud that Aunt June's son had done all right for himself. The Assistant District Attorney, a brisk young Latina in heels, short black skirt, white blouse and a black fitted blazer looked familiar to Charles, and a sick feeling came over him that she might be a former student. There was no hint of recognition on her part, and she read the charges and the police account of Charles' arrest in a cool impersonal voice tinged with a Bronx accent.

"Notices," said the judge, the Honorable H. Baines, who with his white hair and white trimmed beard bore an uncanny resemblance to a black-robed Kris Kringle.

"Seven ten thirty-one A", the Assistant District Attorney said. Charles looked at Stanley for a translation, but Stanley was looking down at his legal pad.

"May it please the court that after discussion with the arresting officer and Detective Nichols and reviewing the facts in the case, the state is dropping the murder charge and reducing the first-degree kidnapping and child abuse charges to kidnapping and child endangerment in the second degree." Stanley seemed surprised. Then pleased.

"May I have a word with my client, your honor?"

"Granted." Stanley turned to Charles and quietly explained, "They're offering you a plea agreement. This is new. They didn't tell me this before I met with you. If you plead guilty to the lesser charges the maximum sentence would be three years."

"I'd go to prison for three years?"

"At the most."

"The most! I am not guilty of any of this. I'm not accepting a plea bargain for phony charges. I want to be exonerated." Stanley nodded but did not look happy.

"How do you plead Mr. Rivers?"

"My client pleads not guilty to the charges," Stanley said. An expression of annoyance passed over the Assistant District Attorney's face.

"What is the state's recommendation?" The judge asked.

"Your honor, we move that the defendant be held in custody without bail."

"Counselor?"

"Your honor, I know these are serious charges, but they are based on a misunderstanding of the circumstances. My client maintains that he was protecting rather than endangering the child after her mother abandoned her on his premises. He did not abduct the child. He took care of the child who was left with him and sought medical attention on her behalf when she needed it. Professor Rivers is a respected member of the community, a long-time university professor who has been known for his service and good reputation and support of causes that enhance the lives of young people. He has never been arrested or had any previous personal encounters with the law and I move that the charges be dropped."

The judge looked down at Charles, and instead of the dispassionate game face Charles expected, he fixed him with a curious human stare as if to ask, "Don't I know you?" Then he scanned the paperwork in front of him.

"The child has been hospitalized. Any further reports on her condition?"

"We just got the hospital report. Although there were no signs of recent physical abuse during this examination, we can't rule out psychological damage," Ms. Rodriguez said dramatically. "The bruising and other symptoms are consistent with a possible diagnosis of leukemia. The child's blood is being cultured." Charles reeled when he heard the word "leukemia."

"Why wasn't the defense given the report," Stanley protested.

"We literally just got it," the A.D.A. answered looking at the man in black.

"No excuse," Stanley grumbled.

"Professor Rivers is released on his own recognizance but shall have no further contact with the child during this time and is ordered to appear in court at the pretrial hearing," the judge pronounced.

Stanley turned to Charles with a victory grin, but Charles was too traumatized by the entire experience and by learning how sick Bianca might be to respond with anything close to jubilation. He took a deep breath that made him realize he had hardly been breathing, and then he stole a glance at the judge to try to figure out why he had looked at him the way he did. As he continued to stare, the creeping realization that "H" stood for Harold and that Harold Baines was the nephew of Mrs. Price, the woman his mother had worked for on Park Avenue for so many years, came to him. Harold was much younger than his cousins and when he was a boy and used to visit the Prices on school holidays, he and Charles would sometimes play with Matchbox cars in the hallway outside the service door to the kitchen. That gray-haired man was the blond boy who used to play with him. His "friend" Harry, who was five years older than Charles and from another world. He glanced towards the bench again, but the judge was occupied with something else.

"I know him," Charles said to Stanley.

"Who?"

"The judge. We played together when we were boys." Stanley raised an eyebrow. "My mother worked for his aunt."

"You got lucky, bro," Stanley said, clapping him on the shoulder. Charles had begun to think his luck had run out, but the fact that he literally knew *the man* or more precisely, *the man* knew him meant that he might get a chance to prevail over the *people.*

"What do I do now?" Charles asked Stanley.

"After you sign the papers you are free to get your belongings and go about your business until the pre-trial hearing. I'm sure they dropped the murder charge because it would be almost impossible to prove. And it's not worth it to them. She had drugs in her system, a history of homelessness and recent arrests for prostitution. The first-degree kidnapping charge is weak, and they know it. And the hospital report disproved the abuse charges. The whole thing will probably get dismissed."

"But what about Bianca?"

"Since her mother is dead, if she has no other relatives, she is a ward of the state."

"The state that took such very good care of her mother so that she ended up dead and I ended up here because I tried to help her child?"

"She'll be assigned a social worker and be put in foster care."

"Yes, that's what happened to her mother."

When he exited the detention center, Charles was surprised to feel cool September air on his face, to smell the faint saline stench of the East and Hudson Rivers and to see life going on as usual for those on the outside —the hotdog vendors under their blue and yellow umbrellas, the government workers, jurors, attorneys, tourists walking on Centre Street. He bought a frank from a vendor whose cart was parked at the curb right outside the courthouse. He ate it quickly while he stood on the street, feeling empty and bruised, intimidated by the imposing municipal buildings surrounding him, aware on a subliminal level of death; the African Burial Ground lay a few blocks away and several streets to the southwest there were gaping holes in the bedrock of New York City where just a year and a few weeks before the World Trade Center once loomed.

Charles was convinced that the hologram of his disgrace was evident to everyone who looked his way. He finished the frank and walked towards the subway entrance at Canal Street. His left leg hurt and threatened to trip him when he descended the stairs. He gripped the steel banister and that's when he became aware of the pain and noticed the abrasions on his wrists. He stopped when he reached the bottom of the staircase, feeling weary and suddenly very old, confused about what to do next. But before he had time to think, he was pushed forward by a throng of subway patrons rushing to make an incoming train. He fished out his wallet and in the first credit card slot he found his blue and yellow MetroCard. When he swiped his card and walked through the turnstile, it felt like the first normal thing he had done in two days. He went down to the lower level. A 6 train was waiting with open doors. He hesitated before stepping into the car, reacting to the bright lights and the thought of confinement. He was convinced that people would look at him and know where he had come from because he was unshaven and empty-handed, no newspaper, brief-case or shopping bag, and his pants were rumpled and stained by something dark that looked like grease and probably made him smell like one of the homeless.

But no one seemed to notice as he sat down in a seat next to the handrail just inside the door. He stared at the advertisements above the seats across from him as if he had never seen them before. A doctor who treated severe acne, his smooth face smiling down on the straphangers as proof of the effectiveness of his cure. A technical school where you could learn to repair refrigerators and air conditioners. A language class that would rid new speakers of English of their foreign accents, a government nutrition program for pregnant women and nursing mothers, and "If you see something, say something," the ubiquitous slogan that began appearing after the World Trade Center attack. The wheels shrieked as the train pulled out of the station and Charles shuddered and involuntarily grabbed the handrail next to his seat. He was sure the other riders witnessed his panic, but when he stealthily shifted his eyes to survey them, not one was looking in his direction. The movement of the train began to calm him. He was a lifelong New Yorker, after all, and subways were home. As the train rumbled, clacked and screeched through the dark tunnels and in and out of the tiled brightness of the stations, Spring Street, Bleeker, Astor Place, Charles began to feel drowsy and in that state he imagined he was moving away from all the bad things that had happened, and that maybe they hadn't really happened at all, and then he slipped into a memory of the last time he had been with Rosetta. "Leave him and marry me," he said. She had shaken her head, the dark curly halo of her loose hair bobbing as she smiled that smile that made her eyes glow. That smile that made him know she loved him. "But then we couldn't have so much fun." The train stopped at 14th Street and Union Square and a crowd of passengers rushed in. Just before the doors closed, one of "New York's Finest" in his midnight blue uniform stepped onto the train commanding a place in front of the door beside Charles. Charles panicked again thinking the cop had somehow come after him. But the officer stared straight ahead with his hands in the pockets of his blue jacket, radiating the authority of his badge but not seeming to pay particular attention to anyone.

Rosetta. He needed to see Rosetta. Stanley had told him he couldn't discuss the case with her. But he couldn't wait to tell her what happened and to find out if she had been able to see Bianca. He needed to switch trains after 34th Street to cross over to the West Side. But what if he didn't? What if he took the train up to where Rosetta lived and got off at 86th Street? What day was it? Will would most likely be at work. The kids would be at school. He pictured Rosetta in slow motion, her smile forming like the sun rising, her arms reaching out pulling him inside her door to safety. He felt them melting into the kind of embrace that took them out of this world and spun them onto a planet where the only thing that existed was their love. Then the train screeched into the 42nd Street Station and the bulk of passengers prepared to exit, and as if propelled by their collective will, Charles stood up himself and left the subway car with them.

Charles walked painfully up the stairs at the 110th Street subway station and emerged from the underground gloom and din into the bright sunlight and sounds of an early fall afternoon in the neighborhood. His eyes were drawn to the green of Central Park. He imagined Rosetta running around the curve of the park drive, and his heart swelled with a love that made it feel too big for his body. An ambulance whined, crows cawed, brakes screeched as the crosstown bus stopped on the corner of 110th Street and Central Park North. A car rocked with loud reggae music as the driver waited for the light to change and a group of children freed from the prison of school lined up for ice cream from the soft serve truck, shouting and laughing. As Charles crossed to 111th Street, a disheveled man with matted dreads and rumpled pants with one side rolled up, propelled himself on one leg in a wheelchair and thrust a dirty paper cup towards him. Charles ignored his entreaty, passing the group of local men who sat on milk crates opposite the liquor store and a confused looking woman with a lopsided wig and hot pants revealing meaty inner thighs. She gripped a beverage in a brown paper bag and said to no one in particular, "I wash my ass; you wear perfume." Harlem residents were alive and kicking, even those with only one leg, and being back in the neighborhood made Charles realize he was too. As he haltingly walked towards 112th Street, troubled by pain in his knees, he made ambitious plans to change into his running shorts and head to the park as soon as he got home.

But his heart nearly stopped and that resolve drained from him when a woman pushing a stroller approached with a girl happily singing and skipping alongside her wearing the same plaid uniform Bianca wore to school. Bianca was in the hospital a little more than ten blocks away, but she might as well have been as far away as Jason, or even as far away as Madeline, who was dead and never coming back. Charles had spent every day with Bianca for a whole year. He had watched her change right before his eyes, and he could not imagine what home would feel like without her now. What would he tell the school? What would he tell the neighbors who thought she was his legitimate foster child? How would he withstand Mrs. Campbell's withering stare?

When he got to his building a group of teenage boys was clowning around on the stoop, play fighting, talking trash, rehearsing rap lyrics, and showing off their hip-hop wear and sneakers. One of them was spitting rhymes and Charles heard, "Peep the style and the way the cops sweat us..." Once again, his heart stopped. He always thought of Jason when he saw the young men in the neighborhood. The youthful exuberance and expressiveness and even innocence of the kids on the stoop, despite all they had witnessed and suffered, made him fear for their freedom and safety in a new way since he had just experienced first-hand the callousness of the police and had seen so many who looked like them caught up in the system.

"Hey, Mr. Rivers," Montie, who had grown up in the building greeted him. "Where you been? Ain't seen you in a minute." *What? Did he know? Charles had been gone for just over 24 hours.* He was unnerved, but he answered in the neutral way he had cultivated over the years to respond to neighbors he did not want getting into his business.

"I've been around. Just working hard."

"Where Bianca? She a mess, that little girl."

"With the babysitter," Charles lied as he fished for his keys to the front door.

"Don't bother. It's broke again," Montie said. The door open."

By the time he walked up the four flights and got inside his apartment, Charles was too exhausted and drained to do anything but strip off his clothes and fall into the bed where he and Rosetta had made love just a few days before. He reached over to his bedside table and dialed her number from the beige princess rotary phone she had teased him about because it was so ancient; somehow just touching it made him feel connected to her. Hearing her voice would soothe him no matter what bad news she might have about Bianca. But his attempt at calling was met with a busy signal. He collapsed on the pillows with the phone in his hand, the tone pulsing like a discordant electronic heartbeat. He wished she had a cellphone. He hadn't bothered to purchase one yet, but some of his students had them. He closed his eyes and was instantly asleep only to be awakened seconds later by a recorded voice issuing from the phone, "If you'd like to make a call, please hang up and dial again. If you need help hang up and then dial your operator." He rolled over and hung up. He caught a hint of Rosetta's scent on the pillow, and as he lay there slowly breathing it in, he fell asleep again. He dreamed he was a huge gray whale barreling through acres of ocean, and he did not wake up until the next morning when the phone rang at around 10 o'clock.

ROSETTA

Rosetta had been up on the couch all night crying into a bloody towel, melting ice and tears running down her face and neck. Ryan was always the first person in the household to wake up, but this morning when he called out, "Mommy" at around 6:45 am instead of going to his room and snuggling with him, Rosetta went into their bedroom to wake up Will, who was snoring heavily in his typical fashion, his large body sprawled across the bed. The covers were in disarray and his calf rested on a portion of the uncovered sheet that had been stained dark red by Rosetta's blood. Rosetta pressed the button on the doorknob to lock the door.

"Ryan is up. Wake up! You have to take them to school." Will rolled his head from side to side and peeled his eyes partway open, yawning groggily.

"Did you hear me?" Will opened his eyes wider and looked towards Rosetta. Then he sat up abruptly, fully awake.

"Oh my god. Oh my god, your face, your face. Rosie, I'm sorry. I'm so sorry." Rosetta went into the bathroom adjoining the bedroom and when she switched on the light she gasped when she saw a crime victim in the vanity mirror. Her face hurt so bad she couldn't think straight, but until now she had been afraid to see what it looked like. She had two black eyes, and her nose and mouth were twisted to the side and swollen to twice their size. Will came into the bathroom and tried to put his arms around her.

"Please. Don't touch me. Just get them ready and get them out of here."

Rosetta was still wearing the bloody tee-shirt and the jeans she had worn the night before. She stripped them off and got into bed pulling the covers over her face to block out the sunlight that had begun to pour through the windows as if this were a day like any other. She wondered where Charles was and what he would think about what Will had done to her. Her bones, her heart—her body were so heavy that she sank down into the mattress as if she could pass right through it. To comfort herself she imagined that Charles was holding her and soon she fell asleep.

She awakened with a jolt when she heard Will's voice, opened her eyes, and pulled the sheet away from her face to see him standing over her.

"I brought you some coffee," he said holding out a blue and white container from the deli on the corner.

"You think I can drink coffee now? Do you see my lips? Do you see my nose?"

"I want to take you to the hospital," Will said, setting the coffee down on the flower print fabric covering the bedside table and sitting in the rocking chair by the side of the bed.

"Fuck off and don't put the coffee on there. It'll stain it."

"I love you," Will said, picking up the coffee container and setting it on the floor.

"You found a great way to show it," Rosetta said lying on her side.

"I'm not the one who was cheating."

"No, you're the one who was drinking beer on the couch."

"What's that supposed to mean? I can't have a beer? Me drinking a beer is grounds for you to fuck some old guy at work?"

"Maybe you drink too much."

"You're saying I have a problem?"

"What do you think?"

"You're *my* wife. You belong to me."

"I don't belong to you. What is this? Slavery? I don't belong to anyone." She said, thinking in her heart that she belonged to Charles.

"There you go bringing race into it."

"Don't talk to me. Why are you even talking to me? Just leave me alone." Rosetta pulled the sheet back over her head.

"You need to see a doctor."

"Oh really? And what am I supposed to say happened to me? You gonna tell them you did this to me?"

"Do you know what *you* did to me? I love you. I've always loved you. And you, you obviously don't give a shit about me."

"You know that's not true."

"Then why did you do it?"

"Maybe it wasn't about you," Rosetta said.

"What's so great about him, anyway? What could you even talk about with him besides work?" Oh, wait. It wasn't about talking. It was about fucking."

"Shut up!"

"I know things have been kind of messed up because of the work situation and everything, but I never expected you to turn on me."

"I didn't turn on you," Rosetta said.

"Turn away from me then," Will said with what sounded like tears in his throat. Rosetta pulled the sheet away from her face and despite herself she felt some sympathy for him as she squinted through the slits of her swollen eyelids.

"It was lonely, Will. I was lonely."

"Lonely? You have me and the kids."

"Really? When's the last time *we* really talked about anything? When's the last time we had sex?"

"What?"

"Do you remember?"

"The last time...I don't know. But you were probably fucking him."

"The fact that you can't remember is a problem."

"This is about the abortion, isn't it? This is payback for me saying we couldn't afford to have another kid." Will stood up abruptly. The rocking chair bumped into the wall. Rosetta immediately thought of their next-door neighbor, Judy, a skinny white middle-aged paralegal who often complained that the kids were making too much noise.

"No," Rosetta said, but she wondered if there was some truth in Will's accusation. She had never felt more distant from him than that day he sat in the waiting room reading the paper while the fertilized egg was sucked out of her womb. Rosetta sat up and saw that Will was red-faced and trembling. He looked like a big piece of timber ready to fall. She was afraid that if she said the wrong thing it would fall and crush her.

"Look, I'm going to go, take myself to the hospital and say, say I was assaulted last night, and that the assailant ran away."

"You're lying."

"Of course, I'm lying. Do you want to get arrested?"

"You're going to see him."

"I'm not going to see him. I can't see him. He's in jail," she blurted out.

"Figures."

"It's a mistake."

"A lot of mistakes," Will said, but hearing that Charles was in jail seemed to diminish some of his anger. "You hate me and now the boys hate me, too. My parents hate me for being with you. My whole family is turned against me." Self-pity creeped in and replaced the fury in his voice. Will left the room. Rosetta knew where he was headed. In her mind's eye she saw him open the refrigerator, twist the beer can out of its plastic collar, pop it open with his index finger, and tilt it to his lips. In the meantime, she got out of bed and took a shower, standing with her back directly under the spray. She felt numb all over except for the excruciating pain around her nose and eyes. She made the water hotter and hotter; it should have burned her, but she felt nothing. She dressed and went into the living room, expecting to see Will slumped on the couch with a can of beer in his hand. But instead he was sitting at the dining room table furiously scribbling.

"What are you doing?"

"Writing a letter."

"A letter? Who are you writing to?"

"To him."

"Wait. What? No."

"I'm writing him a letter. I'm telling him that you're *my* wife and to keep his hands off you."

"You can't do that."

"The hell I can't. The hell I can't. Why can't I, Rosie, Rosie?" From his seat at the far end of the long table, Will looked up at Rosetta who stood at the other end, his eyes pleading and colorless, magnified by tears. "I don't want to lose you." Will began to cry loudly. Rosetta's back stung and it was warm from the heat of the shower, but those words produced a chill that ran down her spine because Charles had said the very same thing. She wasn't about to forgive Will for hitting her or suggesting that she was his property, but for the first time since she'd gotten involved with Charles, Rosetta put herself in Will's position. *I really fucked up*, she said, but not to Will. *This whole thing with Bianca and Charles and now Will is my fault.* She sighed, and it hurt. It really hurt.

"Don't write him a letter. You don't have to write him a letter, okay? I'll just tell him."

"What? What are you gonna tell him? Tell me what you're going to tell him."

"That I can't see him anymore."

CHARLES

Charles rolled over on his side to answer the phone. His head was heavy, and he wasn't sure how his voice would come out when he spoke.

"Hello?"

"Professor Rivers, this is Yolanda. I tried your office but there was no answer. I've got some students here. They went to class, and you weren't there. They want to know if the class is canceled."

"Oh, yes, I'm so sorry, sorry I didn't call. It's a family emergency. I have to cancel class. An issue with my, with my mother."

"I'll put a note on the door. I hope everything's okay. Take care. Bye."

His hand shook as he hung up the phone. It was a new day and he had told a new lie while the strands of his previous yarns were unraveling. He reached for the phone again. He would call Rosetta. Will would be at work by now, so it was safe. The phone hardly rang.

"Hello?" It was Rosetta but it didn't sound like her.

"Hey, I'm out. Are you okay?"

"Just let me talk to him. I'll tell him," he heard Rosetta say in a muffled voice.

"Hello, hello," it was Will shouting into the phone. "You're lucky I don't come over there and beat your ass to a goddamn pulp, motherfucker. You do know who you're talking to, don't you?"

"Give me the phone, Will."

"I am not giving you the phone. Stay away from my wife. Stay away. Do you hear me?"

"Charles," he heard Rosetta say, *"Charles, I'm so sorry, but I can't do this anymore..."*

"Sorry?" Will roared, *"You should be saying you're sorry to me, bitch."*

Charles heard a click. The connection went dead. He held the receiver to his ear, his hand trembling. The recorded voice came on and he slammed down the handset so hard it fell off the cradle. When the voice came on again, he yanked the phone cord out of the wall. What he had feared most had apparently come to pass. He turned onto his back and lay still for a long time as the magnitude of all he had lost soaked through him and made his body heavy as though he had drowned.

DEEP RIVERS

JASON

Jason reached up and felt his face. There was a big bulge between his eyes and his head throbbed like a motherfucker. He was lying against the driver's side door of the minivan. It was on its side in a shallow ditch in the woods beneath the road. He blinked his eyes again because the sun, refracted through the prism of the upside-down windshield seemed to be on a search and destroy mission for his retinas. He tried to sit up, but the angle of the van challenged his balance. He wiggled his toes and gingerly moved his legs. Nothing seemed broken. He pulled himself across the console, crawled onto the passenger seat and grabbed the door handle above him. The door opened like a hatch, and he squeezed through it headfirst crawling down the side of the hot car and tumbling out onto the underbrush, all around him the smell of decaying leaves and dead animals. He stood up and examined his limbs as if he had just newly come into possession of them. There was a scrape on his forearm but otherwise he seemed to be in one piece. He could hear cars on the road and birds screeching in the air above him. He was trying to figure out how he had gotten there, whether he had woken up from a dream or was still having one. He felt in the pocket of his shorts for his phone, flipped it open and saw that he had seven missed calls from Gracie Ellen and one from Frankie. That's when he remembered the money he was supposed to drop off after he sold the pills. He flipped the phone shut and felt in his back pocket for his wallet. It was still there and when he saw the wad of twenties in it, the events of the previous day and night started to come back to him.

He scrambled up the embankment onto the road, weeds and sharp grasses scratching his legs. The sun was high, and the blacktop was hot. He stayed in the shadow of the brush, fearing that the cops might be coming after him, but reasoning that the last thing Gracie Ellen and her mom would do would be to call the police, considering all their shady scams. What he was afraid of was Frankie, who fancied himself a big-time drug dealer, or one of his dumb boys coming after him. Jason still had bad dreams in which he woke up dead and he could still feel the cold hard edge of the gun barrel pressed against his temple the time those guys had tackled him when he was sixteen, accusing him of trying to intrude on their turf. It was after that incident that he used his father's credit card and got on a bus to get out of New York and ended up in Wisconsin with this girl he had been talking to on the Internet.

Jason knew which cars the people who lived in Gracie Ellen's complex drove, and he wanted to stay out of sight in case one of them came by. A black Nissan passed, and then it seemed to slow down as if the driver saw something suspicious in the rearview mirror, but soon it disappeared to be followed by a gray Corolla and then a once red, but now rusty orange Chevy pick-up truck carrying machinery parts in the flatbed and traveling about 30 miles an hour. When Jason saw that the driver was an older Black man, he ran onto the road waving his arms wildly. The driver passed him, but then slowed down, leaning out of the window to get a better look out of his sideview mirror. He backed up slowly.

"What you doing out here, son?"

"Can you take me to the bus station?"

"Bus station? You in trouble?"

"Not really."

"You ain't a ax-murderer, is ya?" The old guy cackled, and Jason saw that he was missing the top row of teeth.

"No, nothing like that, sir," Jason said falling back on his prep school diction.

"You ain't from around here."

"No."

"Where you headed?"

"New York."

"That where you from? Never been myself."

"Yeah, where my dad lives."

"What brought you down here?"

"That's a long story."

"Git in."

ROSETTA

"Oh my god," Tracy shouted when Rosetta opened the apartment door. "Look what that bastard did to you. This is not okay, not okay. Where is he?" Tracy said looking around with anger in her eyes as she stepped into the foyer.

"He picked the boys up from school and took them to the Y. Evan has basketball practice."

"Does Charles know about this?" Rosetta shook her head slightly, but even that small movement made her entire head explode in pain.

"He called; It was his home number. Will snatched the phone. I was feeling so bad. I told him it was over," Rosetta said walking slowly to steady her head, leading Tracy into the living room.

"What? I mean, I get it but..."

"I fucked up."

"More like you got fucked up."

"You want some tea or something."

"No! I mean, this is not the time to play hostess. Sit down and let me look at you." Rosetta obeyed her friend and sat down in the rose-colored wing chair across from the sofa. Tracy was slender and petite, the size of a ten-year old child, but her limbs were sinewy and strong, and she had voluminous dreads, that were almost as long as she was tall, tied back with a strip and yellow and black Kente cloth. Rosetta had learned what it meant to be tough from Tracy, who, when they were growing up, had always been the kind of kid who would not back down. She talked back to teachers. She talked back to the principal. Once she even talked back to the police when she saw them handcuffing a boy at school. Tiny as she was, she fought boys with her fists. Tracy possessed a strong sense of justice and felt compelled to speak out if something was not fair.

Now, she gently grasped Rosetta's chin and examined her face with the probing eyes of a medical practitioner.

"We have to get you to the doctor. I know you called me over here thinking I could help you, and I brought my bag and all, but I can look at you and see that your nose is broken, girl. And no matter what you did and what that motherfucker said, you didn't deserve this. Are you going to press charges?"

"I don't know what to do. I don't know what I thought would happen. I wasn't thinking. I have to teach tonight. Oh, Trace, Trace. What am I going to do?" Rosetta began to cry. Tracy grabbed Rosetta's hands.

"It's gonna be alright, Rosie. You can cancel the class. Come on. Get up. Get your stuff. We'll get a cab. I'm taking you to the hospital."

CHARLES

It was late afternoon when Charles dragged him-self up and staggered into the bathroom wearing the brown leather slippers he always kept by the bed. As he stood at the toilet, his thoughts congealed into the only course of action that seemed to make sense. Refusing to engage the unshaven apparition that passed the medicine cabinet mirror, he left the bathroom. He walked slowly and deliberately down the long hallway, his limp exagger-ated by pain radiating from his lower back. At the end of the hall, he came to the closet where the locked gun case rested on the top shelf above the folded towels and sheets. Charles took down the case. He carried it to the bedroom and placed it on top of the massive mahogany dresser that had once belonged to the Price family. The key to the case was in the back of a small middle drawer stuffed with old bills, random photos, combination locks, and numerous tiny pieces of Lego. When he turned the key, the gun case popped open, but there was no gun inside, just a hollow plastic indentation in the shape of one. Charles howled at the discovery, and like a toddler, or an angry god, he swept the empty gun case off the top of the dresser along with everything else on it. Charles moaned and gripped his head as loose change, a metal razor, pill bottles, sunglasses, keys and the small Polaroid i-Zone camera and miniature strips of photos he and Rosetta had taken of each other naked thudded and clattered as they hit the floor.

He stomped the blue plastic camera until it cracked, kicked the pill bottles and the gun case until his slipper flew off and he stubbed his toe. Then he lost his balance and fell back against the dresser. He cried out in pain, turned, and then shook the dresser as if it were an intentional assailant. The attached mirror wobbled and in its disintegrating silvered glaze he watched tears running down the cheeks and disappearing into the stubble of a dark-skinned, middle-aged man that he barely recognized.

A business card that was stuck between the glass and wood frame of the mirror caught his eye. The foreign words *Nam Myoho Renge Kyo* were printed on it in block letters under a picture of a white lotus flower. A woman gave it to him once in a hospital waiting room. She made him pronounce the strange words and told him that chanting them could change anything. She told him that people who died could be reborn and rejoin their loved ones. He was skeptical; if there was anything he was not, it was a man of faith, but he kept the card all these years because she had a kind smile and a cute ass and had written her number on the back, which he never called.

Charles plucked the card from the mirror and contemplated it through a lens of tears. *For more information call Vicky.* He was tempted to tear up the card, but as he stared it morphed into a tiny screen and Rosetta's face, then Bianca's, then Jason's, and Maddie's and his father's and his mother's appeared on the small rectangle, one fading into another. He laid the card on the dresser and sat down on the bed burying his head in his hands as he mourned the opportunity to take his own life now that it seemed everyone he loved had been taken from him. He willed the walls to close in around him like a coffin, thinking that if he just sat there long enough his consciousness would be obliterated by the intensity of his pain.

But after a while he remembered how to breathe. He inhaled deeply through his nostrils. He exhaled through his mouth. The walls began to recede. His thoughts began to untangle. He got up from the bed and started picking up the items he'd knocked to the floor, putting them back on the dresser. How could he kill himself? Even if it was over with Rosetta, he had to get the charges cleared so he could somehow be there for Bianca. What about Jason? Where would he go when he finally came home?

Charles went into the hallway and stood in the doorway of what had been Jason's and now had become Bianca's room. There was an easel in the far corner with a picture she painted of a pinwheel-shaped flower in pink, yellow and mint green; next to it was the play kitchen with plastic food and miniature aluminum pots and pans that he bought her that first Christmas. A brown cloth-bodied baby doll lay face-down at the foot of the bed, its plastic legs splayed out like a starfish. Charles picked it up and clutched it as if it were some kind of talisman. He tried to pray, but instead of a prayer, lines from a poem came to him, "So boy, don't you turn back/Don't you set down on the steps/'Cause you finds it's kinder hard." They were from "Mother to Son" by Langston Hughes, and it was in that moment that he realized how long it had been since he'd seen his mother. He was so involved with Rosetta and Bianca that he rationalized not visiting her, especially since she didn't recognize him. But how could he have neglected her like that?

He remembered then how his mother cried and begged him not to go to Vietnam. She told him not to choose death over life. She blamed herself for his refusal to open his heart to Carol. She said she and his Daddy did not teach him how to love. But love was why he was hurt-ing so badly now. Maybe *they* hadn't taught him well, but the pain he was feeling was proof that he *had* learned to open his heart. He made up his mind to go see his mother then. Even if she didn't recognize him, even if she didn't understand him, he needed to tell her that he wouldn't "set down on the steps." He needed to tell her that he was choosing life over death. He needed to tell her that his heart was broken but that it was still open.

He laid the doll on Bianca's bed. His back still ached, and his arm felt sore from where he had fallen against the dresser. He went into the bathroom, pulled off his underwear and pushed back the vinyl shower curtain Rosetta bought to replace the old one that had grown stiff and cracked and was coated with years of soap scum. He lifted his shorter and then his longer leg over the curved lip of the claw-footed tub. The pipes screeched when he turned on the tap and arrows of lukewarm water gushed from the wobbling shower head, striking his chest as if they were aiming for his heart.

He was in his bathrobe with shaving cream on his face, picturing the walk to the nursing home, how he would go to 110th and then up the hill to Amsterdam when he heard the hard knock on the apartment door above the rushing sound of the tap. His heart leapt and he dropped the razor.

"Who is it?" he called out as he hurried barefoot into the long hallway, thinking, hoping, wishing that it was Rosetta.

"Dad? Dad, are you home? Can you open the door? It's me, your son. Jason."

Sharon Marshall writes fiction, poetry and essays and lives in New York City. A retired English composition professor and program director, she is an avid photographer and roof-top gardener. She is the author of a previous novel, *Water Child*.

ACKNOWLEDGEMENTS

I would like to thank Edward Willinger, Irene Papoulis, and Douglas Gill for their advice about the manuscript, Jana Roth for her cover suggestions, Christine Logan for her enthusiastic anticipation, and Klay S. Williams for life coaching during the publication process.